ALSO BY ALICE ADAMS

Careless Love

Families and Survivors

Listening to Billie

Beautiful Girl (STORIES)

Rich Rewards

To See You Again (STORIES)

Superior Women

Return Trips (STORIES)

Second Chances

After You've Gone (STORIES)

Caroline's Daughters

Mexico: Some Travels and Travellers There

THIS IS A BORZOI BOOK
PUBLISHED BY ALFRED A. KNOPF, INC.

Library of Congress Cataloging-in-Publication Data

Adams, Alice, [date]
Almost perfect / by Alice Adams.
p. cm.
ISBN 0-679-42398-2
I. Title.
PS3551.D324A74   1993
813'.54—dc20   92-54797
CIP

Manufactured in the United States of America
First Edition

Alice Adams

ALMOST
PERFECT

A NOVEL

Alfred A. Knopf   New York   1993

ALMOST
PERFECT

For G.G. and Larry Green
and
Edwina and Jack Leggett
with much love

ALMOST
PERFECT

1

Stella

Stella Blake, small and dark, huge-eyed, faintly foreign-looking, scared, walks along the broken sidewalk of an unfamiliar street, in an unnatural warm and reddish October dusk. Potrero Hill, San Francisco.

The houses here are small and undistinguished, mostly stucco, one-story, although a couple have been remodelled and sport new brown shingles and broad, aluminum-sashed windows and bright brass plates on their doors.

The wide street is so empty that Stella wonders, Where is everyone? Is something happening that she doesn't know about? but then quite suddenly, planted there on the sidewalk in front of her (how can she have got there?) is a tiny black girl, her hair in cornrows and her dress long and purple, old purple, old velvet. A mother's dress. And this small person, her voice surprisingly loud, demands of Stella, "Do you know what you're going to be on Halloween?"

Thinking, I don't know what I'm going to be tomorrow, or next week, much less on Halloween, Stella simply says, "No. I don't know."

"But you have to know." A tiny scowl. "I be a queen. But I could change my mind. I could. Then I be Michael Jackson."

"I guess I'd better decide too."

"Well, you better. Girl, you better had." And the tiny girl, out of breath and maybe out of bravado too, takes off, running up across a yellowed lawn, disappearing into shadows.

Thinking, It's true, I really don't know what I'll be next week—among other uncertainties, her newspaper job is quite provisional—Stella quite sensibly decides not to make too much of this incident, any more than she would of a random horoscope reading (LEO: Do not engage in expensive activities during this period). She will not even tell anyone about it, despite its obvious anecdotal value.

The immediate cause of Stella's fears and uncertainties is the fact that she is heading toward an interview; her current job includes a lot of interviewing (it is what she is supposed to be good at), and so she should not be frightened—but in this case it is she who is the subject, interviewee rather than interviewer. And the real subject is not herself but her father: Prentice Blake, now dying in Patchen Place, in Greenwich Village. Prentice, a small-time novelist and part-time Stalinist who fought in Spain in the Thirties, was a minor figure himself, but he always knew the important, major figures: Hemingway (of course), and Cummings was a neighbor, Allen Tate, Djuna Barnes—he knew them all. Prentice Blake was known for his great good looks, his "charm," his love affairs and marriages, rather than for his fiction, or for his war record, which was honorable but slight, as his novels were, full of fairly foolish political monologues.

But the very idea of being questioned about her father, being called to account for him, so to speak, scares Stella badly. She is his only child; the other wives, as Prentice likes to point out, were more careful. Stella's mother was Delia, known as Prentice's Mexican beauty—hence Stella's dark Indian eyes, her slightly exotic look.

She stumbles, retrieves her balance, and wishes she had yielded to the actuality of this weather, rather than to some abstract, eastern notion of fall; she should have worn a cotton dress, or jeans. In her sweater and blazer, wool skirt and high-heeled boots, she is hot, and she must look like some Sixties throwback (which in a sense she feels that she is), and she wonders, What have I dressed for? for *whom*?

The interviewer, out from New York, has a name that Stella finds promising: Simon Daniels. She likes the sound of it, and she is also impressed (and frightened) by his credentials, his *New York Review–Critical Inquiry–Raritan* status. But: he will be impossibly tall, small-eyed and bucktoothed, and married and/or gay, Stella tells herself, even as she despises the neediness that adds erotic fantasies to a professional courtesy, and she reminds herself that it is nice of her to take the time to talk to him, when she is both busy and loath to talk about her father, who almost never gave her the time of day, as it were. Who will die soon and will not have left her a cent, despite all his talk of her inheritance. She chides herself for this last greedy thought, so ugly, but it is true that Prentice is very bad about money (rebellious son of New England Republicans, given equally to extravagance and to thrift, both in extremes), and it is true too that Stella at this moment is close to broke.

In any case, this is to be a long day: after Simon Daniels she has to go over to North Beach to do an interview of her own, for the paper. Some advertising jerk, Richard Fallon. Or Dallon. She has to check her notes.

Just now the sunset is blazingly reflected in all the windows of Oakland, across the bay, so that dangerous, problematic Oakland, and Berkeley too, are glorious, golden cities, promising everything. Leading eastward.

Simon Daniels, who opens the door several frightening moments after her knock, is indeed very tall. Bald, spectacled, gentle-voiced and reassuringly rumpled. Possibly gay. In any case, very nice; that comes through at once in his small gestures of leading her into the room and in his thanks that she has troubled, taken the time, to come and talk to him.

But the room itself is bare. Some bentwood chairs, a folding table, and a bookcase in which all the spines of the books are dead upright are all that Stella first sees in that room. Presumably there are other rooms, with beds, a kitchen, some human mess, somewhere. Or so Stella hopes.

Simon has said that he is visiting a painter friend. "Jake is more than a little crazy," he explains, no doubt feeling the shock of her glance at such emptiness. "Have you ever seen his work? The minimalists' minimalist." He smiles. "It's going to be hard on both of us, talking here. I'll feel like an inquisitor, if not a very grand one, and you'll feel . . . I can't quite imagine."

"Like a patient." This quite unintentional remark, once spoken, Stella recognizes as the truth; in her fantasies of visiting a shrink, which she has not so far done, she sits in a bare room with a strange tall man. And talks about her father.

However, as they sit down, facing each other on the hard spare chairs, Simon consciously or not soon dispels this notion— with a great flow of conversation about himself. Which Stella of course recognizes as standard interviewing technique, but she is nevertheless reassured and somewhat seduced, seduced into thinking of him as a trusted old friend.

"My father must have been about the perfect opposite of yours," announces Simon. "Dr. Dull. Harvard, Harvard Med. Beth Israel internship. A stint in the navy, then marriage to a princess from Beverly Hills, and four happy little children. Pediatrics in Pasadena. Aren't doctors strange, don't you think? Such hermetic worlds. And his affection for children borders on the obscene."

"My father can't stand children," Stella tells him, Pavlov-obedient. "I think the competition. That's one of the things he held against my mother, her having a child."

"Well, at least he must have been pretty interesting to have around. My father bores me into screaming fits. I'm sure I turned queer just to get his goat."

Oh. "Well, Prentice could be pretty boring, actually. The same old stories so often, you know. The boasting, which of course got worse as he got older, with less to brag about. The name-drops." Acute anxiety beats in Stella's breast as she speaks of Prentice in this way. But it's all right, she tells herself. Prentice won't know (or will he?).

"Did you like it better living in Mexico with your mother?" asks Simon.

"Sort of. But we were pretty broke. Poor is more like it. Prentice didn't send money when he said he would. And we were in Cuernavaca, among all those rich gringos. My mother's friends. I really dislike that city."

"Actually so do I. No traces of the Lowrys, right? Such an odd place for them to have chosen, I've always thought."

"Cuernavaca's changed a lot. Since I was there, and I'm sure even more since the Thirties, or whenever they were there. But the best part is still those volcanoes. The way you suddenly see them, in different lights."

And so on.

Simon leads her intelligently with his own confessions and observations, to which Stella adds her own, quite forgetting, as she herself has watched and heard her own interviewees forget, that only one side of this conversation will appear in print.

Indeed, as she might have with a shrink, Stella tells this strange man (but so nice, so seductively nice, intelligent and interested—oh, ever so interested), tells him the tales of later wives and girlfriends of Prentice's. And what she herself as a child experienced as non-love. As neglect. Disapproval.

"Prentice has a trick of kicking you when you're down," says Stella to this new friend. "Of saying something to make you feel a lot worse than you already feel." She even says, "I really dread his death. One more body blow."

"He doesn't exactly have a reputation for kindness. But then I guess being kind was held to be a little sissy in his day." Simon laughs.

"I guess. He was really concerned with that macho stuff. 'Not man enough' was one of his favorite expressions. Or taunts. Even to me. He would say that I wasn't 'man enough' for something. Even when I was little I thought that was sort of odd."

"Indeed." He stares at her, and then Simon Daniels says, "Do you have any idea how beautiful you are? No? I didn't think so. And actually not quite yet; I'd put it about ten years off. Some

women are like that, you know. They just have to wait, sometimes for middle age. But the shape of your forehead—lovely!
And those eyes."

Very embarrassed, Stella finds nothing to say in response to
this. She ducks her head, she mutters, "Well, thank you."

"Well, back to old Prentice. Tell me, when you were a kid,
did he talk much about the circumstances of his break with the
Party?"

Because she is running a little late, and because, calculatedly
or not, Simon Daniels has come across so sympathetically (he
even promised to send her the pages in which she figures, a rare
professional courtesy), Stella treats herself to a cab, Potrero Hill
to North Beach, in the darkening, strangely warm evening.

That encounter with Simon Daniels was indeed positive,
thinks Stella, noting too her uncharacteristic lack of guilt at having (to some extent) bad-mouthed Prentice. Her lack of fear. She
even experiences a sort of relief—as though Simon had indeed
been a shrink instead of an interviewer.

Driven through unfamiliar streets, in the broken back seat of
the Yellow Cab, to Stella the city itself seems suddenly strange,
almost foreign. She could be almost anywhere at all, she thinks,
anywhere thousands of miles from San Francisco.

She could be in New York, in the late Sixties, racing toward
an interview with Liam O'Gara, the director, with whom over
the course of several years, the years of her own late teens, she
had a momentous love affair. For several years and over several
continents. Stella, in those days looking barely older than a child,
used to fly with Liam to Rome and to Lisbon for a couple of
days, to Edinburgh and at last to Mexico, where Liam had managed an actual job for her. On the set of *Black Hacienda*, Liam's
last great film, Stella worked in Oaxaca and Morelia and in Zi-
hautanejo, in the crumbling, beautiful Hotel Catalina, where the
last scenes of the film were shot and where Liam and Stella played
out some of their own final hours, among all that brilliant flowing bougainvillea, over too many, too sweet margaritas.

Stella's divided life, in those days, was mad; she was wrenched, almost crazed, by the contrast between her daily "normal" life in a dingy West Side apartment—grubbing along on sparse newspaper assignments and taking classes at Hunter, shopping for bargains, skipping meals—and her precipitous first-class flights to Liam, wherever he was, to Liam and his entourage, all that talk and drinking; some drugs; exotic food flown in. The passion and the sleeplessness (like many geniuses that Stella had read about, Liam had almost no need for sleep). The endless talk, the strange wild presents: flowers, impossible jewelry, brilliant dresses. The love. A queen of nowhere, she had felt herself to be: a small half-Mexican, half-Anglo princess of nothing. Liam's street child. His waif. Then rushing back to her grubby jobs and her classes.

Sheer unreality, though, was helpful in the end; Stella suffered, but what she felt was in a sense literary, an aesthetic pain. She suffered and watched herself suffering, and both were quite apart from her daily life. She broke with Liam, and after a year or so of solitary pain, she had what she thought of as "relationships" with a couple of other men. Not love affairs.

But now, in the taxi that hurries through darkened streets, under freeways, skirting monumental abutments, passing dingy south-of-Market hotels and derelict bars and bright seedy restaurants, despite the generally drab ambiance of the city at night, Stella feels a suddenly recovered sense of adventure, as though she were indeed in a country where Liam was, perhaps even Mexico. Rushing to meet him. Running late, out of breath. She suddenly misses Liam, as she has not missed him for years.

When at last the cab stops, she is surprised, though she quickly sees exactly where they are: on Pacific, where the old International Settlement used to be (Stella once did a feature for the Sunday paper on this particular bit of San Francisco history). Near Jackson Square. But they have stopped at a building that looks to be boarded up. However, this is the right address; getting out of the cab, Stella sees that indeed there is a door, cut into the boarding. And as she looks more closely, she sees a tiny card, rather casually tacked above the knob: R. FALLON.

And a button. She rings, and hears an inner buzz. And then no sounds at all.

And then, as she is about to turn and leave, she hears very

heavy fast footsteps, clearly a man's. The door opens, and a very out-of-breath, very large man stands there, staring down at her— as she looks up to rumpled blond hair that is haloed by the light. His shadowed face is almost invisible. A tall man in a bathrobe, and barefoot, who is saying, "Jesus Christ! I forgot. Oh God!"

A very deep voice, very attractive—perhaps self-consciously so? Somewhere Stella registers vanity.

"I forgot!" he tells her again. "But do you want a drink? I can't talk now," he adds. "Too disorganized."

Angry, and confused (does he mean have a drink now instead of the interview?), Stella tells him that it's perfectly all right. She is tired, is happy just to go home (that much at least is true).

"Can I drive you? My car's right here. I could dress—"

No, she can very easily get a cab on Broadway. And she starts away from him, even as his deep, rounded voice is saying, "Will you call me? At least let me buy you a drink?"

In a pig's eye, is what Stella thinks, as she turns to wave, intending a definitive farewell.

Call him? He must be crazy, she thinks, as she hurries along toward the brighter lights.

So much for Richard Fallon.

2

Richard

Richard woke up feeling beautiful. No other way to put it, and you could never say that to anyone, but that was how he felt, perfectly rested and smooth-skinned, tight and strong. Beautiful. Great to touch.

And his mirror, that morning in the bathroom, confirms what he felt in bed: he looks ... well, perfect. Nowhere near middle-aged. He smiles at himself. This will be a day on which everything will work for him, he can tell, a day that begins so beautifully.

It is also the day that should end with the Stella Blake interview, whoever the hell she is.

* * *

Richard is a commercial artist ("Not quite commercial enough," is his joke), and his studio, in the building where he also lives, is an enormously cluttered two-story brick-walled room. The clutter consists of everything: paintings, vases, wooden sculptures, bronze and marble statuary. Glossy green-leafed plants and feathery ferns. Various chairs, from comfortable broken leather to tiny gilt. Mirrors, several on each wall, some heavy, ornately framed, others plain.

It is an opulent chaos, which, curiously, works; its effect is of an aesthetic whole, a design. "A beautiful accident," was Richard's first wife's description (crazy Marina, with a very mean crazy tongue). "Sort of like you, Rickie." Only Marina ever called him Rickie.

The center of the room, its focus, is Richard's worktable, on which there is further chaos: piles of papers; small bottles of ink, in all colors; jars of pencils and brushes. Above the table is an elaborate cut-glass candelabra, refracting light and frequently shedding bright beams on Richard's light mass of hair.

At the back of the room is a balcony, with stairs leading up to a space that is clear and efficient, surprisingly, with filing cabinets, a drafting table, and various machines: copier, typewriter, computer, adding machine, stereo. Below the balcony, behind a door, is Richard's living suite: his bedroom and bath, a pullman kitchen—all perfectly functional, all small. The bedroom is smallest of all, a tapestried cave, walls lined with coarse brown linen. There is a queen-size bed, a bureau with mirror, an easy chair, a lamp. "It's the sexiest room I've ever seen," snarled Marina, furiously, instantly sure that Richard "brought girls there," as she would put it, which of course he did. Especially beautiful Claudia, rich and married, who after a lot of trouble became his second wife, for a rough two years. Richard will never marry again; it spoils everything, he knows that.

Richard's clothes are in a larger room, a big closet that forms the passageway to his bath and kitchen, the kitchen where on a tall stool Richard now sits over coffee, still smiling, still pleased with the day. Looking back to the passageway at his clothes, he thinks as he often has before that he has too many, far too many clothes—and he determines (as he has before) that he will get a bunch of them together for homeless people. Some shelter. He will definitely do that this week.

Presentation time. That is what this day is for him, what he is almost about to get together—and then at the end of the day that interview, which even now he knows he may forget, what with so much else going on. Big clients coming. Big money involved.

Webster Wines.

Three hours later, at almost noon, the hour of the presentation, Richard's studio is totally transformed. It has become a wonderland of bright glass bubbles: thousands of them—five thousand exactly. He should know; he ordered and paid for them, and they cost the earth, but they are worth it. Tiny glass translucent balls, hung from everywhere in that enormous space, from tiny gilt cornices on mirrors, from tips of philodendron leaves—everywhere bubbles.

And that is the theme of this whole presentation: Bubble time, the campaign for the new champagne from Webster Wines.

"You're an absolute genius, you know that, Dick?"

"Richard, it's so beautiful I could cry."

"Man, you're really a crazy SOB, but this is super, very very super, I mean it."

"What a great party! Rich, when you do it you really do it, you know what I mean?"

Along with the champagne, courtesy Webster Winery, Richard has provided small pastry puffs of caviar ("Well, of course, what else but caviar?"), puffs of cheese, and, for the more abstemious, grapes and melon balls. ("It's all balls, did you notice? Call it bubbles if you want to, but it's basically balls. Right, Rich?")

In his pale-gray blazer, smiling his smile, Richard moves through his party, adoring every minute, every overheard or directly spoken word of praise. Each pat on the back, each kiss. He loves this, this makes it all worthwhile, his often lousy work. He loves all this love and praise, it warms his blood. Love vibrates in his chest.

And it all could vanish in a breath, he knows that. Like soap bubbles vanishing. It's all unreal; he is playing with funny money; it could all be dust tomorrow. As he could be dust, lying dead and dirty in an alley somewhere. What he does is as fake, as phony, as what all the others do, all the people in this room, the art directors and the clients, the hotshot moneybags clients; they could lose it all, as easily as anyone. As easily as he himself could lose it all. As Richard Fallon, Esquire.

But in the meantime he might as well enjoy it, mightn't he?

"Say, Richard man, this is really the greatest."

"Dick, old man, a lot of the time I think you're an asshole, but you're also a fucking genius, you know that?"

"Richard darling, I never saw anything quite so beautiful. You must leave it like this forever!"

Of course all these people are jerks.

On the other hand, a few of them are fairly attractive.

Linda, who wants him to keep his studio like this forever, is not too bad. Hair a little long for her age, and that pink shirt is definitely a mistake, but still, Linda is not too bad.

She is across the room by now and is talking to someone else, some old advertising broad, he's seen her around. Approaching the two women, Richard smiles, he gleams at them both, and then, as the older woman turns for a moment to someone else, into Linda's ear he whispers, "Why don't you ever call me?"

"Call you? Richard, for heaven's sake, why would I?" But she is blushing.

"Because I'd really like it if you did. Isn't that a reason?"

She laughs. "I'll think about it."

She will, he knows she'll call. But why did he have to ask her? Most women just call, and call. Even Claudia, to whom he was recently married, still calls.

And some men call.

Like Andrew Bacci, who in fact did call this very morning to say, "You know, we could just put in a little more together. Hang out. Preferably siesta time, but if not, not. Don't you ever get tired of women? Of—that horrible word you guys use—of 'cunt'? I wouldn't do anything you don't want, I promise. I'll stop the minute you say to. But honestly, kiddo, I think you might like it."

Andrew is very good-looking, if you like that curly, long-lashed Italian look, and Richard sort of does; he has to admit it. Andrew is young, twenty-something, and smart, very smart. A stockbroker. Funny too. Richard always has a lot of laughs on the phone or having a couple of drinks with Andrew. And as far as that other stuff goes ... well, Andrew could be right. He might like it. And that might be a problem.

This quick reverie on Andrew—which, Richard has to admit, has turned him on, it really has—is interrupted by a woman named Margot Carlisle, a dark and extremely chic (there is no other word for Margot's style) older woman, whom Richard distrusts and almost dislikes and is not at all turned on by. Margot in fact is a good friend of Andrew Bacci's. For all Margot's big reputation for sexiness and lovers—she has lived all over the world, known almost everyone and slept with most people—Margot is almost always with gay men, and she seems to like Andrew best of all.

She begins her conversations with a tiny deep-throat laugh, usually. She does so now, the little laugh, before saying, "Darling Richard, you've really outdone yourself. This is truly fantastic." Her manner is somewhat campy, with always too many gestures, eyebrow raisings, like a bad imitation of Garbo.

"Well, dollings," Richard tells her, Bronx style, "thanks. Coming from you ... well, really, thanks."

Margot swings her sheaf of black hair. "I hear a friend of mine is coming to talk to you."

"Oh?" His mind is a blank.

"Yes, the dearest young woman. Stella Blake. Quite a brilliant girl, actually. Hardly your type, no style at all. She's working for some paper. But you be nice to her, Richard. A man I used to know, a big director, wasn't nice to her at all. Although for a while he adored her."

"I'm always nice."

"That's not exactly what I've heard." Margot smirks.

"Anyway the whole idea seems so dumb. An interview. Christ. I don't like to talk."

"It doesn't matter at all what you say, don't worry." Margot pauses to scan the room, plotting her next move, before she turns back to Richard. Then, "I had lunch yesterday with darling Andrew," she tells him, batting her eyelashes. "He's absolutely pining."

"Jesus Christ, Margot. You know perfectly well."

Giving him a long vamp smile, complicit, amused and knowing, Margot slides into the crowd—as from somewhere Richard hears "Dick, phone for you. A lady, naturally."

"I'll take it inside."

Knowing, somehow, that it will be Claudia, and knowing too how the conversation will end, Richard takes his time getting to the phone, noting as he does so that the party is winding down. He'll give it another half hour, but the best part is over, and Richard sighs with great and genuine sadness. What everyone said was true: what he did was really fantastic, almost perfect; in his way he is a sort of genius.

The first time Richard ever saw Claudia—it must be ten years ago now—what he thought was: That's it, that's her. That's the most beautiful woman I ever saw. That's *her*. The perfect one. Stark naked, standing in front of him, in a puddle of red silk.

He had been working all day on his cabin up the coast. He even remembers the colors of that day: an April mauve-pink-blue day, the sky that color all day, and the sea reflective, calm. Richard was up there alone, just working. Marina had stayed home, for some damn reason or other of her own. One of her nutcake intuitions, probably. But he was all alone and working well, on the beautiful house of his own design, his own labor. And he had that day the most marvelous sense of his own good work; he had imagined this house, all out of his head, and made drawings. Got a contractor for the foundation and the frame, a plumber for all that stuff, and here it was, beautiful and almost done. It worked. That day he was shingling the roof, stopping now and then to breathe the clean salt air, to admire the sky and the sea, the swooping gulls.

He barely remembered, in fact, that he had been asked to a

party that night at Sea Ranch; some client had bought a huge spread there recently.

But then he did remember, and he thought it might be fun; he hadn't been to a party alone for a while, what the hell. Marina was unreliable, partywise; sometimes she hated a party on sight and wanted to go home, other times she got fairly drunk and wanted to stay all night. Now he even remembers a lilting sense of expectancy as he drove along the coast in the fresh spring dark, the dark-blue sky star-sprinkled, to the huge low-lying "contemporary" house, with its show-off Frank Lloyd Wright winged roof, its pretentious fancy brass door.

A blast of party hit Richard, opening that door when no one came to his knock. Extreme noise: there must have been two bands, several speaker systems. And people trying to shout above all that sound, as though they had something to say. Richard, whose nose is exceptionally sensitive, smelled garlic and fish and booze, cigarette and cigar smoke and some dope, and about a hundred fabulous French perfumes. Too rich, this is all too rich for my old thin Irish blood, Richard thought, aware of an urgent and private need: I'd like to piss all over this place, he thought, asking someone for directions to the can.

He went down a hall and he opened, as directed, the second door to the right, to a brilliant black-tiled bathroom, in the middle of which was standing, naked as a jaybird, a ravishing golden girl.

Who shrieked and tried to cover her snatch and her tits, but she was laughing too; Richard could feel her looking him over, and he knew how he must look to her, in his white party coat, dark-blue silk scarf. With his hair, and his eyes.

She laughed and laughed, giving up on her body, using her hands to cover her face, and not even succeeding at that too well.

He threw her a towel from the rack on the door. It was all he could do; he couldn't speak.

"So chivalrous!" she cried out. "God, couldn't you knock?"

"I didn't know it would open. Don't you lock doors?"

"Oh, go away!"

Near her feet lay a red silk dress, some lacy red silk underthings, and hose. God knows why she had to take all that stuff off to pee.

"See you later," Richard was barely able to say.

About half an hour later, by which time Richard had found an empty bathroom and had also found his host and the bar, he was introduced to this ravishing girl in red, a girl with a big full mane of dark-blond hair, not far from the color of his own hair (and a dark-blond muff and pink tits), a girl who blushed terrifically as he said to her, "I do think we've met somewhere."

Claudia Farnsworth.

"I never saw you before in my life," she said.

"Would you dance with me anyway?"

"Well, I might."

Claudia was a flirt, very vain and selfish, but she was also smart, in a certain way; even that first night, Richard recognized in her some of his own survival-in-the-jungle qualities. A girl from Salt Lake City, she had sold cosmetics at I. Magnin, modelled a little, until she met and as soon as possible married Bucky Farnsworth, married the quantities of "old money" that made her feel both inferior and secure.

Which was almost how Richard felt, at parties like that one: he knew he was better-looking and probably as smart as anyone there, but at the same time he was very aware of not having gone to their schools, of not having known them for very long. Of being from Paterson, New Jersey, which was not exactly what any of them meant when they said "the East."

"You'll have to come to my house sometime," he said to Claudia, dancing close.

"You mean in the city?"

"No, up here, on the coast."

"Oh, we have a house up here too, and one at Tahoe. But where do you live in the city?"

"Oh, up near Twin Peaks, at the moment. But my studio's in North Beach."

"I've never been to Twin Peaks, I don't think."

"You don't have to. Come to my studio. Call me."

"Oh, you." Her laugh was as pretty as everything about her, high and soft, a little burst of silver.

Later that night Richard met her husband, red-faced Bucky Farnsworth, who mentioned both Exeter and Yale within minutes of their introduction.

Later still, in fact very late, some hours after midnight, Richard managed to get Claudia out onto one of the porches, where through clusters of pines and hemlocks and aspens they could see the blackly glittering sea and an almost clearing new day. Clinging together, they kissed, for Richard a kiss of such sweetness, such innocence (she tasted of apricots). A kiss of true love. He felt that his heart would break.

"I feel like a child," he whispered to her, to lovely Claudia, as they pulled apart.

"Me too—that's how I feel." She shivered. "We'd better go in, though."

After that, for the weeks of spring and into summer, almost everywhere that Richard went he saw her, beautiful Claudia. For at that time he and Marina seemed to be taken up by a certain group, rich people with houses at Tahoe and up on the coast, people who gave a lot of parties. And since Richard's house had turned out so perfectly, a small showplace, really, photographed all over, everyone loved it, and they were invited everywhere, Richard and Marina Fallon, the new smart couple. Richard saw Claudia at all those parties, in all her marvelous clothes—and he thought of her naked, red silk at her pretty feet. He was truly in love with her, he knew that, but he never made a real move in her direction. There were only those rare, intensely sweet and almost innocent kisses.

Until the afternoon when Claudia called him, and she came to his studio and told him that she could not live without him, not another moment. Which was, as Richard now sees it, the beginning of the end. Everything after that was more or less predictable, and more or less downhill: the impassioned afternoons, and evening quarrels at home. Divorce, and marriage to Claudia.

More quarrels. Another divorce.

Not that Richard ever forgot about those early afternoons—they were lovely, and she was indeed a lovely-looking woman. They even had, occasionally, a good conversation; Claudia was almost as mean as he was about the people they both knew, as mean and as ambivalent.

But she was basically a very stupid woman, and vain, and selfish. Richard was almost relieved when she told him, finally, that an old boyfriend from Salt Lake had shown up in her life (terrifically rich, that went without saying). She wanted out. And so Richard moved back into his studio—not, as poor Marina would have liked, to Twin Peaks with her.

And now occasionally Claudia still calls, and sometimes they get together, for a couple of hours in his studio, in bed. He actually misses her children, two nice little boys, much more than he misses Claudia.

Living alone, though, Richard has moments, even days, of the most appalling aloneness, a sense of cold vacancy in his very soul. He worries about Marina, who often acts crazy. He worries about Claudia's boys, believing that she is too stupid to take proper care of them. For all these reasons, he often ends up drinking too much, one way or another, and he spends time with people he does not even much like—stupid people, no life to them. Including, sometimes, Claudia.

"Sometimes I absolutely can't believe that we could fail. I mean, where did we go wrong? You're the most beautiful guy in the world, and I really love us together. I absolutely don't understand it."

Claudia says this as, late that afternoon, on the day of his bubble party, they lie together naked across his bed and she happily fingers the light growth of hair on his chest. But she has said all that before, and Richard has no new answers for her.

"It's just marriage," he says, as he has said before. "Not us."

"But I love you so much, and it's so good with you!"

Richard pats her sleek thigh. "I have to say, today was a big success," he tells her. "They really went for it."

"Darling, of course they did. The room looked fabulous."

"You just saw the remnants." Richard told Claudia very firmly that she must not arrive before three—at which time he knew the last guests would be gone. Which indeed was the case, though he had a little trouble with Linda, who seemed to feel that the afternoon was hers, hers with Richard. "It was really incredible about noon," he tells Claudia, "when people began to show up. And the sun—"

"Oh God, it's almost five. I have to go!" Scrambling from the bed, Claudia stumbles into the bathroom, where she leaves the door open, and goes on talking, while she thoroughly washes herself. This habit, the open door, is one that Richard does not like at all; he does not want to see her doing all that, and even if he closes his eyes he knows. He can see her still.

"And Donny is so impossible," Claudia continues, from the toilet. "Sometimes I think God's punishing me with him. Rich, do you think I should try to gain some weight?"

"Are you serious?"

"Well, sort of. I read somewhere that older women have to sacrifice their figures to their faces."

"Christ. In the first place, you're not an older woman."

"No, but I will be. And so will you. Older, I mean. Can you imagine being middle-aged? Like our parents, when we were kids?"

Any mention of his parents, any stray thought of them, blackens Richard's consciousness, as does the notion of age. "No," he says vehemently—to everything, sitting up in bed and watching Claudia as she brushes on makeup.

He suddenly feels that she has contrived to ruin his day. The day that started with such promise. The day of his big success. The next time she calls he will simply say, No, I don't want to see you, Richard decides. Some women can ruin your life.

After Claudia is gone he simply wanders about the studio, not yet ready to tackle cleaning it up, and noting that it looks like the devastation after Christmas. The catering girls took the food and all that mess, but there are still all those goddam glass bubbles everywhere, many broken, many still rolling around the floor like marbles. Richard imagines weeks and months of stray bits of broken glass.

He feels vague pains in his chest and wonders if he is having a heart attack.

When the doorbell rings, Richard's first thought, curiously, is of Andrew Bacci, although Andrew has never just stopped by like that. Linda? And then he remembers: Jesus, the interview girl.

Stella. Whatever the hell her name was.

He heads toward the door, walking heavily. Fast, with more pain in his chest.

3

Friends

"Actually I guess he forgot. I got there on time; you know me: even when I mean to be late. But he came to the door in a robe, not expecting me."

"Richard can be very careless," Margot tells Stella. "He's rather spoiled, I think. So handsome, though fortunately not at all my type. He's not pretty, you know? I like men to be pretty. But no one was ever so pretty as George, and look how he treated me. Richard should never have married Claudia Farnsworth; the most total mistake. They could have gone on with that super affair forever. Andrew told me the two of them exuded steam. You know my friend Andrew Bacci, don't you, Stell? Talk about pretty. But I guess Marina, Richard's nutcake wife, got some of that steam blown in her face, and she threw him out, just like that. So stupid. Europeans have much more sense about these things."

This is a telephone conversation that some weeks hence Stella will strain to remember in detail, and fortunately journalistic training has given her a memory that records automatically. At the moment, though, she simply reflects on the general uninterestingness of gossip, however steamy, when it concerns people one does not know. And she reflects too on the extremely small-town quality of San Francisco: only last week she did indeed meet Andrew Bacci, Margot's pretty friend. She was covering a fund-raising dinner for AIDS, and Andrew was one of the sponsors. And he was, as Margot said, extremely pretty. And now it seems that both he and Margot are somehow connected to, or friends with, Richard Fallon, her non-interview. In fact Stella is later to think that a seeming web of friends could almost have been conspiring that she and Richard should meet.

But at the moment, how bored she is with Margot! They met more or less through friends when Margot's then husband, George, had just walked out, leaving Margot, who is considerably older than she looks, with no money, no job. With nothing. Stella, touched by this unfair plight, and by some quality in Margot herself, some brave undaunted verve, helped Margot get a job at a gallery out on Jackson Street. Not much of a job, but it helped a lot, and Margot was gracefully grateful. And they became, with limitations, friends, mostly phone friends: Margot, with not much to do but sit at the gallery, calls and talks, and Stella listens—as she has just noted, with decreasing interest.

"In any case, so rude of Richard," Margot now comments.

"Actually he seems to feel very bad about it. He keeps calling to apologize."

"He must want to see you."

"I doubt it, really. And at this point I wouldn't know him if I saw him."

"He's very, very handsome. But of course you don't care about anything so superficial, do you."

Stella laughs. "Of course not. Whether or not they're politically correct and are fond of Wittgenstein, that's my sole criterion."

"You even say you didn't think Liam was handsome."

"Well, I guess he was. Is. Sort of."

"Everyone else certainly seems to think so." And Margot sniffs.

Her history is probably the most interesting thing about Margot; most interesting to Stella is the fact that Margot once knew (or simply met: this is not entirely clear) Liam O'Gara. Also, Margot once wrote a book, a novel that was popular some years ago and is now out of print. She has been married three times (probably), once to a man with whom she lived in England for several years, which is where and when she knew (or simply met) Liam O'Gara. She also lived in Mexico City, where she posed (it is said) for Diego Rivera. She has lived in Turkey, and of course in New York. She is not a name-dropper, not really, but it does come out that she knew various important people: Stephen Spender, Balanchine, Mary McCarthy, John Huston, Jackson Pollock. Halston and Christopher Isherwood. Liam O'Gara.

Stella has said very little to Margot about Liam, their affair, beyond the indisputable fact that she used to see him. Margot of course would like to hear much more, and continually brings him up.

"I hardly think of Liam," Stella now tells her. She laughs. "I might not know him either, if I saw him somewhere. Other than in the tabloids."

"Oh, you." Margot sighs. "Well, I'm glad that Richard at least feels that apologies are in order."

"Too many. I wish he'd knock it off."

That is not entirely true: Richard has actually called only twice, once to apologize hastily and once to set up another meeting, for next week. What is annoying—in fact this is irritating in the extreme—is how much Stella finds that she cares. How much she thinks of him. Imprinted in her consciousness is the shadowed face of that very tall man, with his backlit halo of pale tangled hair. She thinks of that face, and of his deep troubled voice; she thinks obsessively of the room behind him, his studio. All that she could see of it that night was that it was extremely large and full of objects. Looming furniture, plants.

She is waiting for their next contact, the interview that is to take place next Tuesday, and *no one*, especially not Margot (and more especially not Richard Fallon himself), must have the smallest clue as to the excitement she feels. Which has nothing to do with the actual Richard Fallon, Stella tells herself; it was only an accidental small fire set to her overreceptive imagination—or, also likely, to her somewhat starved libido, after an overly long stretch "between beaux," as her Texas friend, Justine Jones, likes to put it.

Undoubtedly, by this time next week the whole obsession, if it is that, will have vanished, blown away. And in the meantime she does not want to talk about it.

She gets Margot off the phone (not always an easy task) and starts to work on a series of interviews with homeless people around Civic Center and a group who want to feed them.

She manages to concentrate, to get a great deal done.

Stella's flat is in the nondescript, amorphous area known as the Richmond District, in roughly the northwest quadrant of the city, and the flat itself is quite nondescript, its two virtues being its size (it is roomy) and its proximity to the Presidio, the Army-owned stretch of land that is mostly woods, dark and deep and very beautiful. Stella's windows look out to these woods; from her narrow bedroom window she sees a sweep of cypress boughs, a grassy hillock, and the black trunks of pines and hemlocks, some wind-bent cypresses.

Her large and clumsily proportioned living room is sparsely furnished, and decorated with somewhat childish souvenirs: posters, silver masks, ceramics. Lots of books. There is also a dining room, and another, very small room, for which she has never found a definite use; she puts things there, and periodically she has to clear them out. Her bathroom is large and papered with cabbage roses, vaguely matched by rose-colored tiles around the shower.

Stella tends to spend time mostly in her bedroom; she reads there, and often works at a long cluttered table across from her bed.

Richard Fallon is unimaginable in these rooms; that is one of the things that Stella thinks that day, after talking to Margot and observing, anew, the unruly piles of books by which she is surrounded. She sighs, and sits down at her desk, and gets to work.

She has two hours before meeting a friend for lunch down-town, and she needs to make the most of them.

This fairly frequent lunchtime friend is Justine Jones, some ten years older than Stella. A very close, maybe her closest friend, from a crossroads down in East Texas. A lean and lanky gray-blonde (a dust-bowl blonde, she terms herself), freckle-faced, in-congruously heavy-breasted. Justine was scooped up into the giant university at Austin, where she prospered and won further scholarships, in journalism, to Columbia. And thence to the job in San Francisco. She is literally Stella's boss, a fact they both tend to forget; Justine is in charge of feature stories, the section for which Stella mostly writes, what used to be called the women's page.

An avid talker, sometimes brilliant, always interesting, and often wise, Justine is monumentally discreet about her own life; she is even discreet about her own opinions. She tends to listen and to comment—in a word, an ideal friend, which is how Stella and quite a few other people view her, including the lovers of whom she does not often speak. Life in New York served to speed up her native delivery, but apparent in her speech are still certain flat vowels, as well as a frequent wry colloquial turn, which she is much too intelligent to overdo. The sounds of her voice are actually very beautiful, like soft sweet bells, sounding an upper range. She spent the past year with a Nieman Fellow-ship at Harvard, but Cambridge seems not to have affected her speech.

Once they settle at their table, Stella tells her friend, "I'm really okay. Just broke and sometimes lonely, but aren't most people both those things?" Stella is aware, still, of having missed Justine for a year, and is anxious, still, to tell her everything—an effect that is frequent with Justine.

"I do worry about Prentice," Stella continues. "It's hard when an ambivalently loved parent is dying."

"It sure is."

They pause delicately, both recognizing the problem: un-loved, unloving Prentice Blake dying.

It is Stella who breaks the silence then, saying, "And then there's Liam. Always lurking somewhere in the tabloids. If a person can *lurk* in tabloids."

The two women laugh, with a small note of sadness, of rue, thrown in.

"Just yesterday something in a gossip column," Stella goes on. Justine is the only person to whom she speaks of Liam.

"I saw it," Justine tells her. "Honestly, baby-girl stars. At his age." And then she asks Stella, "Why are you peering like that? See someone you know?"

Caught out, Stella half lies. "Not really. I just thought I saw someone." The truth is, she is more or less half looking for, half expecting to see, Richard Fallon. Who has, she now feels, insinuated himself into her imagination. She has found herself looking about, as (observably) she now is doing.

Justine is a woman of exceptional intuitive powers; she could almost be counted on to divine the state of mind of her friend. And so it is really to change the subject, again, that Stella remarks, "In addition to dying, Prentice is more than a little strange about money, I think. He keeps going on about what he's leaving me. Sometimes he's apologetic, saying he wishes it were more, other times he makes a big deal about how generous he is."

"He's crazy." Justine says this very gently, very sparingly.

"Yes, but he's also dying." Stella sighs, painfully; almost any thought of her father is for her filled with pain. And this linkage of his death with unspecified but supposedly large sums of money is in every way terrible: a seditious bribe, an evil push toward wishes for his death.

Justine as a rule speaks very little of herself, a quality that Stella has tried and failed to emulate. Justine asks questions and she listens, wonderfully—Justine is one of the great listeners. She speaks about general topics. Thus Stella often knows very little about her current life. It is very surprising, then, to Stella to hear Justine say, "This quite curious thing has come up in my life. A man I know, whom I've been, uh, going out with from time to time, now has decided that we must get married, and I find myself very confused. Totally. Confused."

"Justine, how nice, that's terrific." But even as she says this

Stella wonders, Is it terrific? Why does she make this assumption? Does she herself wish to be married? She would rather have thought that she prided herself on not marrying, on avoiding that particular form of trouble.

"I'm not so sure," says Justine, as though in answer to all of Stella's unspoken questions. "But I must say I'm a little embarrassed at how pleased I am to be asked. And to make it even more embarrassing, he's sort of rich; not really rich but what my poor old mother would call comfortable. And he *is* comfortable. I really like him."

For whatever reasons, possibly including the proposal, Justine is in one of her very young-looking phases. In an old heavy soft-blue sweater, a scarf and jeans (Margot: "Your Okie friend really takes the prize for dowdy"), her light hair tied back with a ribbon, her blue eyes bright, she looks like a friend of Stella's own age, or even a younger friend.

"Funnily enough, he's a contractor," Justine now tells Stella, long, strong fingers toying with her wineglass. "Funnier still, I met him in a bar. I really wish it hadn't happened like that, in a way, but it did. I'd just had a really bad day downtown, and I was so tired, and I thought, How nice just to have a glass of wine at some cheery place. So I went into Le Central, forgetting it was Friday, so crowded—and there he was, this nice fat man moving over to let me get a drink, and then talking to me, and then saying why don't we go and have dinner. And so we did."

Stella laughs. "And so, as they say, one thing led to another."

"Well yes, eventually. In fact very eventually; it was all very slow and deliberate, and so nice; I never felt rushed, or pushed." She smiles at Stella. "Another funny thing—in fact everything about this story is very odd, wouldn't you say? But Collin, my contractor, seems to know that advertising type who stood you up. You remember, Mr. Fallon?"

A strange flush of heat goes through Stella—so stupid; *why?*— even as quite coolly she is saying, "Everyone seems to know him, one way or another. But how does Collin?"

"Collin mostly builds houses. And he was showing me some pictures—he keeps files on them all, of course—and he came to one, rather small but so beautiful, really super, up the coast. And he said it was the best house he'd ever built, and that some advertising type had just drawn it on a cocktail napkin, and he built it from the drawing, and it turned out perfect. A crazy genius, he said, named Richard Fallon. So, you know how I am about names; my old head is literally stuffed with them. And so I thought, Oh, Richard Fallon. Stella's missing interview." Justine smiles, rather pleased with this tidy tying together of things.

"What did it look like, the house?" Asking this, Stella realizes that she is short of breath.

"Like a terribly sophisticated cabin. A pile of upright logs against a steep bank. Big windows. It's hard to describe. Ask him. Did you ever get to the interview?"

"Next week. I think." Stella smiles across at her friend, taking breaths. "So, now. About this marriage idea," she says.

Justine flushes, looking younger yet. And she begins to talk. About Collin Schmidt. And herself.

4

More Friends

Like many men, Richard Fallon is not given to close friendships with other men, although he has, perhaps, more friends than most men do. He has certain teasing intimacies here and there; bantering connections involving silly names and punch lines from old jokes. These friendships, with both straight and gay men, are all lightly flirtatious, in their way.

Richard has names for everyone. His name for Collin Schmidt, whom he has known almost since he first came to town, is Bunny. What he calls Andrew Bacci is Dog Shoes, a senseless name that made Richard smile when he first thought of it and that he likes to use privately, with Andrew. Sometimes, though rarely in public, Andrew calls Richard Dickie Bird.

Andrew does so now, on the phone. Andrew takes his major

risks during phone conversations; he has been known to leave incriminating messages on tapes.

"Dickie Bird," says Andrew, "you're not doing a damn thing this weekend, you said so yourself. You might as well come to this tiny party, up on Potrero. The big love of a friend of mine is in from New York, and my friend wants to impress him with local talent. You can be the token straight."

And that is how Richard finds himself on Potrero Hill, in the very same bare flat in which Stella was interviewed (one more filament in the web that will bind them together). Although today the flat is somewhat less austere. For the party for Simon Daniels, his lover, Jacob has placed what look like tiny test tubes, each containing a single flower, a ranunculus, here and there. And in one corner there is a very discreet table of white wine and Perrier.

Simon Daniels is talking about the interview for which he ostensibly came to San Francisco—this odd woman named Stella Blake. "Quite an amazing young woman," says this New York product, this bald and spectacled Harvard-speaking (Richard imagines these to be Harvard vowels) person. "She grew up in a way that one might romanticize, all those marvelous dead poets, in the last old days in the village. And then there was her mother, the Mexican, Delia, the pal of Frida Kahlo, in fact the old man likes to suggest something going on between those two ladies, but *quién sabe,* and how would he know, any more than his poor biographer does?"

("It was almost as though he was trying to fix us up, advertising you to me," says Richard later to Stella. "But I was just scared.")

At the time, everyone laughs a little, as Richard wonders about all those names just dropped; the only one he caught and knew was Frida Kahlo, whose work he does know a little, sufficiently to arouse violently ambivalent feelings in himself: he sees the terrific skill, even the beauty. But all that blood, all those intensely female wounds—he finds this unbearable. She reminds him of something within himself, something hateful, frightful. Frightening.

However, Richard would like to make it clear to this group

that he knows who Frida Kahlo is. Was. He feels uneasy—not so much because everyone else is gay as because they all seem to have gone to Harvard, or some Ivy place, and although Richard has often been told that he sounds very Ivy, he painfully knows that he is just a good mimic, good with accents. He barely got through junior high, back in Paterson. He just reads a lot, mostly magazines and newspapers. He's good at remembering names and certain facts—usually irrelevant ones.

But before Richard can say "Frida Kahlo," this Simon Daniels is going on about Stella Blake, who certainly seems to have made an impression on the guy.

"Another thing about this little Ms. Blake," says Simon, with his twisted, owlish smile. "I got this from her name-dropping old father, never from herself, but she had a tremendous involvement with Liam O'Gara—you know, the director. All over the world together for a couple of years. The only time she managed to impress her father, I guess. Poor girl. She must have been a child at the time. But you'd never know it to look at her. And you'd think she might have mentioned this to me."

"No, I don't think," says thin-lipped Jacob, the minimalist. Simon's host, and lover.

Unperturbed, Simon smiles and goes on. "At first I was surprised. After all, O'Gara's probably the second coming of John Huston, but then when I met her and looked at her very carefully, I felt there was something, something not quite there yet but somehow present in her—"

"Maybe she's very sexy," Richard interrupts, in his deepest (most Ivy) voice. "I've met her; it could be that. A Mexican sexpot."

He did not mean to sound so crude (and his words now tremble in his own ears, extremely crude). But in this pansy-Ivy atmosphere almost anything he said would have come out sounding gross. And it is not even true; he did not think Stella Blake especially sexy. Or did he? And even to say he met her is an exaggeration; it is hard to remember her at all: someone small and dark at his door, with great huge eyes, looking frightened. He remembers a thin pale face, dark, very heavy but well-curved eyebrows, those big eyes, a small nose and a long mouth. A possibly tender face, vulnerable in the glare of his entrance light. As he concentrates he can see her entirely: the unstylish blazer, the wrong boots. The kind of woman he would never look at twice, except for something, some hint in her face—he is not sure of what. She looked intelligent but very uncertain, scared. Hard to imagine her as the heroine of some high-powered love affair, but maybe Liam O'Gara is really old and can't get the greatest girls anymore.

"An odd-looking woman, not exactly the great beauty her mother was," this Simon Daniels goes on. "But she'll change. Certain women hit their peak quite late."

"Such as they are," says Jacob.

"My dear, you are quite obsessed with this woman," says Andrew Bacci, to Simon.

"Well, hardly. I'm obsessed with this piece I have to write. And I hope her old man doesn't cash in before I can see him again."

And that is all there is about Stella Blake. The conversation dissolves into the usual trivia, discussions of San Francisco versus New York, of weather and of restaurants in both cities.

Homelessness in both cities.

AIDS. Dead friends.

Out of here. I have to get out of here, thinks Richard. It is less a thought than a cry from his blood. I have got to leave this place *now.*

He presses Andrew's arm, he whispers, "Later, Dog Shoes. Got to go. Say goodby for me, okay?"

This is the best he can manage, just before bolting out of the room. Away. Almost free. *Out of there.*

5

Love Affairs, of Sorts

Margot and her friend Andrew Bacci live quite near each other on Russian Hill, but in contrasting quarters. Margot's small, narrow rooms are filled with antiques, delicate woods, gilt frames and satin flounces, especially in the largest room, her bedroom. Lots of flounces in the bedroom. Whereas Andrew's more spacious and much more expensive digs are sleekly "contemporary": pale postmodern colors of wool and textured cotton and heavy, bright lacquered surfaces. Pale leather and high-tech steel.

Andrew really looks best in her apartment, Margot thinks—and would not tell Andrew, not for anything. On a Sunday morning, in his open-necked, broad-striped blue shirt, his black curls crisp above that pale smooth brow, and a few chest hairs just visible (the shirt is unbuttoned perhaps one button too low), as he stands and leans, so gracefully, against her small carved marble table, Andrew is truly ravishing. He should stand there always, he should always just be there for her to look at. Thinking this, Margot smiles as she offers him more coffee.

But Andrew is not smiling; he is talking seriously. (God, why do men always talk so much? Margot has repeatedly wondered this, even of beautiful Andrew, but she has come up with no answer.)

"... real recession," he is saying. "No matter what the feds are calling it. Things are very bad, and my private crystal balls are telling me it's getting worse. Lord, I may have to move."

Very little of this has got through to Margot. She never reads or watches any news, confining herself mostly to fashion magazines and memoirs, preferably of the very rich and sexually active. But she did quite clearly understand Andrew as he said, "... have to move."

"But, darling, wherever would you go?" she asks him, all sympathy.

"Oh, someplace south of Market, probably. Maybe Bluxome Street. Somewhere like that."

"Ugh." Margot shrugs theatrically. "I've never even been there."

"Or maybe Potrero. Richard and I took in a party there."

"Oh, you and Richard?" Margot giggles, believing it permissible to tease Andrew in this way.

But Andrew seems not to take this as teasing. Or to be not in the mood for teasing. "Yes, Richard and I went to a party, is that so odd? Really, Margot, Richard is possibly my closest friend."

He is so deadly serious, so unlike his usual light jokey self, that Margot is silenced, nonplussed, even as her mind records and dissects this exchange, and what she comes up with is a considerable surprise: Andrew actually *loves* Richard Fallon, Andrew is serious, he is in love with Richard, who everyone knows is a flirt but basically straight. Is Andrew mad?

"Well, darling, you mustn't move anywhere dreary like Potrero," she tells Andrew. "You can always move right in here with me." As she says this, Margot silently adds: Why not? I'd adore it. I adore you, beautiful Andrew.

Andrew, however (fatally), laughs. "Come on now, Margot. You're really not old enough to be my mom."

A rage so pure and cold that she almost faints fills Margot, rage and what is for her its inevitable concomitant: a seething lust. Covering her face with her hands, she begins to cough, hiding everything (she hopes). She coughs and coughs, as from behind those long tapering strong jeweled fingers she thinks, You rotten bastard, prick, how dare you, Andrew Bacci? I'll get you for this, you just wait. I'll really get you.

"Sweetie, what is wrong?" asks Andrew. "Are you having some sort of seizure? Can I get you some water?"

"No, darling, I'm really okay, honestly." Margot dabs at her eyes with a scrap of lace and linen, even as she is thinking, Really, how *dare* he? I'll kill him!

She asks, "How is dear Richard?"

In a doting, foolish way, Andrew laughs, confirming Margot's idea. "Oh, the same," Andrew says. "Absolutely brilliant and totally nuts. That guy has a certain streak in him." He smiles, his smile helpless and beautiful, and he pauses, looking marvelous, with those playful onyx eyes and that serious, perfect mouth. He says, "I think Richard's poised on the brink of some very big changes in his life."

"Do you possibly mean he too might move to Potrero Hill?" Margot giggles, knowing perfectly well that that, in a sense, is precisely what Andrew does mean—move along with him, Andrew means. He is the crazy one, perfectly nuts.

Andrew flushes, confirming all suspicions. "Nothing so specific," he mutters.

"Well, my darling Andrew, I think you're probably right on the button. What I see in the future for Richard is a most wonderful new love affair. Something very new for him, this time a truly major passion. One that will really knock him off his pins."

"You think so?" Eager Andrew, his eyes enlarged, mouth unguarded.

"Oh, absolutely. *Sans doute.* The only question is who. What marvelous hitherto unknown woman will deserve him or, more to the point, will get him? Do you think another blonde?"

Andrew smiles unpleasantly. "As you well know, dear Mar-

got, nothing could possibly interest me less than Richard's
blondes."

Understanding him well—and understanding too her own in-
clusion in what does not interest Andrew—Margot again is chilled
through with a trembling rage: Oh God, how dare he—how dare
he? She is forced to fake another coughing fit.

Too slowly, making it clear that he really does not care if
she chokes, Andrew gets up and goes into her tiny kitchen (in
which Margot almost never cooks) and brings her a glass of water. Some minutes after this she has stopped coughing.

And then, still standing, he tells her, "Well, baby, it's tennis
time for me."

Did he mention tennis earlier? Had they not actually planned
a walk, a small venture down to the wharves? Margot ponders
this after Andrew is gone, as she takes the glass and the coffee
cups back to the kitchen—which is worse than untidy, it's dirty,
no doubt making Andrew hate her all the more; she has got to
get a maid. On this especially brilliant day, even the rest of her
apartment looks dingy. She sees small stains and patches in the
gilt, streaks of dust on mahogany and rosewood; she sees shab-
biness and age everywhere. She is old, and everything she owns
is old and shabby. She should throw everything out, get everything better and brighter and more expensive. And get her face
done, all tucked and tightened and smoothed, and then maybe
that rotten Andrew would love her. Adorable Andrew, whom
Margot in her small secret ferocious heart adores.

"He's my kind of guy, absolutely," says Collin Schmidt,
the contractor, to his beloved Justine, as he pours thin rasp-
berry syrup over his large stack of buttermilk pancakes in the
sunny kitchen–dining room of his Mill Valley hillside house, designed and built by Collin and several times featured in various
magazines.

Collin is speaking of Richard Fallon, whom Justine has asked
about. Again. "Why do you ask?" says Collin.

"I just wondered. My friend Stella has an interview coming
up with him." And something in Stella's voice as she has men-

tioned this forthcoming interview has alerted Justine. Stella seems
so "interested." Meaning, in Stella's case, so defensive and vulnerable, and slightly off balance. And so, on behalf of her friend,
Justine probes.

And she thinks how very nice this Collin is. He is so nice
and so unfamiliar in his niceness that Justine hardly knows what
to do with him and thus will do nothing, probably.

"All the guys loved him," says Collin, whose teeth are large
and strong and white, whose mustache is pepper-and-salt, just
now reddened here and there with syrup, which he wipes at with
a very large blue bandanna handkerchief. "The workmen loved
him, I mean. He gets right down into it with them, if you know
what I mean. Rolls up his sleeves and just goes. He can do as
good a job as any of them can, and they know it." Collin laughs,
somewhat self-consciously. "Only thing is, he has this really
dumb name for me. Calls me Bunny. Can you beat that? *Bunny.*"

"Bunny," Justine murmurs, ambiguously. But of course she
is clearly and cruelly aware of what Richard must mean: Collin
is bunny-like, smooth and clean and sweet and good, and (probably) easy to scare off. Whatever else may be said of him, this
Richard is not stupid, Justine decides.

"But I hope your friend doesn't get what we might call a
romantic interest in Richard," cautions Collin, somewhat surprisingly. "He's hell on the ladies. I knew his first wife, Marina;
we go back that far. He really gave her a hard time, although
she's a pretty crazy dame. But she's a real straight shooter, no
fancy talk."

"Was she good-looking?" asks Justine.

"Well, in the early days quite a knockout. A big tall blonde.
His second wife too, tall blonde. I guess that's what he likes."

"Do they look like him?" asks Justine.

"Like Richard?" Collin laughs uncomfortably, slightly disturbed at the notion of male-female resemblance. "Oh no, not a
bit; they were all woman, both of them. But he really gave Marina a bad time over that other one, the one he married after
Marina threw him out. Finally."

"Marina threw him out?"

"Oh yes, right smack on his you-know-what. He didn't know

what hit him. He thought—and he actually told me this—thought Marina'd forgive and forget. Been married to her all those years, and he didn't know the first thing about that woman. I still wouldn't be surprised if he went back to her someday, though. In a way they belong together."

From Collin's hill Justine can see more hills, all scattered with pretty, widely spaced suburban houses. She feels as though she has fallen back into some time warp; at least the externals in this sunny peaceful place have changed so little since the Fifties.

Could she live in such a place, maybe find enough peace to write the novel that is always somewhere in her head? That is the question, and so far Justine has found no answer, although she is sure that the answer lies within her, as clear and definite as a piece of stone. When she finds it she will think, Oh, of course, why didn't I see that before?

Collin even has nice children, of whom he is modestly proud. Two daughters, married now and living somewhere around, and a son, whom Collin describes as "a little too handsome for his own good." The son is a doctor.

Could she, at her age, possibly become a stepmother? Justine almost blushes with discomfort at the thought.

But when she really thinks of Collin, what most frequently comes to mind is not his children or all that sunny Mill Valley peace: what Justine thinks of, often, is Collin in bed. The sexual Collin. And he is, in that regard, quite a piece of work, as Justine puts it to herself, with a small pleased private smile—as she could not say, possibly, to anyone else (not even to Stella, who would certainly be very interested; they just don't talk like that). For Collin, sexually, is something else. Indefatigable, enthusiastic, sensitive, generous and kind—he is truly an amazing lover. Justine does not see how she could ever give him up, and she hopes (sometimes) that this does not mean that she has to marry him.

"Bunny." Collin, beside her in the sun, chuckles. "Can you beat that?"

She leans over to kiss his mouth. "No," says Justine. "I can't."

6

The Interview

"You could sit here. Pretend you're a client," Richard suggests, indicating the small bentwood chair across from his desk, and he smiles at her, radiantly, his private radiance fuelling the magnificence of his room, by which Stella is already both bedazzled and confused. She feels herself diminished, and somehow darkened, dimmed, so large is the scale, so brilliant and beautiful the composition of gilt and oil and wood, of mirror glass, of prisms and polished brass globes. But mostly it is the radiance of Richard himself that dazzles Stella, her sense of his warmth, his energy: he is like a sun.

They have hit on this somewhat odd hour for an interview, nine-thirty at night, as the only one possible for them both for days. Stella on this evening was suddenly sent to cover a convention of social workers at a hotel in Berkeley, a dinner meeting.

And so, having taken BART back from Berkeley, here she is, in this room, almost unable to sit down as she is bidden.

Curiously, as soon as she does sit down she is visited by a very strong longing for a drink, odd, since she barely drinks anything alcoholic. But just now she would give anything for a glass of wine, anything. Apparently, though, she cannot say this to Richard Fallon.

Who almost immediately (telepathically?) says, "What can I offer you to drink? I've got—I've got some champagne on ice, or do you really sophisticated types all dislike champagne?"

"I love champagne," Stella lies. "I'm not all that sophisticated. I don't think I am at all. . . ."

"You sure have it all over me," he tells her. "With your background. I've been really nervous. . . ." The sentence trails off, as he walks into some other area, all darkened.

Minutes later, minutes during which Stella has tried and failed to get used to her surroundings, even in the most casual sense, Richard returns with a champagne bottle and two frosted tulip glasses on a small enamelled tray, which he places on his desk.

More defiantly than she meant to, Stella asks him, "What do you mean, my background?" And then, checking herself, she reminds him, "I'm supposed to be interviewing you, remember?" And she laughs, suddenly fortified by the first small sip of wine—and remembering that somewhere along the line she forgot to eat dinner.

Richard sits down behind his desk, as light from the candelabra feathers his hair. He laughs, very friendly. "I won't be mysterious. This is such a small town. I went to a party with a friend, or not exactly a friend—a guy I know."

Stella wonders, Why all this elaboration about who he went with?

"And there was this man who'd just met and interviewed you, about your old man, I guess. Prentice Blake?"

"Yes. A man called Simon Daniels interviewed me. Sort of."

"Daniels. Right. Nice guy. Thank God I'm not all hung up about gays. I readily admit I could have gone that way myself, under certain circumstances. Say out at sea or something. Anyway I liked Daniels. I like a lot of those guys."

"Sure. Me too." But Stella does not quite know what to make of his tone, or of the peculiar excited energy he seems to emit, with his restless gestures, his glancing, lively eyes, as he leans toward her.

"Anyway," Richard tells her excitedly, "Daniels was really impressed with you. On and on about all the people your folks know, that you grew up with, I guess. Jesus, I can't even remember the names. Not that I recognized most of them. Frida Kahlo?"

A little defensively, Stella explains, "For me it wasn't like growing up with famous people. I thought they were just a bunch of old drunks who hung out with my father. Has-beens. All of them fairly seedy, no money or clothes. To me it just seemed disorderly, and sort of scary." Stella thinks, I must be getting drunk; I never talk so much. And she goes on talking. "There were all these wives all the time, their new wives, and a lot of shouting at the parties. I was scared. I liked it better in Mexico, where I lived with my grandmother, Serena. Sometimes. In Oaxaca. She sold flowers in the market there, and her house was very small and tidy and quiet."

A long pause envelops them both, and then Richard says, very quietly, "You probably don't tell a lot of people about Serena."

"Oh, well, not too many, I guess." Actually Stella rather likes talking about Serena, and she has tried to write about her, the problem being to describe Serena as she was, gnarled dirty feet and smelly aprons and all, without sentimentalizing. But she cannot just now (if ever) explain all that to Richard; she does not want to contradict what seems curiously important to him, or to break the very strange mood between them that now seems to fill this room, like music or the scent of flowers. She smiles, and speaks very gently. "But we're supposed to be talking about you." She pauses. "How about your parents? Do they still live back East?"

Richard stares at her, his face bare and haunted, and then, startlingly, terribly, his face contracts, contorts, his features for one instant twisted, before he covers it with his hands.

Stella feels panic: is he going to cry? Her experience with the weeping of men has been horrifying: it is so violent, and they hate it so. She saw her father cry drunkenly, a couple of times, usually wild ugly tears of rage. And Liam O'Gara once, when his youngest son had drowned in a flood, in Spain.

But when Richard uncovers his face it is pale, dry of tears and empty; Stella has never seen such a frightening blank. "My father killed my mother," he tells her, flat-voiced. "He was drunk and he shot her. I was out with a friend and came home to find all these cops and no parents. Nobody much cared, a drunk Irish bartender and his housekeeper wife. It barely made the papers, and he got put away for thirty years. He's out now, for all I know. But that's why I left town." He stares at Stella—who notes that a little color and some expression have come back into his face. An expression that she is unable to read, however.

"I've never told anyone that before," Richard tells her. "I wonder why you?"

"I don't know." Stella has found this hard to believe, his choosing her to tell; nevertheless she has trouble with her voice, and her breath.

He says, "There must be something that relates us."

"I . . . guess."

"Maybe we'll find out what it is."

For Stella this is both melodramatic and vague. It feels false. B-film, as Liam would have put it. But very likely she is being hard, she thinks; she knows that she tends to be judgmental. This man is in some pain, and he has confided in her, for whatever reasons.

But all this precludes the possibility of an interview, she vaguely feels.

Still staring at her, Richard speaks very slowly. "I think I'll take you home now, if that's okay."

Does he mean take her home and then to bed, to make love? Stella has not the slightest idea of his intention, and Richard gives no clue. She is not at all sure that she wants that, such a sudden collision with a man she does not know, not at all. And does not quite entirely trust: something is wrong; how could she trust him? (And besides, this isn't the Sixties; you're not supposed to do that anymore, just fall into bed with someone new.) But the very idea, the bare small possibility that they might later on make love, is enough to take her breath, as together they stand up and walk out of his studio, and onto the street, to his car.

And all across the city, North Beach to Van Ness Avenue, out Sacramento Street, Clay, and then Lake, to the Richmond, where Stella lives—all that way, Stella wonders what they are up to, just what they are doing together, in this cool fog-ridden night. At the same time her mind crowds with more familiar anxieties: just how clean is her house, should he mean to come in? And more basically, she wonders about her own person: she showered this morning, but is she still all perfectly, fragrantly clean?

These anxieties cloud the more real question of what it is that she really wants to do, assuming that she has some choice. What does she really want of Richard?

His car is an old convertible. Insensitive to cars, a non-driver, Stella has no idea of make or year. But the broad deep seats and cracked leather remind her of her adolescence somewhere. Drives out to Long Island, when she was a New York kid.

"It's a funny old car," remarks Richard, at the exact moment of these thoughts in Stella's mind. A coincidence, undoubtedly, but one that Stella notes: it is when she begins to think that he can read her mind.

"You probably haven't seen a car like this since you were a kid," says Richard.

"That's right; I was thinking that. Though I really don't know much about cars," she tells him.

And a little later, "This is where I live," says Stella.

He stops, and parks, and very chivalrously he comes around to her side of the car and hands her out.

He walks along with her to the half-lit entranceway, where, with a long and deliberate unfolding of himself, he bends down to take her in his arms, to meet her mouth in a kiss of surpassing sweetness. And of, for Stella, the most instant and violent excitement.

Then, very gently disengaging himself, Richard speaks what is obviously meant as a parting note. "You're lovely. I'll call you. Or you call me if you want to."

He turns and goes back to his car, as Stella, fumbling as usual with her key, almost expects to hear his returning steps behind her: he will change his mind?

But what she next hears is the starting up of his car, as she turns to watch him swing out into the street.

And he is gone.

7

Beginning

Fortunately for Stella, in the days and weeks following her "interview" or whatever that was with Richard Fallon, she is busy. The social worker piece led, somewhat circuitously, to another, an interview with a young Mexican-American priest who works with pregnant girls, boys with AIDS—all high school kids, out in the Mission District. A priest who has come into considerable conflict with the Church's higher powers. Reflecting that she has not met a very young priest for a very long time, Stella finds herself very moved by this boy, who cannot be much over twenty, and all that he faces: illness, opprobrium, very possibly excommunication. She guesses that he is gay, which could give him another set of consequences to face.

And she goes down to Stanford to interview two experts on Central America: one from the Hoover Institute, a willowy Yalie type, with a confusing accent compounded of Yale and New Jersey, who speaks clearly and succinctly of the need for a U.S.-backed police force; the other a Salvadoran poet, small and lithe, rather beautiful, who raises his hands very gracefully in sheer despair at the poverty and corruption and sheer ignorance among his people. "I am Mexican," Stella tells him (they have been speaking in Spanish). "My feelings for my own people are as yours are. I see little hope on either of our horizons."

She goes home with a heavy sack of discouraging tapes—and in her dreams that night she compounds all those men, the young priest and the two academics, and herself, the supposedly objective reporter. In the dream she is actually a sort of spy, and she does not know for whom.

Though busy, she thinks of Richard Fallon often, and with a curious discomfort. She feels that he has claimed her somehow—as though he still held her tightly by one wrist. As though by telling her his melodramatic black secret (and was it even true? did his father really kill his mother, as he said?) and then by kissing her, as he did, he had set her aside, in some way, so that now she is forced to wait around, to see what he does next. And she thinks, He can't have been serious when he said that I should call him; why would I? But she looks up his number in the phone book and then is unable to forget it.

She explains to Justine as best she can that she will probably not do the interview with Richard Fallon. "I think he really deserves Malcolm." Malcolm is the paper's aged art critic, brilliant, acerbic and alcoholic, and probably dying of emphysema. "He's not just an advertising type," Stella tells Justine, of Richard. "His studio is really something; it's amazing. I'm not up to it. And besides, it got sort of out of hand. I don't mean he came on to me, it wasn't like that. I mean I think he's a little out of control. Around women. Or maybe it's just me. I don't know."

At all of which Justine smiles wisely and comes to her own conclusions. Which she does not communicate to Stella.

* * *

Stella was waiting to be kissed again. At times it all came to
that, she thought. The sweet pressure of their mouths together,
their bodies, for that long instant. Standing at her door, in the
porch light. It was the kiss that she thought of, remembered, was
somehow imprinted with. It was as though that kiss had begun
some process within her that had to be continued, perhaps con-
cluded. And Stella was not sure that actual sex would be the
logical ending. It could be simply more kissing, she thought.

And she also thought, He really is so vain. That studio of his
is a sort of temple to himself. On the other hand, it is very
beautiful—as he is. Richard Fallon is an exceptionally handsome
man, and if he is somewhat vain about his looks, so what?

Thinking such thoughts, Stella walks through the brilliant
false-green, false-spring woods in the Presidio, near her house. In
November, after one more month of drought. She is struck by
the blackness of the trees, and the bright clear blue of the afternoon, and she thinks, I would like to be in love with someone
again.

That is the night that he calls her. The phone rings just as
she gets in from her walk, as though he knew just when that
would be.

"It's me—Richard," he says, as though he knew that she
would be more or less waiting for his call. "I know it's late, but
I've been away, and I really want to see you before I have to go
away again. Tonight. Could we possibly have dinner?"

Stella's plan for that night was soup and a bath and early
to bed with some magazines. She has already made the soup,
Serena's recipe, a meatball soup, and so, without much thought,
she says to Richard, "I've made a sort of Mexican soup. It's good
if you like cilantro. And some salad. Would that be enough?"

"Sounds great. I love cilantro. You really cook?" He laughs.
"Actually I do too. But my wives never cooked."

I'm not your wife, and I have no plans along those lines,
Stella thinks of pointing out. She is suddenly tired of him and
wishes that she had not asked him to dinner. A drink would
have been sufficient. But she only says, "I sometimes cook."

"Great," he repeats. "I'll bring some wine, okay? Anything else?"

Again, without calculation, Stella tells him what is true. "I need some scallions for the salad. If you could."

"Of course, nothing easier than scallions. Or lighter, for that matter." Again the laugh—deep, almost theatrical.

And so he arrives, with a small domestic-looking paper bag, scallion tops just prettily showing (arranged to show?), two bottles of wine in another bag. A small sheaf of purple irises.

He comes in and puts the things down without kissing her, Stella notes. He only smiles. They could have been married for years.

He looks very odd in her surroundings, Stella thinks, over their pre-dinner glasses of wine. So fair, so composed, in his perfect just-shabby old tweed jacket and trim gray flannels, he seems another order of physical presence, as though the molecules and atoms that make up his being have no connection with anything else in the room. (With her.)

But their conversation at dinner seems ordinary enough. Divorced-man talk, of the sort that Stella has heard before, with variants. Several times.

"I was totally knocked out," he says, speaking of the time when his first wife, Marina, asked him for a divorce. "You know, the old saw: I thought it couldn't happen to me. I thought Marina and I were forever, no matter what. I thought I could talk her out of it, and so I suggested a weekend in La Jolla, where we used to go on vacations sometimes, and she said that was just like me, appealing to her weakness. Sex."

Saying that last word, "sex," Richard's eyes flick up at Stella: is he asking how she feels about it? She gives him the tiniest frown, thinking all this a little obvious, and very bluntly she asks him, "Did Marina know about Claudia?"

His frown is deeper than hers. "You really get right at it, don't you. Well, she sort of knew. Strongly suspected. Jesus, she wasn't blind. But she could have been wrong, you know what I mean? And that wouldn't have made any difference to her. She's a really punitive woman. Eyes for eyes and teeth for teeth."

Stella does see what he means, but she finds his logic a little skewed.

He gets up and brings in another bottle of wine. Admiring his walk, and his deft hands and the grace of his wrists, Stella also thinks, This is too much wine, but it tastes marvelous, such fun to have so much. She tells him, "This is really good wine."

"I don't know the first thing about wine. You probably do. Claudia did. Jesus, she was a walking wine encyclopedia."

"I'm not; I don't know much about it either." And Stella notes the old male trick, often observed before: the setting up of women against each other. Inciting them to compete. She will not do that, she vows, no matter how many ex-wives he trots out.

She notes too that his eyes are perhaps one centimeter too close together; they are large and beautiful and blue-gray, with an odd shading of yellow. Beautiful eyes but, yes, too close.

"I don't know much about anything is the truth of it," he tells her. "I may be the most ignorant person you ever met, bookwise."

"I haven't read all that much myself." But actually she has; Stella has read a great deal, by most standards. Why with Richard does she feel that she has to apologize for all that reading?

"You must let me cook for you next time," he then says. "I'm not too bad at cooking. Jesus, I had to be good. Marina couldn't cook worth a damn; she's basically not interested in food—anorexic, I suspected. And Claudia, she thought it was something maids did. Her kids loved my cooking. That's something I still miss, cooking for Claudia's boys. I even made their box lunches."

"My father could cook," Stella tells him, and then wishes she had not. She adds, "Just a few things."

"Do you go back to New York to see him very much?"

"Not much, but I should go soon. He's pretty sick, and he's really old. In his eighties now."

"I never go back there. I despise New York." Richard's violence comes as a shock; it is even a little scary. Stella represses an impulse to calm him by saying that she too hates New York, which would have been a lie. She loves the city; she would like to go there more often—if she had more money. And if she did not have to see Prentice and her stepmother, mean Alexandra, on each visit. Her mother, Delia, died while Stella was in college.

"I think you look a little younger than you are," Richard tells her quite suddenly, staring at her. "You have a sort of child's face; just at this moment you look like a child, you could be a little girl. All flat surfaces, like children have. Not quite beautiful but interesting, very."

Feeling herself flush, Stella gets up. "I'll bring in the salad," she tells him.

Throughout all that more or less inconsequential conversation, the air between them has been heavily charged: with sexuality, of course, but also with some other quality. They are like two people walking through a thick fog, close together, feeling their way. Unable to separate but at the same time aware of the accident that has placed them together, and they wonder, Why us? why us together?

This charge between them, this tension, becomes more marked as they leave the dinner table and go into the living room, with the after-dinner bourbons that are Richard's idea.

They stop talking, there on the dark lumpy sofa, and they look at each other, still wondering. To break that look, to break something, Richard smiles, a small shy smile, and he gets up to fix more bourbon.

Returning, handing her the drink, he then asks, "Shall we fall madly in love, do you think? Have a really tremendous affair?"

This makes no sense, has no context, but it is so much what Stella has wanted to hear—no man for a long time in her life has mentioned love—that she forgets that for stretches of this evening she has not liked Richard very much. Her heart dances out to him as she dizzily smiles, as she moves toward his kiss.

He is clumsier, more boyish than Stella would have imagined, pulling at her blouse, holding her too hard, but he is still very arousing, especially his mouth, which never leaves her mouth. An endless kiss.

After a long time of this sweet kissing, touching, groping at each other (how long it was, Stella could have no clear idea), in the midst of their breathy, steaming silence, with what seems terrific abruptness, Richard announces, "This is crazy, but I have to leave for Carmel. I mean right now. They're shooting a big spread on Point Lobos, some damn thing. . . ."

Gently disengaging himself, he stands up, and Stella stands too. For more kissing. A long farewell.

"Try to think of me," he says, with his smile. "I'll call you. Whenever I can."

Unused to drinking (in the old days with Liam she always drank diet Cokes, which for him was part of her childish charm), Stella spends the next two or three days in the throes of a fiendish hangover. Streaks of pain attack her eyes, her throat; her stomach is held in a twisting vise.

Fortunately this is a weekend for which she did not have urgent plans, and so she can simply lie about in bed. And wait for the phone to ring.

Richard calls several times a day, but it is mostly to tell her about the shoot. "Wouldn't you know, the heaviest fog of the year," he tells her. "You can't see your own face, much less anything out in front of it. And the birds are totally refusing cooperation; they'd rather sleep." And he says, "Oh, I can't wait to see you! Do you miss me at all?"

"All the time. I feel terrible."

He laughs, sounding pleased. "You're in love. Those are the signs. You can't eat, right?"

"Yes. No."

Perhaps she is—in love. Is love the true meaning of this illness that she experiences? This sick derangement, this inability to eat or sleep? Surely those are the classic symptoms, as he says, if slightly schoolgirlish ones. But Stella tends to yield to the feeling. She thinks of storybook-handsome Richard, and she thinks, Oh, I love him!

Two days later, Sunday night, having called from South Palo Alto ("Can you believe there is such a place?"), Richard arrives at her door, tired and unshaven. Incredibly beautiful.

And again Stella feeds him some soup and bread and wine—between kisses, endearments, small laughs of astonishment.

And at last, amid cries of love and of sheer wonder at their luck at finding each other, in being together so freely, they go off to bed. And at last they make love. All night.

At some point in the middle of that long night Stella awakens from a dream—a dream of flowers, of lovely pale-pink plum blossoms on a dark twisted bough. She smiles to herself at the triteness, the corny metaphor, but that is what she dreamed. Of the loveliest flowers.

8

A New Romance

After that first night of love, Stella and Richard begin to see each other every night, and the pattern of their evenings together rarely varies from what they so early on established:

Richard arrives, bearing wine and sometimes bourbon, often flowers, and after an endless, languishing kiss at the door they settle in the living room for several drinks, for talking and kissing. Next they proceed to the kitchen for whatever needs to be done in terms of cooking. Richard takes an active part; he makes salads, or a mustard sauce for salmon steaks, he peels potatoes and chops up parsley.

With dinner they drink a lot of wine, but before quite having finished either their food or their wine they rush off to bed. To love.

In the morning Richard brings orange juice to Stella, who is still in bed. She gets up, and while he shaves and showers she does a few dishes, clearing up some of the mess from the night before. Then she makes coffee and toast, often bacon and eggs: Richard thinks all the fuss about cholesterol is silly.

There is no time in all that for Stella to wash and dress, and besides, Richard is in the bathroom. By the time he leaves she feels somewhat frowsy, and eager for her shower, her own clean clothes and makeup. But generally she does not have to be at the paper at a specified time; she and Richard both lead more or less free-lance lives, which for the moment seems to work out well. It does not matter at what precise time they start their days, although sometimes Stella does wish that hers could begin a little earlier.

When they talk, it is mostly about how they feel about each other, the wonder of it all—including invidious comparisons with others. And they give much mutual praise, endless praise. Richard finds odd and interesting things to praise in Stella: "Your knees are so beautiful, I love your knees. I love the way you move around in the kitchen, all your motions are so vague. I never saw anyone slice a tomato in midair before."

This marvelous particularity as much as anything that he says convinces Stella of love (or almost), but sometimes she thinks that she would rather have been a woman to whom he said, You're so beautiful, I love your face (as he must have said to Claudia, and possibly to Marina). Sometimes in the mornings he will gently whisper to her, "Oh! you were so lovely last night," with great feeling; but this refers, she feels, to how she makes love rather than to her person.

It is not so much that he makes her feel non-beautiful (whereas with Liam she always felt very beautiful, his beautiful child) as that, with Richard, she becomes so concentrated on how she looks. In an obsessive way she thinks of her face, her body, and particularly her clothes, for suddenly nothing that she owns seems right, seems worthy. The skirts and pants, the sweaters and shirts that she normally wears all seem so dowdy and old.

To remedy this, Stella goes downtown one afternoon just for shopping, but she can find nothing—or nothing that she can be sure Richard will like.

Outside the store, on Sutter Street, she suddenly sees Richard's unmistakable old convertible, with Richard driving, alone. In an instant she could have hailed him, but she does not, and so he passes on, not seeing her.

Heavyhearted, Stella continues on to the newspaper office, in her old boots, old skirt and blazer. She is aware that if she had been wearing something smart and new she would have called out to Richard, and they could have gone out to lunch, in a festive way.

Or is all this disapproval only in her own head? Some neurotic transference of disapproval from disapproving Prentice, her (mostly) mean father? Stella simply does not know.

That night she says to Richard, "Oh, I saw you driving by today on Sutter Street, and I almost called out to you, but I was in such a hurry."

"Oh, me too, sweetie. God, what a day!"

But this is all wrong, Stella knows it is. If she had seen Justine in her car on Sutter Street, or even Margot, any friend, she would have called out, Hi! She would have been pleased at the chance that put them together at that moment downtown. Why could she not call out to Richard?

This concentration on the surface of herself is all wrong, she knows that it is wrong.

For a couple of days, and into the nights, there is suddenly a heat wave; unseasonal, everyone says unseasonal, and the papers carry articles about the untoward effects of the winter heat: people fainting, swimming in the highly polluted bay. And there are pictures of sunbathers, strewn all over the city's high green parks. Many trees, mistaking the season, put forth great bursts of generous pink blossoms.

What to wear?

Reaching into her closet, Stella finds a long bright-pink cotton dress from Oaxaca. She puts it on, before hurrying into the kitchen for the last touches on a special cold fish soup that she is making, with red peppers and cilantro.

"Sweetie, you look—oh! you look so beautiful," Richard exclaims as he enters, then he holds her off to look at. Before kissing her, again and again. "Beautiful!" he repeats, and he laughs. "Funny I never quite saw it before."

She asks him, "It's the pink you like?" She is thinking, I could buy everything pink from now on.

"I guess, although I wouldn't have thought so. But that particular shade, it's perfect for you." A deep laugh. "When I'm in a position to pick out all your clothes, I'll keep that shade in mind."

Does he mean that he plans to marry her, that he wants them to get married? At least half aware that she does not want to marry Richard—although much in love, she sees that marriage would be a mistake—Stella is still made anxious by this ambiguity. What could he mean?

"You know, you could do a lot with this place." Richard gestures at the somewhat dingy, mostly empty space around them: Stella's flat, on a Saturday afternoon that Richard has devoted, househusband-like, to washing windows.

"Really? How?" But even asking this, Stella is apprehensive: he will mean that she should spend a lot of money, buy good furniture, rugs, big plants, gold-framed mirrors. Like some of the things in his studio. And she is so broke, always doing small sums in her head for survival: pay MasterCard so much, so much to Macy's, a lot to her dentist. Richard probably has no idea how little money she has; he would be horrified if he knew. Maybe love her less.

But he does not say furniture. "If you opened it out," he says, with large gestures (always in the core of his gestures there is a gentle turn of his wrists, which Stella finds infinitely moving). "All these walls," he says. "And that tiny window. It should be open across that whole wall, so you'd see all the green out there.

Then you could just throw out all your furniture. Buy a few big cushions from Cost Plus, and sit around and admire your view. But don't throw out your bed; we need that."

This is all so evidently, eminently impractical that Stella laughs. "Oh great, just knock out a few walls and cut some big picture windows. Mr. Wong would really go for that."

Pleased with himself, Richard smiles. "Have you ever asked him? He just might. Improve his property."

"He scares me. I don't even dare ask him if I could get a cat, which I used to want."

"Before you got me, right?" He takes her into his arms. "Do you know what I love about your face? The way your forehead curves. It's so nice. I could sculpt it, if I could sculpt."

They laugh, and kiss, and decide it's time for a nap.

They drink a lot, but for the moment this is not worrying to Stella. It is simply so much fun. Old-fashioneds before dinner, and each night some good new California wine with the meal, and maybe more wine, or maybe bourbon highballs after dinner. Which they often take to bed and do not get around to drinking. (Horrible, though, is the smell of bourbon in the morning.)

And there are other, more surprising times of drinking, invented by Richard: Bloody Marys at breakfast (not exactly original, but something Stella has never done before). Or bullshots. A bottle of champagne in the middle of a Sunday afternoon, for no reason at all. Margaritas for lunch, beer for breakfast. Gin and tonic in a dark cool bar on a hot afternoon. Not all of this every day, of course not, but almost every day, in one way or another, they do a lot of drinking. And for the moment it seems very festive, a way of heightening their pleasure in each other. Even of intensifying their love.

We don't go out very much, Stella sometimes thinks. No concerts or plays or even neighborhood movies. At most, on a weekend, they may go for a drive to look at the ocean; on rare occasions they go to restaurants. But dinners out are less successful, generally, than eating at home; they both feel this. They are happier cooking together, eating and hurrying off to bed.

This is their pattern—their shtick, as Richard sometimes calls it—and they are both somewhat afraid to break it.

9

Friends of Friends

"Your friends won't necessarily love me as much as you do,"
Richard tells Stella, one Saturday at breakfast. They are eating
late, and eating too much: bullshots, and then bagels and lox and
scrambled eggs and too much coffee. Stella has just come back
from the telephone with an invitation to a cocktail party at Justine's. A week from Sunday.

"I should hope not." Stella laughs, but inwardly she acknowl-
edges that he is right. What she herself loves in Richard—and
even now she would have a hard time defining it, finding any
words for what seems pure feeling—what she is in love with in
Richard, might not appeal or even be apparent to her friends. He
is not their type would be one way to put it. He is extremely
bright; in his own way he may well be a genius (Stella thinks he
is), but his brilliance is not the sort that her friends are used to.

And he is much too handsome, and he dresses too well, is too conscious of his clothes. "Superficial" would be the easiest word for a dismissal of Richard. (Can a person be deeply superficial? Disloyally, Stella has wondered.)

And then there is the question of Richard's own friends, about whom Stella has no fixed notion. From what she can make out, he seems to know people from two distinct groups: work-men compose the first. He is especially close to a cabinetmaker named Tony Russo, whom Richard inexplicably calls Cats. Tony has a new girlfriend, named Valerie; apparently Richard and Tony discuss their love affairs with each other—unusual for men, in Stella's experience.

"But why do you call him Cats?"

Richard laughs. "He looks like a cat. A small brown cat."

"Oh."

"Don't you like cats? You could get one."

"I meant to get a dog or a cat, I've told you. Actually I don't know too much about cats."

"You'll have to meet my Cats."

Richard's other group of friends could be described as "so-cial." Rich and stylish types, addicted to parties, openings, boats and skiing. People, Stella gathers, whom he knew through Clau-dia and now does not see very much. But there is something in his voice when Richard mentions these people, their houses and parties and trips, that Stella finds disturbing. Ostensibly he puts them down, he makes jokes about how dumb and silly they are, but still Stella feels that on some level he misses his life in that group, and for all she knows he misses Claudia. She wonders too just how accepting all those people, including Claudia, really were of her handsome Richard: did they possibly find him beautiful but not quite right, in their own terms? The clothes a little too much, the accent slightly off?

And just why is Stella herself having such thoughts as these, projecting snobberies worthy of her father at his worst? (Pren-tice, in what have literally been his declining years, has begun to sound much as his Edwardian mother must have sounded: full of complaints and comments about accents and clothes—observations that in better and stronger times he would have considered beneath his notice.) Why does Stella at this point sound like her father? Is she herself, underneath it all, as much of a snob as he?

"This is our enchanted cottage," Richard tells her. "We're probably wise not to let anyone else come in."

But that can't last very long, has been one of Stella's reactions. And is that what he really has in mind—something very intense (God knows they are intense) and brief?

The very next day Richard calls Stella at the paper to ask her, "How would you feel about meeting Cats and Valerie for dinner? He's found some place out in the Mission with fabulous food and great music. Want to give it a try?"

Fighting anxiety—an unaccountable wave of panic has hit her at the mention of this innocent plan—Stella says, "Sure! Great."

Tony Russo, Richard's Cats, is indeed a small brown man, with brown hair and weathered brown skin, brown beard, and long serious brown eyes. Stella does not see the cat resemblance, but then, as she has told Richard, she does not know much about cats. Cats's new girlfriend, Valerie, is a very large blonde, with big teeth and prominent breasts, huge blue eyes that are blackly lined and lashed. She wears a tight white sweater, a short black skirt that shows long legs in black net stockings. They have just met, just fallen in love, she and Tony—Cats—and they are all over each other, hands clutching and groping, unchaste kisses exchanged. As the two couples face each other in a green plastic booth. In the Jump Room, in the Outer Mission.

They are drinking margaritas. This is a Mexican place; at one end of the room, an enthusiastic mariachi group, in taut black pants, flowing ties and large black hats, is singing an endless ballad of love and betrayal and blood. From the ceiling, Christmas decorations are still suspended, tinfoil angels and stars, dusty green plastic wreaths.

"You feel right at home here?" Richard whispered this to Stella as they first came in and sat down. His smile was teasing.

"Well, not exactly." But she smiled too, as though she really liked it anyway.

In any case, she does not feel at home with Tony and Valerie. She tells herself that they are very good, nice, kind and generally well-intentioned people (probably), especially Tony; she can see how Richard would like him and feel at home with him. But they express themselves in ways that she is unused to, that she cannot fall in with.

"You're Mexican?" Tony asks her, early on, having clearly been primed by Richard (but she wonders: Exactly what did Richard say, explaining her to Tony?).

"Uh, yes. My mother's Mexican."

"I love Mexicans." Tony beams.

"Me too." Saying this, Valerie looks at Tony. "They're so— so *real.*"

But my mother wasn't real at all, Stella does not say. My mother, Delia, had dyed-blond hair and did not even look very Mexican, not in one of the thousands of ways of looking "Mexican." My mother was ashamed of her own mother, Serena, the vendor of flowers; when we visited Serena in Oaxaca, my mother pretended to be a tourist. And going to Dalton and Hunter College did not exactly fill me with national pride. But none of this seems possible to explain, certainly not now, in this group.

"These drinks are just so good," says Valerie, beaming, to Tony. "I just don't care if they make me drunk. Or fat."

"Baby, I love every ounce you've got." Tony beams back.

"These are good margaritas," Stella tells Richard. A lie: the drinks are much too sweet.

"You don't think they're a little too sweet?" he counters, frowning.

"Well, I guess."

Across the table Tony and Valerie are kissing—again. Do they love each other more than we do? Stella wonders. Accept each other more? She feels very stiff and uncomfortable. Lost. Unconnected to Richard, as though whatever bond had drawn and bound them together had dissolved in this smoky, noisy air. Or perhaps had never existed; perhaps it was false and all wrong from the start.

They all drink more margaritas, and eventually they eat: platters of shrimp, some beans and enchiladas, which Tony proclaims the best, the most authentic, he ever had. To which Richard shouts agreement (everyone seems to have forgotten the supposed Mexican among them, Stella notes). In fact Tony and Valerie do not address Stella at all; they talk between themselves, and occasionally one or the other of them will toss a small speech across the table in Richard's general direction—a speech having to do with their own love affair, their grand passion.

Valerie: "Can you believe this guy? The first time we went out, I thought if he didn't kiss me I'd die."

Tony: "This little girl's got the greatest singing voice you ever heard, I'm telling you. She's going places. She's something else."

And so on, all night.

"Because you're a fucking snob, and they could feel it. What do you think they are, insensitive?"

Richard, lurching and accusatory, holds to the frame of the door, Stella's door, which they have just come through. Any minute he will leave, will rush back out into the night, rush dangerously across the city, in his open car. Gone. Maybe dead. She will never see him again.

Stella experiences ferocious anxiety. Panic. A huge bird caged in her chest beats its wings against her ribs. Insufferable. She cannot let him go.

"Well, actually I'm not really snobbish, or I don't think I am. I liked them a lot, I really did. I think they're very nice," she chatters, in a whisper. "I really did like them."

"You did not like them, and they felt it. I'm not so sure you like me either." Richard's face is swollen, darkened, his eyes a glowering dark gray, the color of storm clouds, of storms.

And then, more suddenly than seems possible, he is gone, gone faster than Stella could imagine. No way to run after him now. She hears the slam of his car door, the engine's start into motion, as her heart beats more loudly than any other sound.

Quite irrationally—he could be anywhere now but in his studio—almost at once she begins to dial his number. Perhaps because she can think of nothing else whatsoever to do. And so she must do this crazy thing. Call Richard, who is not there, who could not be there.

And that is what she does all night, or almost. She dials Richard's number, and listens to the hollow rhythmic rings, and she thinks, This is craziness, I am acting truly crazily.

She does not get Richard on the phone until almost noon on the following day, when she calls him from work. For the tenth or possibly the fifteenth time.

"Well, uh, that was not exactly one of our great nights," he says.

"But you ran out. I was so upset. You could have been killed—"

He laughs. "Of course I could have, but I wasn't."

She is dead serious. As well as dead tired. Dead. "Please," she tells him. "Please never do that again. Please, whatever's wrong, talk to me."

"I don't much like talking, haven't you noticed? I tend to run. But I'll try hard not to with you. Okay?"

She settles for that as the best she can do at the time.

That night despite resolutions they do not talk very much. Disturbances of the night before are expressed in intensified passion. Greater love.

And deep within Stella there is nascent panic, which is never to be far from her, in all her time with Richard.

Going to Justine's party is considerably more successful. In Justine's pretty rooms, on Belmont Street, on the northern slope of Twin Peaks, Richard looks perfectly at home. Justine's furniture, her "things," are old and worn, but they possess a quality that Richard would recognize; they are "good," collected with care and taste. As Richard later puts it to Stella, Justine has style, a quality he knows and values.

And Justine's friends, although not stylish in the Margot sense, have quality; they are good, smart and interesting. Left-leaning professionals, most of them, professors and social workers and do-good doctors and lefty lawyers. Richard is curiously impressed.

And of course there is Justine's new love, Collin Schmidt, the contractor. The admirer of Richard. His Bunny. Although, as the party works out, Stella spends more time with Bunny than Richard does. Richard has involved himself with a group of doctors who are working on AIDS in Africa. ("I don't know anything! I've never done anything worthwhile, and what they're doing is so magnificent, so great and hopeless!" Richard cries out to Stella later on, drunk and almost tearful.) While Stella talks to Bunny and Justine—Justine a somewhat dizzy hostess in green velvet pants and long loose hair that makes her look about sixteen.

Bunny tells Stella, in effect, what he has already told Justine. That Justine has repeated. His opinion that Richard is a genius. He seems to believe that Stella plans to marry Richard (is this because he himself wishes to marry Justine?), and he extols Richard's virtues, overdoing it more than a little. "And not only that, the guy's the world's greatest cook," he finishes. "When we were up on the coast, the meals he used to put on. I'm telling you. Do you let him do the cooking much?"

"Sure. Whenever I can."

A pause. "You been up to the cabin yet?"

"No. Not yet."

"We'll have to invite my Bunny and your Justine to the cabin very soon," says Richard on the way home; in his enthusiasm he seems to have forgotten that Stella herself has never been there. "What a great woman! What breasts! I think we could really be friends. You know, even in business I've never really had women friends. There's always"—he smiles, self-lovingly (Stella feels), suggestively (or is she too harsh? too jealous?)—"there's always, you know, some suggestion that if things were different we'd really be going at each other."

"Oh really? I have quite a few men friends, straight as well as gay."

"Well, you would. That's different. Your Justine must have

been something else a few years back. Lucky for you I don't go for older women."

"Oh, Richard, for Christ's sake."

"Now now, don't sound like that. Can't you take a joke?"

"Richard, you're driving . . ." His driving is slow and erratic. Any cop would pick up on it instantly, Stella is sure.

"Look, I'm an excellent driver."

"I know you are—"

"Then stop bitching. You make things worse."

They spend that night together, and in the morning everything is okay, or at least as okay as usual, although Stella is more and more fearful and unhappy: can they indeed not spend any time with other people? not go to parties? Is Richard an alcoholic or just someone who sometimes drinks too much?

For a very long twenty-four hours after that Richard does not call—nor does Stella call him. She stays alone with her unhappy thoughts but finds to her considerable surprise that she is able to work. Anyway.

And then she does call, and as though nothing had happened they begin to talk about what to have for dinner.

10

Richard on the Phone

Richard.

Richard.

Richard Richard Richard. Richard.

He loves his name, the way people say it. Women; men too. He loves the Rich of Richard, and the hard, or heart, depending. Richard, Richard: his mother made that sound, and an early high school girlfriend, Celestina—a Puerto Rican and not so good at English, a dirty family but a beautiful girl, really lovely. "Rich-heart," she would say, not knowing why he laughed. And she would take his cock in her mouth, so beautifully. Lovely Celestina.

Rich. A lot of people just call him that, of course. Very different in different voices. So abrupt and scolding the way Marina said it when they were married, and afterwards, quarrelling. When she loved him she called him Rickie.

Rich. So classy in Claudia's voice, short and peremptory. Cats calls him Rich—"Reech," nice and warm.

Stella says Richard, as though the word were golden. Full of love, too full, and she says his name a little too often, Richard feels—or sometimes feels; often he loves his name in Stella's mouth. He often loves Stella. (And sometimes he hates her. Jesus, the blackness! he could hit her. Kill.)

But really, seriously, Stella is an exceptionally nice woman, intelligent (maybe a little too intelligent?) and kind. And not pretty or beautiful, really, but special. His Stella. With her lovely forehead, lovely tastes of fish. (Claudia tastes of alcohol, something antiseptic, alcohol based. "How can you do that, there?" he has asked her, making her laugh.) Stella's wide flat mouth is so vulnerable (too vulnerable?), taking him in.

Richard. Andrew Bacci says it mockingly, two syllables full of implication. Richard, whodoyouthinkyouare, playing at being "Richard," when I know you, I know who you are, and I'm waiting. But in the meantime, it's all pretty funny, no? Richard?

He is sitting at his desk, trying to draw (trying to think of something to draw) and waiting for the phone to ring. Nothing special, he just needs some distraction. Interruption. Although it is just as apt to be bad news.

And it is.

"Mr. Richard Fallon?"

"So sorry, not in at moment," says Richard, imitating Chinese diction (old-style movie Chinese). "Say who call?"

A pause, and then, "Would you please tell him to call Mrs. Elvira Jenkins, at 555-3728?"

"Will do: 555-3728."

Elvira Jenkins, a collection agency name if he ever heard one. *Elvira Jenkins.* And her voice had that prim reproving sound, tight. The cunt. How dare she? Interrupting him, demanding: how dare any of them, hounding, tracking him down?

When the phone rings again he lets it go, as he thinks, Elvira again, and this time she'll pretend to be someone else, maybe call him Dick—that's always a tip-off; anyone calling him Dick is either some non-friend pretending, like Elvira, or else some total jerk that he knows but does not want to see.

His answering machine clicks on, and he hears not Elvira Jenkins but Stella, Stella sobbing, her voice almost unrecognizable. "Richard, it's me. I had this terrible news. It's Prentice, my father. He—he's dead." More sobs. "Call me right away, okay?"

Jesus. All he needs. Stella on his hands like this. Tears, sobbing. Jesus. No control. Women *like* to cry.

But at the same time that he thinks of her so angrily, Richard's stomach clenches in sympathy for Stella, his Stella. Oh, poor Stella, and her father always such a shit to her, and now dead. Poor Stella! Tears come to his own eyes as he reaches for the phone to call her back.

And then does not. No reason to call her right away; for all she knows, he's out. Out of town, he could be. And then the phone rings again.

He answers. Hello.

"Richard." It's Marina. "Richard, I've got this pile of bills that I can hardly see over, so many. You know you're responsible! Often sick. Don't you ever? I can't think. I remember everything, I'm trying to write it all down. I know this terrific guy, he used to be a policeman. Sick! Bills!"

Hanging up, having said almost nothing in response to Marina (that's the best thing to do with her, say nothing; it drives her crazy: crazier), Richard finds that he is shaking. Cold. Crazy women, all over him. *Jesus.*

He dials Andrew's number, gets Andrew's jaunty recorded message. Hi! In no mood for jauntiness, Richard hangs up.

He sits there fuming, breathing heavily. His morning ruined, ruined with women. All wanting too much. Oh Christ! their demands!

When the phone rings again he does not answer it, and over his machine he hears Stella's voice (again!), still tearful but now more controlled. Somewhat more controlled. "Oh damn, Richard. You're still not there. God, what a day. You know, I knew Prentice was sick, he wouldn't last forever, but still. The finality. I have to admit, I feel awful. Almost worse than when Delia died, I think. And of course Alexandra is being horrible." (Who is Alexandra? and then Richard remembers: stepmother of Stella. Wife, now widow, of Prentice Blake. Used to be some kind of an actress. Fancy women he went for, old Prentice.) "Alexandra is saying I mustn't come back there, there isn't even going to be a memorial service. He didn't want one. Not that I'd want to go back, with her around, but still. Oh, Richard darling, I do need to see you. Call me. . . ."

Well, he can't call her right away. Obviously not, or she'd know that he was there in his studio, had been there all along, just listening, not answering her pleas. Not helping. Besides, later on he has a meeting with a client. A possible new client, and he could really use one (ask Marina). Some woman from a new German magazine, said to be very, very solvent. The woman is coming to the studio in about an hour. A Kraut, apt to be prompt. So he had better get ready. No time now, really none, to call Stella.

But as he gets into some tidying up, some very light house-keeping, Richard does give some thought to poor old Prentice Blake, now dead. Poor Stella's dad. Stella seems not to have any pictures of her parents, or if she has, she has not shown them to Richard, and so he has pictured Prentice in terms of old black-and-white movies, some old guy like William Powell, or Gary Cooper, maybe even Cary Grant. Someone lean and dapper and vaguely English. And always mixed up with some woman, or women; nothing monogamous about those guys. And for the first time it occurs to Richard that they might even have liked each other, he and old Prentice. A pity that won't happen. He is certain that Prentice was a better man than that cheap-shot phony Liam, the so-called director, the big love of Stella's life. Big love before Richard, that is.

Richard can only think of Prentice Blake in that somewhat removed, movie way, though; he cannot imagine a man at home, having supper with his wife and his little girl, little Stella. And come to think of it, maybe that's what's wrong with Stella, maybe Prentice was never just an ordinary father, taking her on his lap and mildly feeling her up, the way fathers can do with little girls. Sometimes Richard wishes he had a lot of little girls, his daughters; at other times he longs for sons. He was crazy about Claudia's two boys; he misses them, he longs for their warm little bodies on his lap.

Marina never got pregnant; he used to blame her, but secretly he wonders if he could be sterile.

He does not want to have kids with Stella; mostly he cannot imagine Stella as a mom. Sometimes he thinks she's as crazy as Marina. Even, more darkly, he has this idea that it's really him, that he has some mysterious black disease that affects all women who come near him with craziness. And he can't stand it, he really can't, their wild female insanity. Their dangerous eyes and their voices.

But he must call Stella, so in love with him, and her father just dead.

He looks at his watch. Five of eleven, and the Kraut is due in five minutes, but she wouldn't be right on time, would she? He can call Stella, talk briefly, strongly, comfortingly. But what on earth will he say?

He is sitting there, biting a pencil and scowling, when the doorbell rings.

Going across the room to the door, he feels her aura. He feels something deep and disturbing. As though he might open the door to an earthquake, a cyclone. To black light.

Instead there is a woman so tall and beautiful that Richard gasps, as though in pain ("like someone hit me in the gut," he later tells Andrew Bacci, his confidant). But she doesn't know it! This dumb Kraut does not know how incredibly, how perfectly beautiful she is; Richard takes this in at once, in her hesitant smile, her light blush. ("Or maybe she comes from some town where all the women look like that. Jesus, I'm emigrating!")

"I have maybe the wrong place?" she says. "I come for Mr. Richard Fallon." She smiles, and Richard sees that he was wrong: she knows she is beautiful; she is just very classy about it, playing it down. But of course she knows.

"No; you're right; that's me." Richard's smile answers hers, as he does not say, as he would like to: Just please please repeat my name over several times, in that incredibly low throaty shadowy voice?

She has pale brown-blond hair, pale tan skin, and light sea-green eyes. Hollow cheeks (she must be really thin), a small, somewhat austere nose, and a mouth of surprising sweetness, soft and full. He could stare forever, just at her mouth. Hard not to imagine slipping it into her mouth.

"I'm Eva Wulfman." She extends a hand, which Richard eagerly takes—and which is smaller and softer than he would have imagined.

"Well!" he says, feeling totally helpless; all his usual ploys have disappeared. "Come in! Sit down! Can I make you some coffee?"

"Some coffee would in fact be wonderful. Last night, I had some problems with sleep. I believe, a new city—"

They seem unable to stop smiling at each other, both of them, smiling and smiling. She has lovely small white glistening teeth, and the tip of her tongue is pointed, pink.

"Where you are here, your studio is most beautiful," says Eva, staring at Richard.

If we had children together they would be the most beautiful people in the world, is what Richard thinks, and he thinks it so strongly that she must hear his thought. And she does, doesn't she? He whispers, "Did you feel what I just thought?"

Very softly, "I think so," she tells him, as a faint rose color deepens her tan, in the long hollows of her cheeks.

"Well! I'll make coffee. You just sit there."

In his tiny kitchen Richard manages to make the coffee, trying as he does so to achieve some control, some vestige of calm. (And he must call Stella! God, her father dead. She must feel terrible.)

When Richard reenters the room with his neat lacquered tray of coffee, sugar and milk, he sees that Eva is spreading layouts, presumably from her magazine, across his table, from a large red portfolio that in his dazzlement, his haste to do everything, he did not even see. He puts down the tray and goes over to stand beside her, controlling his breath.

But she turns, this ravishing tall blond German woman turns, and she looks at him, and with a little smile she says to him, "Please, Richard, do we kiss each other now?"

* * *

"Stella darling, I couldn't. Really, all day. I really could not, and of course I've been thinking of you. I'm so sorry about your dad, Stella. But just thinking about it won't—Stella, I'm really busy. These German types, they just left, and I have to have dinner with them later, worst luck. But it's a big deal; I can't afford not to. Stella, I'm sorry. But I'm leaving right now. I'll be there in twenty minutes, okay? I'm leaving right now."

But he hasn't brought her anything, no wine or flowers, just himself. Himself just out of the shower and just, just crazy, out of his mind in love with the most beautiful, most exciting, most everything woman. He could cry, for the sheer enormity of his love, his whole heart turning on one name, his whole soul crying out Eva. Eva, very softly. Eva, a whisper.

Strangely (and this is really crazy, probably), he would like to tell Stella about this great new adventure of his: this fantastic rich young woman from the Munich magazine who is basing herself here in San Francisco for the next three months. This wild, world-class, state-of-the-art, internationally sophisticated fabulous person who fell madly in love with him, Richard Fallon, from Nowhere, New Jersey, at first sight. Who had to have him, she said, right away. Right after kissing. In his small sexy bedroom that they almost tore apart.

If this were a story that he could tell about someone else, Stella would love it, she would be extremely interested. She likes stories, gossip; after all, it's more or less what she does. Reporting. "Human interest." He can imagine her eager face listening, with that absorbed look she gets, imagining and feeling what she hears. But of course it is not a story about someone else—and in fact this is probably the very last story in the world that Stella would like to hear. Especially today.

Driving slowly along Union Street (and why has he chosen to come this slow way?), Richard is still thinking that he should have brought something. Some present. What might be a sort of diversion, as well as a token of sympathy and love, a sort of love.

Then, at the same moment, he sees both a parking space, a good one, and, next to it, a pet store. Not having been thinking of pets, Richard nevertheless brakes, stops, gets out and walks into the store. And there it is, the perfect solution to his problem: the palest-brown, wide-blue-eyed, most beautiful small cat. Three hundred dollars; well, what the hell—if his MasterCard can stand it, he can. For good measure he also buys a peaked-roof cardboard cat carrier, four cans of cat food, and a bag of kitty litter.

"Well. Richard, she's so beautiful. I never saw such a lovely cat. But Mr. Wong. Are you sure?"

"I talked to Wong. It's okay." What Richard means is, he will talk to Mr. Wong. Very soon. Before that Chink has any idea about the cat.

"She's lovely." Kneeling down to the cat, Stella strokes her back, and the cat (thank God!) responds, arching her back against the friendly hand, beginning to purr. "What's her name?" asks Stella.

"Who? The cat? Oh, Eva. I mean Eve."

"Eve. I like that." Sitting on the floor, Stella cradles the small cat in her lap.

She looks bad, Stella does. Un-made-up, disheveled, in her old jeans and old green Shetland sweater, her tattered brown espadrilles. Richard feels a small, quick flash of resentment at how she looks: doesn't she know that if she pulled herself together to look a little better, put on lipstick, she would feel better too? How can she expect to be loved—by him?

"I'm really sorry about your dad," Richard says.

Her eyes tear up. "Thanks. I feel worse than I should feel, I think."

For an instant Richard's heart contorts with tenderness for this wounded woman, his Stella, his love. And then he thinks, Oh Christ, how could I? How could I make love to someone else, someone new, on the very day that her father died?

But then he remembers Eva; he recalls her totally, her skin and her smells.

He looks at his watch. "I'm really sorry about dinner," he says.

"Do you really have to? I mean, could you come over later or something?"

"Uh, I don't really think so, sweetie. Just not a good idea." He grins. "For one thing I may be drunk."

"Oh Jesus, Richard." She frowns, fighting tears.

"Stella honey, why don't you call Justine, or even Margot?"

"I don't particularly feel like seeing either of them. That's why."

If he doesn't get out of there right away there'll be terrible trouble, Richard can smell it coming. He can hear it in Stella's voice, the rising note of hysteria, rage. He can feel accusations. (He can hear his mother's voice, and the note that all women sound, sooner or later.)

He reaches down to pat the cat, now curled, sleeping and purring, against Stella's inner thigh. Such a beautiful cat. Small Eve. In almost the same gesture Richard kisses Stella warmly and gently on her soft and needy mouth.

He says, "I'll call you tomorrow," and he smiles.

And is gone.

Out of there.

11

Margot's Weapon

Sometimes, in her narrow, often-dark apartment, overcrowded with her treasures—her books and her silver and her porcelain, her "things"—sometimes, despite everything that is or is not going on in her life, Margot is perfectly happy. On a sunny morning, say, when she takes a delicious cup of coffee back to bed, with the papers, then she is happy. In the mirror across the room she does not look too bad; she looks, in fact, like a most elegant and interesting woman; someone told her so at a party last night, the new French cultural attaché. Of course she knows—their hostess told her before the party—that this man, this small and bald but handsome M. Pineau, has a wife and family at home in Paris, who will join him momentarily, but in the meantime it was very nice to hear him say, "You are a woman I would much like to know more, a most beautiful and elegant woman. You must tell me, is it possible?" Well, maybe. But what he said was quite true: especially here in her own boudoir, leaning into a froth of ruffled pillows, her dark hair falling just right, eyes large and clear, a suggestion of pale-pink silk beneath her rose silk robe. She looks great; well, if not great, very good, very good indeed for a woman of—of her years (even in her own mind Margot does not like to be too specific). The point is, probably, that today Margot feels truly happy, both because she is looking good and because she is possessed of her favorite thing: a perfect piece of gossip. A jewel of gossip, so valuable that Margot is not quite sure what to do with it; she plans to show it around in tiny glimpses, perhaps to bargain with it.

This is how it came about, her possession of this marvelous piece of news: three nights ago she was having dinner with Denny, a young friend (her hairdresser, in fact, but very presentable; they go to the opera together). In any case, she and Denny had gone to dinner at a rather stylish place on Jackson Street, and there, in a booth not far from theirs, Margot saw: Richard Fallon and an absolute knockout of a woman, one of those giant European blondes, with their perfect skin and teeth (but the skin is always tanned and will surely be leather, if not something worse, by the time they're fifty). But definitely Richard, and definitely Another Woman. About as far from dark dowdy little Stella as you could get. Ah, delicious! Margot instantly thought of uses for this development: how could Stella be so smug, imagining that Richard Fallon was in love with her?

First off she thought of telling Andrew, of course, and she thought of what they, she and Andrew, could do with this piece of news. Very *Liaisons Dangereuses,* Margot thought.

And in the meantime she watched. Oh, how she watched every gesture that passed between those two, who were fortunately seated in a booth more or less in front of Margot and Denny's booth, so that she could observe without being herself observed; she was quite sure that Richard had not seen her.

That woman, that huge blonde, was all over Richard, Margot saw that right away. Her hands—and such very large hands too— were touching Richard's hands, her face was leaning forward, close to Richard's face. She was huge but extremely thin, the blonde was, and wearing a super dress of dark ruffled silk. Ungaro, Margot thought.

Suppose she told Stella? Margot for an instant wondered that. Would that be a bad or a good thing to do? Not that she is a feminist, of course not, but what is the feminist line on such things: are you supposed to tell a friend about a man who cheats? It does seem wrong, in a way, to let Stella continue in this dazzled dream of love, to let Stella believe that Richard really and truly loves her, and only her. On the other hand, it would be cruel indeed to tell her. Margot would have to discuss it with Andrew, she decided. She could hardly wait.

In the meantime she could not resist mentioning to Denny that she knew that couple over there, who were making rather a spectacle of themselves.

"Oh, I know Richard Fallon, I mean I've heard of him, I mean who hasn't?" Denny told her. He laughed. "Once at a party there was this big, fierce argument, a fight, I guess you could call it, about who was the handsomest man in town, and your Richard certainly had his supporters."

Margot giggled. "Hardly my Richard, thank heaven. But what about Andrew Bacci? Don't you think he's pretty?"

Margot could have sworn that Denny blushed as he said, "I sure do."

Margot paused, and then asked him, "That woman, the one with Richard, with all that blond hair—is that all hers, that color?"

Denny squinted forward. "Sorry, babes, it's hers, and it's real. She's some kind of northern Kraut, I'd bet on it."

"You can tell from hair color?"

"Sometimes. Some places. You know. Some guys are good at accents. I'm hair." And he grinned up at Margot.

Cute little Denny. Her pixie. A sudden out-of-character gust of kindliness induced Margot to say, "You know you're really one of the cutest of all, darling Dens."

She looked up to observe a long passionate kiss between Richard Fallon and his German blonde.

* * *

Now, in bed with her coffee, in its beautiful French cup, Margot turns over possible uses of this gossip; not even gossip, actually—this is fact. Richard Fallon is cheating on Stella.

She would like to tell Andrew right off, but at the same time she wonders, Would telling Andrew make him mad at her, for telling? would he somehow blame her for Richard's bad character? Men can be like that, as Margot is well aware—even queer ones, or maybe especially queers; they can be very eager to team up with each other ("bonding," she thinks it's now called). They like to blame poor women for everything bad in the world.

Also, there is the risk that Andrew might tell Richard himself, as a way of uniting himself, Andrew, with Richard, which Margot well knows is what Andrew would most like to do. So that there would be Andrew and Richard, bonded, combined against Margot and even against poor Stella, whom Richard of course will blame for making him feel guilty. Men!

Margot runs over alternatives to telling Andrew, other places to spend her currency of gossip, so to speak. The trouble is, as she soon realizes, that no one else would much care: Richard Fallon is cheating on Stella Blake, so what? What else is new? Don't you know what's going on in Somalia, or right here in San Francisco General Hospital, in the AIDS ward? (Margot has only the vaguest knowledge of these things herself, but at least she knows the names.)

There is obviously nothing for it but to call Andrew, which of course is what Margot has all along pined to do, just to see him. Beautiful Andrew. She forgets that their last encounter was less than pleasant; in fact Margot has a most useful capacity for forgetting what is inconvenient, or what in any way thwarts her purpose, or purposes.

However (amazing!), just as she is pulling herself together to telephone Andrew, arranging sentences in her head and arranging herself more comfortably on her bed, the phone rings, and it is Andrew himself!

Who, with no preliminaries, says to her, "Margot, baby doll, I'd like to come over. Okay?"

"But, darling, I'm not dressed. Give me twenty—"

"Who gives a shit if you're dressed. I'll be right there."

Bridling—she loathes ugly language—Margot nevertheless jumps out of bed and hurries into her bathroom. At least there is time to do something with her face—she hopes.

As she might have known, there is more than enough time: much more—at least an hour before Andrew shows up.

And when he finally does he is so . . . so *odd* that Margot almost wishes he had not come.

First off, and totally out of character for Andrew, he asks for a drink. A drink! at ten-thirty in the morning. Margot very much dislikes drinking, she thinks it smells, and so often it makes men boorish, and God knows it interferes with sex. An occasional perfectly chilled glass of champagne is her idea of pleasant drinking—and even then she takes only a few small sips. And so she cannot help saying, "But, Andrew darling, so early?"

"Don't be so fucking conventional."

A horrified "Oh" from Margot.

"And, baby, I can't believe you haven't heard that very word in your parlor before."

A stiff pause, and then Margot asks, "Well. What kind of a drink would you like, Andrew?"

"Some gin. On ice. Please, ma'm."

Is it possible that Andrew has had a drink, or drinks, already this morning? He looks much the same as always, but then again, not quite: his shirt and his hair are not quite as perfect as usual; both show some muss.

Oh, queers, thinks Margot. Why do I spend all my time with them? They're so utterly unreliable. Just when you think how nice and pretty they are, they go off and do some horrible butch thing, like drinking. Using ugly words.

Back in her living room, she hands Andrew his drink, in a heavy (Bohemian) glass, with a tiny linen napkin.

"Honestly, Margot, you'd think you were giving me medicine. Thanks, Mom," and he grins in an evil way, before gulping down the gin.

"Well, you don't have to drink it like medicine." Margot could not help saying this, and wishes she had not.

"You're wrong, I do have to. Can't you tell?" Andrew stares out at her, from gorgeous dark long-lashed eyes. Italian. Ravishing. And even though his hair is indeed a little messy, and his shirt not perfectly fresh, he is so beautiful, and so distracting to Margot, that she finds it hard to concentrate on a conversation. With an effort she asks him, "You're not feeling well?"

"Oh, I feel fine. I feel randy-dandy so far. But I had to go and take the test, you see? I had to be *tested.*"

"Tested?" Margot knows that she has lost some important thread. This tends to happen when she and Andrew try to talk seriously.

"The HIV test. Good Christ, Margot, surely you've heard it's around?"

"But, darling, you don't have AIDS." Only lower-class people get AIDS, has been Margot's thought. Awful men who go out to public baths. Polk Street prostitutes.

Andrew laughs in a horrible shrill way. "We don't know that. We won't know that until next week. But I'm sure a prime candidate." He turns on her. "And what will you do then, Miss Garbo? When I'm covered with big dark blotches and gone half blind and lame? Will you still be thrusting your offers of hospitality on me? How about it, Margot? Are you up for a stint of nursing?"

Margot forces a laugh. "Well, in the first place you don't have it, of course you don't. And in the second I'm a much nicer person than you think. Of course I'd always take care of a friend who was sick. A good friend, I mean. But, Andrew, you're not sick."

Andrew laughs, a short ugly bitter sound. "If you say so, lady. A more expert view might be that if I'm not, I'm goddam lucky so far."

And before Margot can say anything to stop him—though what it would have been she is not at all sure—Andrew is out of his seat and up and gone.

Why, then, did he come over? Margot has a puzzled sense that Andrew wanted something of her, something that she most clearly failed to provide. She has disappointed Andrew, gorgeous Andrew. Margot frowns, then remembers how bad frowns are for your face, and stops.

Well, she thinks, if (God forbid!) Andrew does get sick, sick with anything at all, even with that horrible plague that he surely will not get, not only will she take care of him but she will insist that he stay right there with her. She will buy all the right clothes for nursing, and she will buy lovely fruits, and she will make delicious soups to make him well. She will be the best nurse, the most devoted, that anyone ever heard of. She will show everyone what she is really like.

Happier now, as in the kitchen she washes out Andrew's glass, Margot reflects too with some pleasure that she did manage not to tell Andrew about Richard and his German blonde after all; she kept that bit of news to herself, and so she has it still to tell, at some opportune time. Like having money to spend.

Just to test herself, she decides to call Justine, who after all is Stella's very big friend. She will call Justine and not tell the awful news of Richard, not even hint.

But almost the first thing that Justine tells her is that Stella's father is dead; or rather, Justine asks if Margot has heard this news.

"Well, no. You know how bad I am about reading the papers." Not reading the papers is actually a pose of Margot's, part of her air of not quite participating in the contemporary world, of which she in so many ways disapproves. The truth is, she spends a lot of time reading newspapers, though in a very selective way: she does not read about famines, wars, or pestilence (and thus she is somewhat ill-informed about AIDS). She often skips the obituaries; too depressing. And so she easily missed the news of the death of Prentice Blake. (But why didn't Stella call her? Does Stella think she is not really a sympathetic person? She resolves to send Stella some very expensive flowers.)

"Oh, poor darling Stella," she says to Justine. "Poor girl. But I hope he's left her something nice; he must have a little money, and she was his only daughter, wasn't she? I think actually an only child. Oh, poor Stella! I must call her, and of course I'll send flowers. So lucky she has that handsome Richard to take care of her, don't you think?" And then, as an afterthought, she asks, "Tell me, Justine. I know you're a true-blue feminist. If you know that some man's been cheating on his wife, or his lover, are you supposed to tell the wife, or the lover? . . . Well,

Justine, I honestly can't see why you think this is funny. I meant it as a very serious question."

Hanging up, annoyed by the burst of laughter with which her really serious question was greeted, Margot senses that all her earlier moments of happiness have evaporated like morning mists—and through no fault of her own!

Andrew was so cross with her, and so mean, so selfishly pre-occupied. And if he does get sick he would probably not even want Margot to take care of him.

And with Stella's father just dead, of course there can be no question of telling anyone about Richard's big affair. It would be just too awful if it did get back to Stella, and naturally everyone would blame Margot, as though it were all her fault that Richard Fallon was a cheat and that Stella was too dumb to see it.

12

Bad Times

The summer that Stella was later to remember as the summer when her father died (and when she had pneumonia, and when she broke with Richard in a way that seemed to be permanent)— that summer was also the coldest, darkest, windiest San Francisco summer that anyone remembered. Black fog billowed in through the Golden Gate, enshrouding the bridge, slowing early-morning traffic; blackness lay like a pall over all the trees in the Presidio— where Stella lived, and mourned, and tried to cheer up, to pull herself together and get well and get to work.

But in the mornings as she left her dark string of rooms to walk to the bus stop, wind cut into her head like knives, exposing the hopeless, anguished muddle of her brain, where all was con- fusion: pain at the loss of her father, and hurt at his will; then pain at lack of love from Richard when she felt that she most needed love from him, and then his loss; and her prolonged, insufferable cold. And all those conditions seemed to fuel each other, each making the others more severe, more unbearable.

Some years earlier—about ten years before the summer when he died—when Stella went out with her father in New York, everyone always stared, which vain Prentice interpreted in his own way: he believed himself to be both famous and handsome. Although, those days, in a comparative sense he was neither— especially at the Algonquin, where he liked to go for drinks; no one in that place was likely to have heard of him, and so many stars of varying degrees of beauty and fame had hung out there: rock stars, movie stars, handsome young writers—Prentice earned all those stares with sheer oddity: his sheaf of yellow-white hair, his ranging wild blue eyes. He looked very odd indeed in his battered old black clothes; there was always the possibility that he might be someone. But savoring all the attention, he leaned back in his leather chair and continued to lecture his erring daughter.

"The point is," he told her (often), "I know guys like Liam O'Gara, and you don't. You just don't. They use women up, those guys. To them a woman of twenty-one is old, a discard. We had guys like him in the Brigade, going crazy over very young Spanish girls, and I mean girls: those kids were all well under twenty, some of them only about fourteen or fifteen. Jail- bait, we used to call them in the States. Liam thinks he's some kind of an Errol Flynn. And I have to tell you, Stell, it's down- right embarrassing for me to have my daughter connected with his name. Not to mention pictures in a vulgar newsmagazine."

The vulgar magazine in question was *Time*, which had run a picture of Liam O'Gara "on location in Ásolo, north of Venice, with his current companion, unidentified." Unidentified Stella, looking even younger than she was, in an old bathing suit that made her look undeveloped, childish, her long black hair in a single girlish braid. "They didn't even use my name," Stella told her father, for the dozenth time. "Who'd know? Who'd care?"

"I, for one," intoned Prentice. "The capitalist press at its worst. Always has been the most terrible magazine. The China lobby. Henry Luce. Look what they did to Paul Robeson." Although his politics had predictably veered right, Prentice still sounded, usually, like a Thirties Stalinist.

"Oh, Daddy, really." The old childish name had slipped out; more often Stella called her father Prentice, which he preferred.

"And my friends. They knew you. In fact a woman you've not even met, name of Alexandra, an exceptional type, asked me if that girl with Liam O'Gara could possibly be my daughter. Thought she saw some resemblance to some pictures I had around."

Which is how Stella first heard of her new stepmother, Alexandra Minsky, an actress—even as she digested Prentice's clear lie: he did not keep pictures of his daughter lying about. The stepmother-before-last, Rachel, had been visibly surprised to find that Prentice had an almost grown-up daughter. (Rachel, the antiquarian book dealer for whom Prentice had ditched Delia, mother of Stella.) Her father lied; Stella had known and reluctantly admitted that fact to herself for some time, and excused it in various ways: he's a writer, he deals in fictions—or, his life has been disappointing, all his friends are more famous and successful than he is. But still, the sense that she could not trust him made Stella queasy; she was embarrassed for even his smallest lies. A man who fought in Spain should be a hero, Stella once believed. Or, having been heroic early, he should have remained so.

As though he had read her mind and been amused by its stupid innocence, Prentice laughed. "Prentice the silly old Commie—is that how you see your old man? Although I suppose some might say that only a very strong father fixation would lead you to a jerk like Liam O'Gara." He leaned back with a challenging, happy smile.

"Actually you couldn't be more different." Blushing as she said this, Stella still believed it to be true, and often (to herself) she had cited instances of difference: Liam's quiet, implacable self-assurance and his upright, severe Scottish conscience—perhaps as odd in a movie director as were Prentice's quite opposite qualities in a hero. Stella had so often made this contrast that at times she wondered if Prentice and Liam could actually be two opposing halves of the same person, a classic schizophrenic.

The room in which they sat and drank, with its low, inviting chairs and nice round tables, was crowded; Prentice, always inattentive to his daughter, kept craning his conspicuous old head around, always searching: there always might be someone. But turning back to Stella, he announced, "Well, if you don't shape up, I just may stop making those insurance payments. Think of that—to have me kick off without any compensation!"

"Oh, Prentice."

"But don't you worry, my girl. I'll keep up that rotten expensive policy until my dying day. Literally. And I want you to do something sensible with the money. Like buy a house." He looked at his watch. "Well, time I was shoving along, old dear. I have to meet the aforesaid Alexandra even farther uptown."

Having imagined that they were to have dinner together (or did she imagine it? didn't Prentice say dinner?), Stella gave a moment's thought to the refrigerator of the friend with whom she was staying, also uptown but West Side: surely she saw some eggs?

"I suppose you'll be meeting Mr. O'Gara somewhere very grand." This was a statement from Prentice, not a question.

"Well, I guess not, not tonight." This seemed hardly the time to tell him that she and Mr. O'Gara were through: the fact that he always, conscientiously, told her about his other, newer and younger loves (younger than twenty-one: Prentice of course was right) made them no easier to bear, Stella had finally, forcefully said to Liam.

Prentice made these unseemly references to an insurance policy fairly often, along with instructions, which were sometimes facetious: "Your first face-lift, if you're your mother's daughter." Or, more sensibly if much more extravagantly, "Buy a house." The house advice surely suggested a lot of money, and the face-lift less, but still, it meant something substantial.

And now, on Prentice's death, there had been the actual will—and nothing from an insurance company. A copy of the will, mailed out by Alexandra, stated clearly that all Prentice's worldly goods went to his beloved wife, Alexandra Minsky Blake; or, should that wife predecease him, everything went to the Libertarian Party of New York, with a street address. (Libertarians! This seemed strange news indeed.) But all in all the will was painful to read; telling no one, Stella crumpled those papers into her garbage can, along with the kitty litter, dead flowers and coffee grounds.

But after several weeks of no further word from Alexandra, much less from an insurance company (Stella had no idea how those things work), she said to Justine, "Prentice kept talking about this insurance policy. For me, I mean. What do you think I should do?"

Laughing, Justine told her, "Honey, I think you have to know which insurance company. You can't just write to them all. But there must be a policy around somewhere."

"You don't know Prentice. I mean, there wasn't necessarily any policy at all. Or he could have taken one out a long time ago in some manic fit and then not paid it."

Obviously, she would have to call Alexandra. Who told her, "Really, Stella, you know how Prentice was. Promises, promises. He thought big. Honestly, if I had a nickel for every imaginary present. Pie in the sky. Or, new stereo locked in the head of Prentice Blake. Naturally, if any insurance company comes around I'll let you know, but, sweetie, I frankly doubt it."

And so, probably, neither a face-lift nor a house. Nor a paying off of debts. Doctors and dentists, Macy's, credit cards. Much less a trip to New York.

Stella tried very hard not to mind, but she did mind. She felt as though she had received a posthumous letter from Prentice, saying, I never cared about you at all. I didn't love you. I only pretended sometimes.

She told herself, It's only the money. Or alternately, It isn't really the money that I mind. But she did mind about the money; she could have used even a small amount. And she minded even more what she felt was the message of uncaringness from Prentice.

Her cold got worse.

And Richard acted worse.

* * *

One night he arrived at her house for dinner a little after seven, already drunk. A big lunch with clients, he said. His new Germans. His face was red and swollen, and he blinked a lot, as though trying to focus. He looked ugly, and threatening.

"You know, I don't really feel too well," Stella whispered. "Maybe . . . I just don't feel like making dinner. Could you . . . do you think . . ."

"Oh Christ." He stared at her, enraged, his face bull-red and coarse. "I think you're asking me to leave. You don't want to have dinner with me, I can tell."

"I guess not," she whispered.

"Well, in that case." He lurched to his feet. "But you don't have to worry about the Germans anymore," she heard him say. "All gone."

Instead of rushing over to him, as she sometimes did, to cling to him and beg him please to stay, Stella leaned back against the sofa and closed her eyes. She was so vastly tired, she ached all over. Dimly, from behind closed lids, she heard Richard heading for the door. The opening, the slam.

And that time, instead of anguish and hysteria, her usual response to Richard's departures, what Stella felt was mostly physical in nature: heat, and an ache in her heart, and some tightening of her breath.

"Richard and I have broken up," she announces to Justine the next morning, on the phone, partly to test the saying of this sentence: Is it true? have they in fact broken up? "He was so drunk and terrible," Stella says to her friend. "But you know, this goddam cold that I have is so bad that I really don't care. Odd logic: I think when I get over the cold I'll be over Richard too."

"Honey, I think you should call your doctor. Honestly, though, this weather is enough to put anyone under. So cold, and the wind. Days like these, I think more kindly than usual of Texas."

Neither her cold nor the pain of breaking with Richard seems to diminish. Stella can barely make it to work; she sniffles and coughs all day, and her chest hurts. In bed at night she finds it hard to breathe.

Piercing memories of Richard make sleep impossible. He seems then, at night, to exist in her mind more vividly than in actual life; she can hear his voice, can see his face, smell his skin more sharply than if he were actually there. And crazily, all that she recalls of him is good; the only Richard in her mind is loving and warm, and kind and laughing, strong and passionately in love with her. And saying so, all night.

Finally she does call her doctor, who says that he would like to see her. That afternoon. And in his office, after listening to her chest, checking pulse and heart rate, he tells her, "I just don't much like what I see. And from what you say, this has gone on for much too long. The hospital. Tests. Check in as soon as you can. I'm sure your insurance. I'll see you there around six."

Stella calls Justine, arranges for some sick leave from the office ("God, I hope he's right about my insurance") and arranges for Mr. Wong to feed the cat, pretty Eve. (Mr. Wong has turned out to be a secret lover of cats; he is crazy about Eve—or so Richard once reported. Richard who himself was getting very thick with Mr. Wong.) And Stella, even more sick than she is terrified, checks into the hospital, which is not far from where she lives.

For several days (and nights: the nights are terrible) she does not get better at all—despite a barrage of drugs, and tests, and doctor visits. What she has, she is told, is a particularly resistant strain of pneumonia. (What people used to die of, Stella thinks.)

During those nights, in her noisy, low-lit room, Stella becomes a total prey to terror. She dreams of, or half imagines, giant wild animals, rustling down the corridors. She hears the mammoth wheels of plundering tanks, smells the killer world of night.

In the daytime, awakened for tests, for gurney trips down to X-ray, she thinks, This is more than an illness, I am obviously having some sort of breakdown. Prentice dying, and then the breakup with Richard, and this pneumonia—everything at once has been too much.

And she does not succeed in separating out those elements; too often she lapses back into tears, and panic, an awful debilitation.

Sometimes during the day she has a few rational moments, though. When Justine comes to visit she even speaks more or less rationally about Richard. What happened. "It's lucky we weren't together much longer," she says. "The addiction or whatever it was could have got worse. And I'm sure it would have."

"That's probably true," says Justine.

A pause, and then Stella asks, "How're things at work?"

"About the same." Justine relates some gossip, a few new rumors of takeovers, dismissals.

"And you and Collin?"

Justine laughs, very shortly. "About the same."

But after that visit Stella notes that she is better.

Margot arrives with a great sheaf of purple flowers. She tells Stella their name, but Stella instantly forgets it.

Even in her own unreal state, Stella can see that Margot is not herself; she looks older, and distracted; even her hair is awry, disheveled. And she talks in a brittle, unconvincing way (as though she were trying not to cry, it occurs to Stella).

There is even some chatter about feminism, vaguely linked to Justine, that Stella, befogged, has trouble following. "Feminists don't really seem to have things sorted out any better than the rest of us," Margot babbles. "Oh, darling, of course I know you are one, but not like Justine, she can be awfully strident. And I asked her the simplest question, and she had absolutely no feminist answer. Well, let me try it out on you."

"Okay." Stella finds that she very much wishes Margot would just go away, or just be quiet.

"Tell me, if you were involved with some guy who was cheating on you, would you want to know about it?"

Half understanding the question, but having grasped that Margot herself is very disturbed, Stella says, "No, I don't think so. But, Margot, are you okay? You just don't look ... like yourself."

Evidently unused to sympathy, Margot bridles. "Why? You must mean my hair. I know it's a mess, but Andrew called just as I was doing it, and he can be so upsetting. Honestly, he's such a hypochondriac."

"I hardly know him," Stella whispers; by now she is truly exhausted. Dimly she is glad that she has not told Margot about Richard. Breaking up with Richard. Richard gone.

She must have fallen asleep, for when she next is conscious Margot is gone and the purple flowers are drooping in their vase. And a nurse is waking her up for another test.

That night she dreams, or imagines, or hallucinates, that Richard is there in the room with her, at some unreal past-midnight hour. Richard is standing at the foot of her bed, holding three pale, very full-blown roses. She can even smell the roses, so vivid is this dream. But Richard's voice is strange, as he tells her, "Oh, Stella, I've been so terrible, I never meant to. I love you, I love *you*, you can't imagine how much I love you. Stella, please don't leave me, I need you." Was he crying? Was this Richard?

He comes toward her, in this incredible dream, he stands beside her and bends down to kiss her forehead. He even laughs! "Christ," he says. "Hospital smells. I've got to get you out of here. I love you!"

Stella seems then to fall asleep, and when she wakes again Richard is gone. Of course he is; the dream is over. Stella sleeps again, very soundly; her best sleep for weeks.

She sleeps until she is awakened by a nurse, who is saying, "What lovely roses you have here. Honey, can you smell them? Lovely! But they're so full, the petals are falling off."

13

Happy Days of Love

Richard does not exactly move into Stella's house, and at no time do they ever admit to each other that they are living together; but after Stella comes home from the hospital—Richard collects her there, bundling her and her clothes and flowers into his open car and handing her out like a prize—he is always at her house. Living there.

In the late afternoons, usually, Stella hears him call out, "Anybody home?" and the sound of his saying that always makes her smile: Where else would she be but at home, expecting him? But she rushes to where he is, in the entranceway.

She has sometimes wondered: Is that what he heard as a boy? Did his father use to enter the house in that way, at night? Calling out, Anybody home? (Did he do that on the night he killed his wife, Richard's mother?)

* * *

During the first few days of Stella's convalescence, Richard usually arrives with great sacks of groceries—food that they somehow, together, turn into a dinner, or two or three dinners, with wine and booze. And flowers; he almost always brings flowers.

And Stella gets much better very quickly; even her doctor agrees that her progress is remarkable. So that soon she is able to do at least some of the shopping; she plans meals and cooks for Richard, with love and high ambitions and considerable nervousness; Richard sets a high standard with his own cooking and prides himself on his palate. Thus the "Anybody home" may find Stella with her hands all floured or smelling violently of garlic. Then she rushes to kiss him with upraised hands and arms, laughing, and he seizes her the more violently, laughing at her, at her semi-fake distress.

Cooking goes well with the work that she is trying to do, Stella finds. The writing. Going back and forth, from her typewriter to the chopping board, the stove, the sink, she feels vastly fulfilled. She believes that she did indeed have some sort of breakdown (which she now attributes mostly to the death of Prentice and to pneumonia, her "resistant strain") and that she recovered to greater strength. She has, for perhaps the first time in her life, a sense of working to capacity—or of all or almost all of her capacities in use at once. Her capacities for work and for love, in ways that are new.

Interruptions from the demands of cooking are not as jarring, as disturbing as other interruptions are, Stella finds. Some culinary need is nowhere near as bad or as importunate as a phone call, nor as some salesman at her door. To remember suddenly that a chicken should be basted, a soup stirred, some bread pushed down, does not distract her from work in a way that makes it difficult to go back to work—just as certain gentle interruptions to one's sleep make it possible to sleep again, to continue with one's dream, while others do not.

* * *

Richard fixes things around the house, to Stella's surprise: she has never known a man before who could fix anything. Prentice felt that any domestic problem was the province of wives; and Liam hired people to do all that. But Stella gradually realizes that Richard not only fixes things, he likes to do so, in the way that he likes to cook. He takes all her knives to be sharpened; he oils the hinge on a door that has always been noisy; he makes a new rack for the kitchen implements, nearer the stove. So wonderful: Stella has tended to accept certain conditions as inevitable, like a noisy door, dull knives and inconveniently placed kitchen tools. To have all that changed seems to her almost miraculous.

Richard downplays his helpfulness, though. "Cosmetic stuff. What I'm good at, I guess." He looks around and sighs. "What this place needs . . . Jesus, it's endless."

That is how their days mostly go, these days. Love and cooking and small domestic conversations and chores. A lot of laughing at silly mutual jokes. A lot of cat jokes. Eve, whose name Richard seems to have changed to Legs ("Eve is really too serious a name for a cat, don't you think?")—Legs is growing up to be quite ungainly; she has, for a cat, a curious lack of grace. She stumbles about on long thin legs, as Stella and Richard watch her, laughing gently and softly. ("It's as though we didn't want to hurt her feelings." "Well, we don't, do we.") Legs the cat, formerly Eve.

Sometimes Richard brings home flowers quite unfamiliar to Stella. Ranunculuses. Poppy-like, with their limp silk petals, they seem to bloom in a marvelous spectrum of colors, mostly yellow, pale oranges, but sometimes purple, or red. Richard loves them, he fills the house with ranunculuses with bright petals, bowls and vases everywhere of these flowers, with mirrors reflecting them back, multiplying flowers. Or he often brings home roses. Richard knows a special shop on Union Street; their roses are all grown somewhere down on the Peninsula—for scent, these are roses that smell like roses. Richard brings home lovely pale bouquets; the rooms smell of roses. And he has a special trick with dried rose petals, bowls of them, here and there. Or freesias. Or stock. Stella so often arrives home to the sight and the scent of flowers that they come to seem a part of the atmosphere in which she and Richard live.

Sometimes, in the night, waking next to Richard, Stella is aware of greater sheer happiness than she can bear. It seems undeserved, and almost unreal, this joy at his presence in her bed, his smooth and fleshy back, the flesh padding large bones and muscles, pulsing blood. His masses of pale fine hair. As she presses her dark skinny body there, to his back, an arm circling his chest, her hand just grazes a small patch of light crinkly hair. It is too much for her, the pleasure that suffuses her heart at such moments, these mornings of sunlight. Of Richard, in bed.

She even sometimes thinks, This is not real, it cannot last. (These are dark whispers from an inner, old familiar voice.) This is out of tune with my life, says this voice. I was not intended for happy love with a man of surpassing beauty.

When Liam loved her, then too Stella experienced a sense of unreality; but that affair was almost all unreal, with its backdrops of exotic cities, expensive hotels. It was obvious that none of that could last. And she herself, Stella always well knew, would not always be the child whom Liam adored. She was only eighteen at the start of that affair; at twenty she would look too old for him, she knew. And she did.

But Richard's back feels real, and instead of thinking, This can't last, Stella often thinks, This is how life is supposed to be, filled with love and the scent of a loved person's flesh—and roses— on a sunny morning, in bed.

"This is great, but we have to let in some air, you know?"
Stella does not quite know, not yet, what he means; she would

like nothing to change. But still, she likes the idea that he is paying attention, is taking them seriously. He sounds so sane and healthy, and wise; quite unlike the other person, or persons, who are also Richard, who have sometimes scared her and seemed to her quite mad.

"We tend to be a little hysterical," Richard tells her, continuing in this vein. "We need to calm down and act like ordinary people. Work a lot, get more sleep." He grins, beautifully. "Probably cut down on the booze. A little."

She tells him, "You're right," still not entirely sure what he has in mind.

"We've got a great thing going, but it needs some concrete implementation, do you see what I mean?"

"I think so."

He laughs. "In the meantime, let's have a drink."

And even though this is the last that Stella ever hears of this semi-plan of Richard's, she continues to cherish this rarely seen side of him: the sensible person, taking charge. Calling a halt to excess and unreality. She needs that, she knows.

Stella notices that Richard and Mr. Wong are spending a lot of time together, on Richard's way in and out. They look somewhat conspiratorial, she thinks, and she next thinks, Lord, I hope Richard is not talking about getting another cat, or cats. Legs is fine. I love her, but she's enough, in this small place.

"Isn't it time we checked out my place up the coast?"

Stella's still-convalescent heart leaps at the question, but she manages to say, "Well, sure. You mean this weekend?"

"I had some longer period in mind, actually. How about this: you add a little work leave to your sick time, and we can go up for ten days or so? My new best friend, Standish Wong, is going to take care of Legs."

"I don't know if I could, but that sounds . . . terrific."

"You'll take work along? I'll have to go back and forth to the city. A little."

* * *

Richard's house is so perfectly a part of its landscape, the surrounding sand, gray dunes, as to be almost invisible. It is indeed a moment before Stella recognizes that this is a house, this is *the* house, before which they have stopped. What at first she sees is a pile of timbers, smooth and as gray as the sand; some horizontal, neatly piled, some upright. Until she realizes that she is looking at a wall and a narrow door.

She says, "What a hideaway! You're perfectly camouflaged."

"It's my bunker. I could just hole up here. Sometimes I think I may."

As he opens the door, though, and she follows him in, Stella gasps in sheer and spontaneous amazement: she sees a beautiful long bright room, with broad high windows that frame a view of the sea. Fortuitously they have arrived just at sunset (or could Richard have planned it that way, timing it perfectly?); pale red light streams into the room, illuminating polished wood, falling softly on velvet cushions, a deep tapestry-covered couch. A large gray-stone fireplace, long refectory table. Some pewter things, brass lamps. Almost fearfully Stella turns to Richard, she hides her face in his chest. "It's just so beautiful," she whispers. "Incredible."

"Well, it really came out okay." But she can hear the pride in his voice, his excitement about his house. "Old Bunny did a first-rate job," he adds.

"But he said it was all you."

Richard laughs. "Well, I guess I was the idea guy. That's my shtick, I guess. But it took a little doing."

The kitchen area is at one end of that long room, then dining, then the sofa and chairs, and the fireplace. Through doors, at either end, are bedrooms and baths. "You see?" says Richard, showing her around. "The simplest design in the world. A kid could do it."

He really means this, Stella in a flash of insight understands; he sees his house as something that a kid, himself, has drawn and constructed. "A genius kid, I think," she tells him, meaning it.

He laughs again. "You're prejudiced. You have no judgment."

* * *

After a couple of days, even though she is becoming more familiar with the house, Stella, walking along the beach, feels something close to panic. Richard is in San Francisco, not much more than an hour away—but as she remembers the drive (so beautiful, such meadows and woods and sweet low-lying farms) it seems farther away, almost impossibly distant. And Richard is so unreliable, in terms of time; he might be really late. She hates the vision of herself waiting there, with the darkening sky all about. It is as though being anything but a very short distance from Richard were unbearable to her; and as Stella recognizes and examines this feeling, it seems ominous. She feels as though some very sane person were telling her, You are not supposed to feel this way, you don't have to, neither your happiness nor your sanity should depend on Richard's presence; come on, you're a feminist. And Stella has to answer that woman (maybe Justine?): But so much does depend on Richard, for me. I am hooked. I am madly in love. Madly hooked.

But perhaps it is the unfriendly beach itself that is causing this mood of darkness in Stella. From the water's edge, where she walks, Stella looks back to the forbidding dunes, and then, at the beach's end, to the high, deeply crevassed cliffs of clay. The sand itself is coarse and cold, brown-gray, and there at her feet among the dirty bits of foam lie squashed-out orange rinds, here and there a dead fish—which brings her back to "hooked," that cruelly accurate metaphor.

Also, her work is not going very well. She brought along her processor, all the information is there, at her fingertips, but it seems as knotted as fishing lines, impenetrable as knots. So that she stares with hatred at her expensive, efficient machine, once her old friend, her helper.

Richard is dangerous. That is a sentence sometimes whispered by that same sane (feminist) woman of Stella's imagination. However, since she knows her imagination to be fairly wild and unreliable, and also since she deals in words all day, it is no small wonder that various random sentences enter her mind. Probably she has thought "Richard is dangerous" simply to make her life more dramatic and exciting. Whereas, closer to the truth, she believes (she believes this most of the time), is the pleasant surprise of Richard as a warm, healthy and loving man, a man who likes to cook and eat and drink and make love. Who is good at carpentry, at things connected with houses. A domestic person. A man whose slightest touch is thrilling to her skin, to her bones.

What is dangerous is her own imagination, as Stella should know by now. It has got her into trouble before.

Out on the horizon, great long black boats, oil tankers, seem not to move at all. Impossible to calculate their direction: Seattle? Mazatlán, for Mexican oil? Stella, her mind returning to her work, sighs with sadness then for Mexico, a country that in a way she considers her own. It is just so ruined, poor Mexico, she thinks. Corruption like an acid everywhere, and the country exploding with babies, always babies, the single, simple pleasure of the poor.

An hour or so later Stella admits to herself that she really does not like being in this house alone. Its beautiful bare bones reproach her somehow. Dead bones, needing Richard's lively presence to revive them.

As Stella needs that presence.

Although since her pneumonia she and Richard have returned to an earlier, sunnier, almost perfectly idyllic time (in fact even happier than their earliest days), Stella still thinks, more or less in spite of herself, of those dark weeks preceding her illness. When Richard was always with those German clients, getting drunk with them, coming late or not at all to her house. And not only drunk but angry, abusive, *terrible*.

Remembering those black and awful weeks, Stella sometimes further thinks that she could and quite possibly should have broken with Richard then. For good. If Prentice had not died at just that time, or if Prentice had left her some liberating cash—or if she had not got so sick just then—she might have been strong enough to say to him, I'm sorry, but we have to end all this. You don't make me happy. You drink too much. I'm in love with you, I know I am, but sometimes I don't think I like you very much. And sometimes I think you don't like me either.

She knows that Prentice's death, and his will, and her pneumonia, are no real excuse; even when Richard came to see her in the hospital, with roses, she could have said those things.

These thoughts, these revisions of circumstance and act, with accompanying self-accusations, are rare and fleeting, though. More often the very thought of a permanent break with Richard is intolerable to Stella—especially now, when she is alone and tired, in a darkened seacoast house, at night.

From the windows she sees no remnants of the sunset, only black. And the sea's salt smell invades the house, and the chill damp winds, and the pounding, pounding roar of the heavy waves. (How could she face being permanently alone?)

The waves drown out almost everything. If the phone rang— Richard saying he'd be late, or maybe not coming at all—would she hear it? Of course she would, but did it possibly ring earlier, when she was taking her bath? (There is no answering machine in this house; Richard likes the idea of relative inaccessibility.)

Stella sits there, shivering, forgetting to turn the heater on. In Richard's beautiful house. In her clean warm pretty clothes.

When suddenly she is aroused by a bursting blast, a sound and a voice, as the door breaks open: *Anybody home?*

She runs to him. They kiss.

14

Richard's Plans

Richard is working hard on a great surprise for Stella; it is so great that his heart warms, his blood quickens, when he thinks of it. So marvelous! so exciting! He can't wait to see her face when she sees it for the first time. He will work even harder and harder; he will get it all finished for her very soon.

Or (maybe) he will fly to Venice to meet Eva. In hours, on the Concorde. Does the Concorde go to Italy? He isn't sure, but probably.

His mania for Venice is an important secret of Richard's. Venice, where he has never been. (Shit, he has never been to Europe at all, and not even to Mexico, or Canada. Christ, *Canada.*) But Venice is the shimmering pinnacle of all his heart's desires. He has read all the books he can find—James Morris, Mary McCarthy—but mostly he has looked at pictures, so that fixed in his inner vision are small gray squares, little arched stone bridges over dark smooth canals; and restaurant terraces, full of handsome and lively people who gaze out across vistas of stone and water; a small obscure church, full of lovely Carpaccios; and the Academy itself, with its marvelous Bellinis, Canalettos. And all the grander, more obvious monuments—Piazza San Marco, Ducal Palace, the Grand Canal. The stones and waters of Venice.

It strikes him as very trite, this passion of his. Christ, everyone loves Venice (but not as he does). He is almost ashamed, which is one reason for his never having told anyone at all, and perhaps a reason too for never seriously planning a trip to Venice. It might disappoint him, just possibly, like a lovely woman who turns out to smell, in some awful way.

But: Venice with Eva! the most perfectly beautiful, perfect (almost perfect) woman of all. Great love with Eva, in a hotel overlooking the water and lovely carved stone. His loveliest Eva.

One night he almost called her. She is now in Berlin, or he thinks she is in Berlin. He did dial her, and he got into some trouble with the overseas operator (that bitch!). Got nowhere. No Eva.

And Eva after all went away mad (Richard tends often to forget this). "You seem curiously unavailable, my darling handsome Richard. Could there just possibly be another woman in your life? I get almost a smell of marriage. Or maybe some boy, as beautiful as you are yourself? That does not strike me as out of the question for you." Eva said all that.

At least Stella has never accused him of being queer. He loves Stella, loves her very much, almost all the time. He loves her knees, and the sweet round curve of her forehead, and the dumb way she slices tomatoes in the air. She makes him smile inside. He can't wait to see her face when she comes back from his house on the coast. When she sees what he's done. Her surprise.

Would he ever go to Venice with Stella? No. No. Well, possibly; under certain circumstances he could.

Stella of course has been to Venice and to all those other places already, been everywhere. Venice and Paris and Cairo and

Amsterdam and Mexico. He's not sure about Canada, but probably. She went everywhere with that Liam, that low-class John Huston type, as Richard thinks of him. That child-molester. No wonder Stella doesn't want to talk about him: she was the molested child. On the other hand, eighteen years old, old enough to know a little better. But she was just this poor spick kid, a relative innocent. He hates to think of Stella with that Liam: he thinks of them all the time. In detail. Stella, the unblemished little girl, dragged all over the world by that old prick. No wonder Stella never talks about those travels, does not talk about Liam. Has certainly never specifically mentioned Venice with Liam.

Richard straightens his back and works his shoulders up and down a few times, feeling their strength, his own muscular power. Working off all those bad thoughts. He tells himself that none of that is important, not even Eva-in-Venice. And God knows not the child Stella with old man ugly, Liam O'Gara.

Today, along with the great surprise for Stella, Richard is thinking about a certain project, or the rumor of a project, for which he has been approached. A project that is so great, so cut to the shape of Richard Fallon, that if he gets it, gets what was totally made for him, it will be like claiming an inheritance. He, little Richard from Nowhere, New Jersey, will be rich and famous for life, forever, everywhere. Or at least he will be very famous in the ad world, and maybe a little in the art world too; those guys are not unknown to take certain talents seriously, so maybe a show sometime, maybe. Some drawings in the Achenbach?

Because the project is California itself. Richard's place, his beautiful discovery, his golden state. The project is for a hotel chain, the Fillmore, hotels all over northern California, plans for expansion down south, and it looks like they may very well want him to do it. Him, Richard Fallon himself. There will be no photos, nowhere photos; it's against their policy. Drawings. Watercolors. Pure sheer design. He can already see them: white rooms hung with rows of bright mounted white-on-white, white-

framed watercolors. *His,* of everything. Freeways (he'll show
Wayne Thiebaud a thing or two) and beaches and lakes and poppies and state parks on the coast, and Victorian gingerbreads, and
contemporary offices, rows of houses, ski scenes (he'll get to ski
again; maybe take Claudia—meet her somewhere?). And everything, everything by Richard Fallon.

As he thinks of these pictures, this plan, the project, the
money—as he thinks of actually doing it, Richard feels the strain
of wild blood flooding his heart, his veins, his lungs, flooding his
very soul with excitement.

He got on well with the account executive, who he more or
less expects will call today. Al Bolling. They really did get on.
Bolling liked him, he could tell. Al Bolling, from Mamaroneck,
New York, a town that Richard remembers driving by, seeing
boats, yacht clubs, mansion-type houses. Many rich Jews, but
Bolling is not a Jew. A preppy WASP, Yale, but nice, a very nice
guy. A little stiff, a little heavy, looks like he doesn't sleep too
well, maybe hits the sauce sometimes. Maybe when they know
each other better, after Richard has the job, they could do some
drinking together, and talk.

" 'Al' doesn't seem quite right for you," Richard imagines
himself saying, with his laugh. "Maybe . . . how about Marbles?"

"Marbles? Why on earth?"

"I don't know." More laughing; they both are laughing. "It
just came to me. Marbles."

And then, in this imagined time of drinks together, dinner,
more drinks, they would really get down to it, talk, the way men
are supposed to do these days.

"It's my kids," Bolling might say. "They really get to me.
Brought up with everything, you know, and they hardly give me
the time of day. The boys are bad enough, but the girl, my
daughter, she's thirty next month and gorgeous, built like Mon-
roe, and she does not like men. My daughter the dyke. I hate to
say it, but it's true, she digs women. I mean, what can they . . . ?
Ever think about it, Richard?"

"Well, of course I have," Richard would tell him, in a comforting, knowing way, even though Al must be a good fifteen
years older than he is. "But it's not the worst thing in the world,

the gay thing. Several guys I know, queers, I guess you'd call them, but they're really nice. You can talk to them."

Richard suddenly laughs, exploding the fantasy, the imagined conversation. And in a firm, realistic way he tells himself that first he has to get the job—before getting into these intimate talks with Al Bolling. *Marbles.* Thinking the nickname, though, Richard laughs again, seated there at his studio desk. He has to admit, he is good with these names for people.

But first he has to get the job.

When the phone rings he first thinks, of course, that it must be Bolling. But it isn't. Claudia.

Sure that she wants to get together, since that is the usual reason for her calls, Richard chats inconsequentially with her for a while: friends, parties, the nice summer camp where both her boys are (those boys whom Richard still misses so badly). As they talk he is planning to turn her down; the very idea of saying no to Claudia fills him with virtuous pleasure, as though he were being faithful both to Stella and, obscurely, to Al Bolling. And actually he does not want any time with Claudia right now; he is in fact too busy, and he really is in love with Stella. Today. He has a somewhat unclear idea that fidelity to Stella would certify him as a good person, a man of rectitude (Bolling's kind of man).

Claudia goes on and on. Richard is almost afraid that she will not get to the point, but at last, of course, she does. "I'd love to see you," she says, with her particular sexy emphasis. "Do you think we could, some afternoon *soon*?"

And so he does get to say it, to say what he has, in a way, always wanted to say to Claudia: "I'm sorry, babes, but these days I just can't. I'm busy, and I'm in love. I think."

A pause, and then a somewhat tremulous "Well, okay, darling handsome Rich. Whatever you say."

Can she possibly be about to cry? He could hear tears in her voice, he would swear to tears, and so Richard has to say, "Only half kidding, sweetheart. But right now I am busy as hell. Let me call you very soon, okay?" He says all that very gently.

"Well, sure," says Claudia. She is feeling better, he can tell. No more tears.

But at least he gave it a try. Tried it on, so to speak. And he did, for today, turn her down.

The next call is from Marina, who sounds as crazy as usual. Maybe more so. Manic. "The greatest guy," she says. "His ex-wife is a policeman. Policewoman. And he's an ex-cop himself. Is that not a kick? Is that not funny? You know, Rickie, some-times I think I'll write a book. About us, the things we went through. Still are going through, wouldn't you say? Sometimes I pretend that you're still here. But this new guy is remarkable. A cop. His former wife, or did I tell you that? Rickie, are you listening?"

God. Women. Sometimes he envies gay men, he really does. And if he were ever off on a ship somewhere, isolated with just men, well, there's no doubt in Richard's mind what would hap-pen. Which is not a thing he would admit to Andrew Bacci. On the other hand, maybe he would admit it to Andrew. He sort of loves Andrew, in a way. He can talk to Andrew.

"Marina, I've got to get to work," he tells his former wife. "I'll call you, okay?" Women like promises. Sometimes he thinks that's what they live on, like fish with those tiny wafers.

"Okay," says Marina.

But what if he doesn't get the Fillmore job, with Bolling? At this thought Richard's spirits plunge downward, like a huge stone into water—a splash, and then gone, down to the bottom. Cold. He shivers, imagining himself a street person. Dirty and cold and friendless. Hopeless. Dying of something. Where in a way he has always known he would be. He will end up on the street. He knows that, sometimes.

"Hello?" He answers the phone again, knowing that his voice is odd: he is still a beggar, out on the street.

"Richard? Richard Fallon? You don't sound quite like your-self. Al Bolling here. I wondered, I know it's late, but could you make lunch today? There're some things I'd like to go over."

Could he!

All energized now, and thinking that he must have known this would happen—he dressed this morning in his best new gray flannel blazer—Richard calculates his time. Exactly an hour and a half before he should leave to meet Al. Marbles. He smiles and gets to work.

He makes some calls, first off. One to Standish Wong. (No nicknames for Standish somehow, although they're getting along really well, as he knew they would.) "Standish? Fallon here. I'll be a little late, got a business lunch, but I'll be along, okay? That's great, Standish, just great."

He hangs up happily, with thoughts of pleasure for Stella. He feels both virtuous and effective, generous and efficient and kind. Himself at his best. Superenergetic. *Charged.*

He makes two more calls, these having to do with business of his own. Work projects, boring and overdue, that now seem dwarfed. Insignificant and annoying, beside the Fillmore thing. But he needs the bread. As always.

When the phone rings again he is on his feet and moving toward the door, but he answers anyway. Knowing it will be Stella.

But her sound is unexpected, unfamiliar: she is so excited over something that at first Richard does not quite understand. Something about an agent in New York and a piece she's been working on.

He breaks in as gently as he can. "Baby, that's terrific, but honestly, I was halfway out the door. Oh, that's great! And do I have a surprise for you! Maybe two surprises. Maybe really great news. Okay, tonight. I'll get up there as early as I possibly can."

He still hasn't entirely understood what Stella was talking about, but it's nice to hear her so cheerful; staying up there on the coast by herself has been getting her down. It's not easy to keep women happy.

Outside, walking fast along the sunny, dirty street, Richard can hardly contain himself. He wants to run, or to skip along, like a kid. Feeling marvelous!

He is stopped almost dead in his tracks, though, by the eyes of a street man, a homeless person, dark and filthy-haired, in rags, with great dark haunted eyes and ugly skin. The eyes stop Richard cold. They seem planted there in front of him, to stop him.

Reaching into his pocket, Richard pulls out the first bill that comes to his hand. A twenty. Good. Payoff money. He hands it to the dirty hand. To the eyes.

And walks along, more slowly now, less securely. To meet Al Bolling.

15

Celebrations

"I can't believe it!" Stella cries out, aware of banality but helpless.

For what she says is the literal truth: she cannot believe the transformation of her apartment. As she enters what were her rooms, the space in which she stands (quite tentatively, clutching at Richard's arm) is no space that she ever saw before. It is large and fairly bare, with huge wide windows, giving onto the deep-green, ferny Presidio woods. Where there were walls, now only a few supporting pillars remain, all painted a rich high-gloss dark brown. The floors have been stripped down to beautiful plain wide planks. In a far corner Stella sees her old bed, now discreetly covered in something thick and brown, and here and there about the room she recognizes objects that are hers: some wooden chairs, a small marble-topped table. But the long broad gray soft leather sofa—she never saw that before, nor the rich scatter of small Oriental rugs. Even, on the walls, new pictures, strange sepia photographs of what looks to be Venice, late nineteenth century (she thinks).

It is a beautiful room; Stella can hardly connect it with herself, can hardly believe that she lives here, that she is intended to live here.

Also, in a sinking, inadmissible way, she is thinking: What must all this have cost? Shouldn't she offer to pay? But that would be impossible: she is as always very broke, and also she and Richard have no language in which money could be discussed. Nevertheless, she does say to him, "But all this new stuff . . ."

Which of course he understands. "Just stuff I had lying around." He stares at her, smiling impatiently. "What's the matter, don't you like it?"

"Oh, Richard, I love it, I can't tell you. It's fantastic." But even as she speaks the truth—she *does* love what he has done, it *is* fantastic—Stella is aware of a deep and squirming discomfort, an unease to which she can give no name and that, as best she can, she rejects.

". . . and listen," Richard is saying, staring into her face, gripping both her arms (a new gesture with him: it would make more sense if she were a very tall woman). "This new job, baby, wait till you hear." He laughs. "It's only the best job any hack in advertising ever had."

"Oh, that's marvelous." And she listens, as Richard tells her about the Fillmore job, Al Bolling, the projected watercolors. California poppies, skiing at Tahoe, the north coast, redwoods, rivers, streams, city parks. The trips the two of them will take, to everywhere.

"It's marvelous!" she tells him, again.

But Richard, with his uncannily attuned intuition, must sense her unease. Her problem is that she would like to tell him about her good news: Gloria Bergstein, her new agent (and impossible to explain to non-literary Richard the particular power and prestige of Gloria), has said that *The Gotham,* a very new, high-paying, high-visibility magazine (whose editor, it is rumored, is Gloria's lover), is very interested in a piece that Stella wrote about the San Francisco homeless. *Very* interested. But this moment seems inappropriate for such news; this moment is Richard's.

"You don't look absolutely happy," Richard accuses, as she almost knew that he would. "Jesus Christ, what would it take?"

"Oh, darling—" Tears, from whatever useful source, flood her eyes. Her hands reach to cover her face, as her shoulders convulse, and Richard takes her in his arms.

"Baby, baby, I'm sorry," he whispers in her ear. "I didn't mean— Christ, you're so sensitive! You're lovely."

"It's just so beautiful, what you've done," Stella (falsely) explains. "I'm not very good at receiving things," she (truthfully) adds.

"I guess you're not." He laughs. "But it didn't come out too bad, really, did it. I brought Al Bolling around to see it yesterday, and I have to admit, he was pretty fucking impressed."

"But—" But I've never met Al Bolling, and he saw my house before I did? Stella does not say this.

"He can't wait to meet you. In fact we've got to have a party, don't you think? A real blast. Pull out all the stops. To celebrate everything."

"Great—"

"Now, about this job I've almost got."

"Richard, I love my house, it's beautiful—"

"Sketching trips, all over the state—"

"Richard, that's so great—"

"Skiing trips—"

"I don't ski—"

"You'll learn!"

Looking down just then, Richard observes, "Legs looks even prettier here now, don't you think? She loves it. More sun." As though flattered, the small cat stretches, and rubs against Richard's feet. And then yawns.

"This house reminds me of some book I read when I was a child," Stella tells him, musingly. "One of my father's childhood books. Called *Sara Crewe*, I think. It was about a poor Victorian orphan girl who's out in the rain one night, all cold and unloved, and she goes back up to her room and someone has filled it all with flowers and presents. An Indian prince, I think."

"Sounds like you have total recall." He laughs. "You read too much."

Briefly, then, they kiss, and Richard tells her, "I have to go now. Later."

Alone in her (their) old-new apartment, with Richard's (her) cat, Stella tries to orient herself. Familiarity may come later on; now she simply has to find out where things are.

She starts by just standing where she was when Richard left—more or less in the middle of the room—and staring about. Then she begins slowly to walk around, to open a door here and there. She finds that things are more as they were than at first they looked to be: her clothes in their closets and chests of drawers; linens and towels and paper supplies in their closet. Wine and booze, cans and boxes of food on new-painted kitchen shelves. Her desk and typewriter in their place, in their corner.

But where is the little chest in which she always kept certain letters and notes—her most important things? Where is that chest?

She hurries all over the still-strange space, as she thinks, terribly: Of course, the chest was ugly and awkward. Richard just threw it out. He saw some old papers, maybe he shoved them into a drawer somewhere. How like him, so intolerant of anything not beautiful. He's so selfish. This whole performance was some ego trip. His ego. *Where is my chest, and my papers?*

Trembling, quite frantic now, she dials Richard's number, but gets his recorded voice. "You have reached—" Not wanting even to hear him, she hangs up.

That little chest, now presumably lost to her, becomes in Stella's lively mind a metaphor for everything wrong between them. A small and ugly paradigm. But this startles her; she had not often before articulated to herself the notion that anything was wrong between them.

Next to her bed (their bed), with its new deep-brown coarse wool cover, onto which Stella has just flung herself, there is a tall new bright brass reading lamp, elegantly resting on a brilliant-blue small lacquered chest. Almost idly, expecting nothing, Stella tries the top drawer of the chest—which opens easily, revealing a packet of letters, carefully wrapped in tissue paper. Her letters.

And the same is true of the next two small drawers, an easy opening to her things, all meticulously wrapped. And Stella, straining through bewilderment, recognizes in this bright-blue lacquered stranger her ugly old chest, miraculously transformed. And the tissue paper suggests an almost reverent regard for her possessions—precisely the reverse of her enraged suspicions, her suppositions.

Stella is as deeply embarrassed as if Richard could have known what was in her mind.

"Anybody home?"

At that sound, that night, Stella rushes toward the door, guilt and gratitude combining to fuel her ardor.

"Say, what'd I do?" he teases, familiarly.

"Oh, you're only talented and brilliant and sensitive and generous and extremely handsome," Stella tells him, laughing.

"Oh."

There are so many versions of Richard, and she lives with all those different men. It is no wonder, Stella sometimes thinks, that she is frequently confused. There is the near genius in visual matters, who could imagine such openness, such bare-boned elegance in her ratty, awkwardly divided, small-scale apartment—and the generous, sensitive person who put it all together, for her. (For the moment she ignores the slight presumption, maybe a little more than slight, of his never having asked or consulted with her about such a radical projected change.) And then there is the plain ordinary man who comes home for dinner at night, tired and hungry, with not a lot to say. And then the raging furious stranger who sometimes, terrifyingly, emerges—the horrible drunk.

And: the most beautiful, fine-skinned, fair fresh flesh-smelling lover, whom she kisses, endlessly. (Does she kiss more than he does, more eagerly, fervently, strongly? Stella will not let this thought occur. Not yet.)

But it is true that she lives with all those people. And that she is often confused.

* * *

What Stella and Richard will do, they decide, is invite everyone they know to their party. An open house for Stella's new apartment. And the subtext, so to speak, is a celebration of Richard's new job; of course Al Bolling will be among those invited.

And Andrew Bacci and Margot and Justine and Collin Schmidt, and Tony Russo, Cats, and his Valerie. ("If they're still together. I haven't heard from him for a while," Richard cautions. Stella refers to Valerie as Tits Galore, which Richard does not think is very funny.) Plus a number of friends from both their places of work, as well as from their former, other lives. Unstated is the fact that this is their first joint effort at party giving; some sort of statement about themselves as a couple is implicitly being made.

But it begins fairly soon to seem, to Stella, more Richard's party. They call his caterer (the same pretty girls who did the bubble party). His florist. Stella, left to herself, would have done it all more simply: buy lots of cheese and cold cuts in North Beach, and flowers from Bloomers.

"Can't I even pay for some of this?" she asks at some point.

"Oh no. I'll let you give a party later on, when I go broke. Right now I'm really okay that way."

Which in a way is all right with Stella; she is as broke as ever, maybe a little more so. She often buys a lot of fairly fancy food for their dinners, even though Richard shops too and almost always brings home wine and booze, not to mention all those flowers.

Still, in another way this does not seem quite right; they should share the expense of this party. It's her party too, is it not?

The day before the party, a Friday, Stella stays at home to clean, and to think of and cope with last-minute details, like cocktail napkins, so far unmentioned, and Perrier, tomato juice, whatever, for the possible non-drinkers. Lemons and limes.

In the midst of her coping with most of that (she is just back from the neighborhood supermarket), the phone rings, and Stella answers—to hear an unfamiliar, very enthusiastic woman's voice.

"Hi, Stell, how's tricks? Listen, hons, I've got some almost unbelievable good news for you, kiddo. Oh, by the way, this is Gloria. Gloria Bergstein—I'm your agent, remember?" A harsh cigarette laugh, which Stella is to come to recognize as readily as the exuberant voice. "Well, *The Gotham* is just nuts about your squatter piece, those people around Civic Center, or whatever you people call it. They love it. They're offering ten for first North American rights, and maybe I can get them up, or maybe do better somewhere else, but I have to tell you I'm tempted just to go with it. What do you think? It's long, of course, but they like that. Spread over two issues, they think."

It is several minutes before Stella is able to understand that this flashy new New York magazine is buying her piece, a long rambling mess, as she thought of it, a mélange of interviews and opinions (mostly her own) about some people camped out at the UN Plaza and some other people, who insisted on feeding them. And that she is being paid ten thousand dollars.

Her first impulse, or one of the first, is to split the money, somehow, with all those people, the squatters and the feeders, all of whom she more or less got to know (several in both groups were Mexicans, with whom she found a special rapport). She dismisses this impulse, or almost dismisses it, as somewhat hysterical. But she will give them a big chunk of the money.

Her second impulse is to call Richard—of course!

"Baby, that's great, that's just really, really great. I always knew you had it in you, kid. This is super! Ten grand? Wow, you can start keeping me anytime. How much of that does your agent get? You don't know? Well, honestly, Stell. Find out. Call her back and ask her. But, honey, I'm so pleased, I'm so proud of you. Now we have even more to celebrate at our party, don't we. Stell, I love you."

He arrives home that night with a huge sheaf of flowers, beautiful, white stock (so sweet-smelling) and purple iris. This is for Stella, as well as for their party.

* * *

I have never been so happy in my life.

That sentence dances through Stella's mind on the night of their party, as she moves through the celebrating, admiring guests, in her new red silk dress in her beautiful new rooms. As she catches sight of Richard here and there, or as he joins her momentarily, now and then, for a small whispered joke, a quick kiss. She thinks, Never so happy. The room is full of flowers, of scents of roses and perfumes and sharp spicy foods, full of bright silk clothes, shining silver and glasses, pale yellow or deep red wines. She is so happy, Stella feels, that her chest might burst. It is one of those rare moments (she could hardly think of another one) when everywhere her mind alights seems propitious, and *good.*

Even her work is going well. She has talked on the phone with her new editor at *The Gotham* and has felt extreme intelligence, along with enthusiasm.

And she has wonderful friends.

And a lovely love affair.

Richard as a host is extremely energetic. He is everywhere at once, as a host is supposed to be. He neither drinks too much nor tells too many long jokes (Stella has observed him doing both those things too often at parties). But now he is too busy for drinking or for jokes; he talks quickly, vividly, to everyone there. He keeps glasses filled, he urges food.

Al Bolling dislikes white wine, he has made that clear—and by implication, people who drink it. His drink is Scotch. "I assume you have some, old man?" Fortunately they do. A tall, somewhat paunchy man with thick dark hair, very pale skin, shadowed eyes, Bolling, for most of the party, seems to keep to himself, resisting efforts by both Richard and Stella to draw him in. "I'm not much of a mingler," he at one point says to Richard. "Observation is more in my line."

"Well, observe away." Blithe Richard.

"I like your lady. I hope you don't mind my saying so."

"Not at all, I'm delighted to hear it, I like her too!" And Richard gives Bolling his warmest good-guy smile.

* * *

Margot has come to the party alone. She meant to come with Andrew, of course, but he is at home with a bad summer cold. Nothing more (Margot is sure), but having tested HIV positive (as he more or less knew he would), Andrew is sent into panic (not unreasonably) by any ailment. Margot has decided to pretend not to take him seriously, in terms of health, and to hide her own panic in sheer silliness. "You're just afraid you don't look cute with a cold," she chided Andrew. "So Richard will love you less."

"Oh, Margot, come on."

Having watched Richard with this new man, this Al Bolling, Margot comes to several conclusions. One is that Richard is overdoing it; he must need Bolling badly for something or other, and his famous charm is not quite working. Bolling is not quite as charmed by Richard as Richard thinks he is. This connection will not end well for either of them, Margot feels.

She also senses that Bolling has at least some incipient interest in her. Later, probably, he will ask her to go out to dinner; will she go? She is not at all sure that she will. He is attractive, but he looks very unhappy, and he looks like a drunk. Not her type at all. Not pretty. And she should go home early, to check on Andrew.

Justine, who has also come alone, without Bunny, is likewise casing the party; and trying to define, for herself, the considerable unease into which this scene has propelled her. Perhaps, she tries to tell herself, she simply cannot get used to, cannot accept, such a smart surround for her insouciant old friend, her dear old Stella. But should she not be glad for such an improvement? The place used to look so shabby. Or is it the slightly manic glint in the eyes of both Stella and Richard, the faint edge of hysteria, of hyper, unreal joy, that she senses? She frowns to herself at the unpleasantly probing, analytic quality of her own mind—and then looks up to see before her an extremely attractive small dark man.

"Hi," he says. "I'm Tony Russo. Richard calls me Cats. Are you a friend of his too?"

Oblivious to almost everything but her own great pleasure in this occasion (she is also getting a little drunk, as Richard now is), Stella still thinks in stray moments of *The Gotham,* her article being there. Her money. Can she do it again? she wonders. She believes that she can. Her head is so full of ideas, of plans; she is dizzy with her own words. She will write more and more and be more and more successful, Stella believes on this night of the party.

She can almost believe that she deserves a man as radiant as Richard is. Looking across the room to where he stands, she feels her heart contract at the very sight of him—as, sensing her glance, he looks up at her and smiles, dazzlingly.

16

Successful Stella

About three weeks after the celebration party, Gloria Bergstein calls early one morning to say that *The Gotham* has taken another piece of Stella's, one that she has worked on off and on for a couple of years, about volunteer workers in local hospices, burnout, all that; it is somewhat grim, and the paper turned it down, finally, on the grounds that no one would want to read it. It is fairly short, and this time *The Gotham* is offering $7,500. "The best I could do, babycakes," rasps Gloria, inhaling an early cigarette; it is 9:00 a.m. in New York, 6:00 in California. "But I'll get them back up to ten next time, or else spit in their eyes."

"God, Gloria, that's okay, seventy-five hundred is terrific, I can't believe it. That's marvelous!"

"Just keep working, kiddo. We'll be in touch."

Stella hangs up the phone and turns to Richard, lying beside her in bed. Now wide-awake and propped up to listen, Stella asks him, "Did you hear that—can you believe it?" She is almost in tears.

"Why didn't you hold out for ten? why are you so grateful?" But he is smiling and happy and warm, kissing and embracing her, telling her then, "You're so lovely, 'I'm so happy you're happy."

"Where shall we go for dinner?" asks Stella. "Let me take you. Somewhere great."

They settle on the Nob Hill, the grandest restaurant they know; they agree to meet there at seven.

All that day long Stella is smiling. This is what happiness is, she thinks. To have love in your life, and especially love in the beautiful form of Richard. And some success in your work, people saying that what you do is really okay, is in fact quite good. And lots of money. Oh, those three things are really enough to make her (or anyone!) entirely happy. How lucky she is! Even if *The Gotham* never takes another piece by her, she will still be very happy, Stella thinks, and for the moment she believes that this is true.

At work everyone congratulates her. "*The Gotham,* wow!" "That's really the best in the business right now. As good as *The New Yorker* used to be." "That's super! How lucky those old fools upstairs turned it down." "That's great!"

Stella is struck by the real warmth in all those reactions; today she feels that everyone genuinely wishes her well, that everyone is pleased for her.

"It's partly because they know you've paid your dues," says Justine, over a quick but celebratory lunchtime salad. "They all know you've been working very hard and you've been as underpaid as they are."

"And I'm not twenty-one. Not some bumptious suddenly successful kid," says Stella, very seriously.

"No. It's lucky you're so old. Otherwise everyone would be very mean and envious."

They laugh, and then Justine asks, very lightly, "Richard's pleased?"

"Of course. Really pleased. But why? You'd think he wouldn't be?"

"Well, it's supposed to be very hard on men. The success of women."

"I know, but Richard isn't like that. Not a dumb macho bone in his body. He's very 'in touch with his femaleness,' you know? And with mine. I think." But this exchange is making her just slightly anxious, Stella notes; she feels a small, painful thrust of worry, a tiny shadow cast on her sunny day. Which almost instantly passes.

"The fact that Richard is so intensely creative too, and successful at it, that must make a big difference. If he were just some ordinary advertising jerk . . . ," says Justine.

"But in that case we wouldn't be together at all," Stella points out, laughing, her happiness restored.

Dinner at the Nob Hill is a great success. Two happy and successful people. Eating and drinking much too much good food and wine. And going home, amazingly, to love. To amazing love.

"You're really hot at *The Gotham*," Gloria Bergstein has told Stella. "And they've got money to burn. Send them anything. Your high school essay contest entry, maybe."

"I don't really have a thing right now, but I'll think."

What Stella does have is an entirely private project, undertaken more or less as therapy after Prentice died when she was trying so hard to shake off all the anger and hurt around his death. At that time she began a sort of reminiscence of some good times with Prentice, in his parents' house in New Hampshire: the wonderful library there of Victorian children's books (including *Sara Crewe*); the attic full of toys. And the lake, the beaches and rocks, and canoes, and picnics. The grandparents getting drunk and singing hymns. Prentice cooking steaks like a regular father. Prentice kind and affectionate with her.

She has written all that, but it makes her shy to think of sending it to *The Gotham.*

She could show it to Justine, she thinks, and ask her opinion, but Stella decides instead (she is not sure just why) to show the piece to Richard. To ask him what he thinks.

"You read it to me," he tells her. "You know how I hate to read. I'm the illiterate lover."

And so, after dinner, she does read the whole fairly long piece to Richard, who listens with great intentness, smiling, with a small laugh here and there. And then, *"Well,"* he tells her. "That's really super. I think it's the best thing you've done; I know they'll take it." Rather hesitantly he adds, "But wouldn't it maybe be a little better if you started with the picnic?—I don't know—and then the books and the dolls?"

"That sounds right—in fact I know you're right. Richard, you are a genius!"

"All the girls tell me that."

But he is very pleased, she can tell. And actually his was a brilliant suggestion; the piece now has a dramatic structure, a form that it lacked before. "You're absolutely brilliant," Stella tells him, when she has printed out her piece and sent it off to Gloria.

"A whole new career for me." Richard laughs. "Illiterate boy finds work as literary critic."

The Gotham buys the piece. This time for twelve thousand.

With Richard, Stella admits only to the wildest happiness, and she credits him with the success of this latest piece. "It was all in the way you shifted things around. Honestly, that made all the difference."

"Stell, come on! But where shall we go to celebrate?"

To Simon Daniels, who calls, as he sometimes does, to give a sort of progress report on the Prentice Blake project, Stella admits a somewhat less positive reaction. "It scares me," she says to Simon. "I know it's silly, but it does. I don't do well with success."

"That's not so silly," Simon tells her. "It is scary. The slightest success. Especially in this crazy country we live in, where every day we see how dangerous it is. Success *or* failure, I think. I do wonder if that's true anywhere else, or as true. I would rather guess not, but it would be interesting to know, don't you think?"

"Extremely," Stella tells him—though she is actually thinking less about success in England or France or China than about her own trepidations. But Simon's question has been interesting, and she forces herself to carry on with it. "You'd think we'd know," she says to Simon. "Or at least that someone would."

"Actually I have a pal in London I can ask about how things are there, success-wise. He's really on the fringe himself, so he'd be the first to know."

Stella then asks how the Prentice book is going, and Simon tells her, "Hard work. Everyone contradicts everyone else. It's honestly hard to believe they're all talking about the same guy."

"Well, he was pretty complicated," Stella tries to reassure him.

"But his politics! Really schizo."

"I know."

"I've begun to think he could have been CIA."

"Oh Lord!"

"Justine, what on earth, what've you done to your hair?"

"Calm down, Stella. It's just a rinse. It'll go away." But Justine frowns a little, and very slightly blushes, as she explains, "Don't you ever think a person could get tired of plain old gray-blond hair?"

Stella laughs. "Oh sure, but I loved it, Justine. Your gray is really beautiful." And then, her voice darkening with suspicion, "Did you do this for Collin? I mean, did he—"

At which her friend in her turn laughs. "No, I actually did it sort of against Collin. He kept going on and on about my beautiful gray hair, and I began to think it was a sort of wifely attribute for him."

"Come on, Justine. All you had to do was say no. You don't have to dye your hair. What is this, some sort of semiotics?"

This conversation is proceeding on a dirty bench in Union Square, at lunchtime. The two women have seated themselves among the new and old homeless, the visibly alcoholic and/or drugged—and the others, who are simply people with nowhere to live. And a scattering of middle-class people more or less like themselves, people with houses and jobs. With lives. At the far end of the square some sort of protest is going on, pitifully small: fifteen or twenty struggling men and women, a few tattered posters, which Stella and Justine are unable to read. They wonder to each other about those people: who? for what cause? Both women, knee-jerk liberals, find their sympathies almost automatically aroused.

Justine's bright new blond hair, in the bright new sunlight, seems to make her look older than the softening gray did—or so Stella thinks. Justine is still very attractive, but also more ordinary. "You look like someone who lives in Burlingame, very Peninsula," is what she says to her friend.

"Well, thanks a lot. A Peninsula matron, my favorite role model. Is success going to make you mean, do you think?"

At which Stella, unaccountably, almost cries; there are tears in her eyes, which she just manages to blink away. "Damn," is all that she says, more or less to herself. And then, to Justine, "This new sale is somehow making me terrifically nervous."

"Well, I can sort of see how that might be." As always, Justine has given her whole attention to what has been said to her; she enters the world of another person with remarkable ease.

And so Stella tells her more. "When I sold that first piece, it just seemed a purely marvelous fluke. And then the second, icing on the cake. But now three. It's like I'm committed to something. I have to keep doing it."

Justine laughs, though gently. "Like after three dates it's a love affair."

"More like taking three steps out onto the tightrope," Stella tells her.

Having taken that in, Justine frowns. "Oh dear." And then she says, "I do see what you mean. You have to keep on going, or fall. You can't just go back to being a newspaper hack. I felt a little that way after the Nieman."

"Exactly."

They are quiet then for a while, both somewhat inattentively watching as the small group in the corner begins to disperse, its banners and placards still unreadable but having a foreign look. And the band of marchers themselves, departing, look alien, very dark.

"Iraqis, maybe?" suggests Justine.

"Maybe. I know they're not Mexican. Pakistanis?"

"Could be." And then Justine, with an air of pulling herself together, of getting down to business, says to Stella, "I have to tell you, babes, I've been getting a little static from upstairs concerning you."

"Oh?"

"Yes. You know what those old boys are like. I'm hearing phrases like 'taking advantage' and 'not serious journalism.' "

"Oh Jesus."

"Yes. Indeed. But easy enough to fix. Just show up around the shop a little more. Make your presence felt. You know, the more busy women around, the more important they all feel."

"So they won't think I'm writing for New York on their precious time."

"Right. You've got it."

Stella's mood of anxiety, though, persists into the afternoon. Despite all Justine's intelligent sympathy. She would even like to call Richard and say to him, Look, I don't really feel like celebrating. I know it's sort of neurotic, but couldn't we just have a quiet dinner at home? However, she does not call.

"That Bolling. Some Marbles. Honestly, I really wonder." These ambiguous phrases, more or less muttered into his martini, are Richard's first utterances of the evening, as, drink from the bar in hand, he slides into the booth beside Stella. Scowling. And then the scowl goes, and he kisses her. (But martinis? Richard never drinks martinis.)

She asks, "What's the matter with Al—acting up?" She has tried to make it a joke.

"Oh, I don't know. It could be just me. I'm not the easiest guy in the world to get along with. Or so I've been told." He flashes a familiar smile.

"Now, who would say a thing like that?"

They both laugh, a little uneasily. In the last week or so they have had a couple of almost major fights, which were her fault quite as much as his, Stella believes.

Does he want to talk about Bolling? As is so often the case, Richard's signals are ambiguous. And so, tentatively, Stella tries. "You mean Bolling's being difficult?"

Richard makes a sound that is half laugh, half snort. Derisory of both herself and Bolling, Stella at that instant feels.

"You could put it like that," says Richard. And then he adds, "Don't ask."

"This place was a good idea," Stella tells him, brightly, after a somber pause. "It's so good-looking, I've been wanting to come here. Have you seen it before?"

"No, never," he says (too quickly?). "I mean yes, I came once with Bolling, actually, and we had a drink at the bar." (It is in fact the place where, observed by Margot, Richard first had dinner with Eva.)

"Oh." Obscurely disturbed, Stella decides that perhaps she should at least try to talk more openly to Richard, more honestly than she usually does. In a friendly way (she hopes), she begins, "I don't know why, but selling this new piece has upset me in some curious way. It's hard to understand. You'd think—"

Richard has been staring at her as she speaks. Unsympathetically; his look is almost hostile, Stella feels. In any case, it is totally without comprehension. And he says, "I sure don't get it. I just don't. Tell that to one of your literary friends. Jesus Christ. Ten grand."

"We could go to Europe," says Stella suddenly. Desperately.

"Europe. Good Christ, Stella, get real. I've got work to do." But then he smiles and reaches for her hand. "Thanks for the offer, though. Well, shall we order? The food's really good here, as I remember."

But (Stella starts to say and does not) you said you just had a drink here.

She has not said this, but Richard seems to have felt or sensed the question. "Bolling and I had a few hors d'oeuvres at the bar," he tells her. "Damned hearty hors d'oeuvres, and damned good."

"Damned" is not a word that Richard uses in that way. Is he suddenly sounding like Al Bolling? And if so, why?

Dinner is good, though, and they drink a lot of good wine. *Quite* a lot. By the time they get home they are tired and merry, and faintly amorous. For a while.

Later Stella cannot even remember what they were talking about—only that suddenly the ground between them flared into fury, inflammable as an oil spill. Boiling blood. Pure rage. *Crazy!* they scream at each other. *You're crazy!* As, in some small part of her mind, Stella sickly thinks, We're both right, we both are crazy. If I were not crazy I would not be living with Richard, and maybe that is true of him too.

Richard's face is red and swollen with anger and hatred. His wild eyes dart about. How he longs to be away from her! Stella can see that. Perhaps he longs to kill her?

She begins to scream like a child, a very sick child. Rushing toward him, she beats on Richard with small clenched fists, hitting against his chest. How she longs to hurt him! But how horrible, how incredible! What she is doing is mad. Hitting and screaming. Crazy!

"Crazy fucking bitch." Richard has grasped her wrists and holds them hard.

Stella bursts into tears. "You're hurting me," she tells him. Although actually he is not, not hurting her wrists. But the tears (perhaps it is the tears) serve to prevent his running away. He drops her wrists, and she falls against him. And they fall together.

Fall, somehow, into bed.

A few hours later they wake, simultaneously. Both thirsty. Both needing to use the bathroom. "You go first," Stella tells him.

After her turn, creeping back into bed, she asks him, "Do you think we're both crazy?"

He mutters, "I guess."

"I think we've got to drink less. For one thing."

"I guess."

He turns on his side, away from her, and Stella clings to his back, as though for life.

17

Richard's Relationships

"Yes indeed. I think Stella's going to be very, very successful,"
says Richard to Bolling one lunchtime that fall. They are in one
of the few remaining old North Beach Italian restaurants, sitting
at the long, dark, high-polished bar (a bar that they are agreed is
a classic, perfect). Drinking Negronis.

"But I'm not at all sure that Stella's equipped to handle success," Richard continues.

Al is not especially interested in hearing about Stella, Richard
can tell—and actually why should he be? Richard was only talking to keep the ball rolling, so to speak; otherwise Al is given to
long black sullen lapses. But now he seems to respond. "That's
a problem with my daughter, Alexis," he tells Richard. "Such
a will to fail. I honestly believe that affected her, uh, sexual
direction. Afraid of failing with men. Which was all my fault.
Naturally."

Bolling's litanies of self-reproach and self-pity are very boring, very repetitive, but Richard forces himself to listen supportively, since—Christ!—if this job fails he will really, really, really be up shit creek without a paddle. "It's hard to understand about your daughter," he says to Bolling, as he has more than once before. "Such a beautiful girl, from her pictures." And then he adds, obliquely, "It's not exactly the same problem with Stella."

"I suppose not."

Bolling is drinking more than usual, as he has been for several weeks, which is one of the things that are worrying to Richard. Bolling is such a somber drinker; he talks and talks, but never jokes. No fun and games. Or else that silence. And sometimes when he talks he makes very little sense.

And it's very hard to get him to focus back on business, when Richard very much needs to do just that.

"A real touch of fall in the air today," he next attempts.

"Not surprising. October." Bolling frowns into his drink.

"I guess not. But about now's when I always start to think of skiing."

"Almost November. I think of the Day of the Dead," says Bolling. "Mexico. So interesting, their celebrations of death. Decorating skeletons, all that. The processions. Didn't you tell me your girlfriend had some Mexican connection?"

"Yes, her mother—"

"I'd like to talk to her sometime. Does she have special feelings about death, would you say?"

"She doesn't talk about it much. Stella's pretty young, you know." And so am I, you gloomy old crock, Richard does not say. But he forces himself to go on. "She's thinking of taking up skiing this year," he lies; Stella has admitted to a severe fear of heights, but said she'd be happy to go along on a trip to wherever for skiing.

"What would you say was the basis for her problem with success?" Bolling unexpectedly asks. Just like him, Richard bitterly reflects: you think he isn't paying attention when he is, and vice versa.

"Well, uh, it's hard to say. Something to do with her father, probably. I guess he was pretty hard on her, most of the time."

Bolling scowls. "It's a tough road, being a father."

"Oh, for sure," agrees Richard—at that moment passionately hating Al Bolling. How he longs to tell Al what he can do with his whole fucking project, and with his ugly dyke daughter. "Sometimes I think I'm very lucky not to have kids," he states piously.

This seems to work.

"You're quite right there," says Bolling. "Stupidest thing I ever did. Siring children." And then, with what Richard thinks of as one of his lapses into sanity, Bolling says, "I take it that you've got some idea about ski pictures, for the Fillmore?"

"Oh, do I!" Richard almost shouts and laughs with relief, but he forces himself to remain very serious and sober. "Only the greatest idea I ever had," he says.

"Meet me in Reno!" Richard shouts into the telephone, across thousands and thousands of miles. To Eva, in Madrid. "In Nevada! Reno! I'll meet you, and we'll go to Squaw Valley. Ski. It's marvelous there. I have to see you. I can't live like this, without you . . ."

The Prado is just across the street from the Ritz, where she is, Eva is saying. She is sitting there in her suite, looking across to the Prado. So wonderful, the most marvelous collection of Flemish. Memling. Bosch. He should come there, Eva tells him; in fact why not right away? She too cannot wait.

"Christ, Eva. I can't come right now. But in a month or so, early snow, come to Reno. I'll meet you."

She has heard of Reno, Eva tells him, her harsh, shadowed voice throbbing across all that distance. Reno is where, she understands, Americans go to divorce? This is perhaps his intention? She laughs deeply, almost gutturally.

"Eva, you know I'm not married. Jesus Christ, I'm talking about skiing. I love you!"

She too does, does love him, her handsomest Richard, says Eva. But at this moment she is most terrifically tired. Does he know that it is almost midnight where she is? (In the Ritz, across from the Prado.)

Oh. He could kill her. Bitch! Kraut cunt! with her perfect teeth and skin and breasts and—Christ!—everything! with her *body*, that length of grace. Her scents of intimacy. Oh Jesus, her intimate blond hair! How he wishes her dead. His sister. His twin. His mirror image.

At first, an hour or so later, Richard does not recognize the female voice on the phone, although of all women's voices in the world, he knows this one best—or has known it longest: it is Marina, his former and his first and in a sense his only wife (Claudia never counted as a wife). But this voice is low and deep: at first for a wild moment he thinks it could be Stella imitating Eva—but how . . . ?

"I think you'd better come over," this woman says. "Rickie, I need you. I'm over on Jersey Street, near the Castro." And Marina gives him a number.

The tone of her voice has left Richard no choice at all: she is sick, or crazy, or both. She needs him.

Panic encircles Richard, as he drives up Castro. All those boys on corners, leather-jacketed gay couples, feeling each other's asses as they walk. The stores, all full of kinky gay merchandise. Even the movie house, the Castro, with its Hepburn revival week. Is everyone staring at him as he drives along? Do they imagine that he belongs here, among *them*? Richard feels eyes watching, observing him, and looks rigidly ahead.

Arrived at the number on Jersey Street, he presses a bell. At which nothing happens. He stands there, in the baking October sunlight, still a little drunk from lunch. And it is so hot, it will never snow. He is thinking that he must have been wrong, must have heard it wrong, or else crazy Marina gave him the wrong house number, maybe even the wrong street. *Jesus.*

But the next thing he knows, there is Marina, coming out the front door to stand beside him. Or he guesses it must be Marina. She looks so terrible, he could have passed her on the street. Nothing pretty about her anymore, or young. Drab long dirty-blond hair, and an awful too-long rag of a dress. Not quite looking up at him, she says, "I'm really sick. Just take me somewhere, would you?"

"Sick how? what kind of sick?" he asks her, even as he dreads her telling him something, some female detail that he does not want to hear. Cannot hear.

But instead she laughs. "Oh, I don't know. Maybe I just wanted to see you, lovely Rickie."

Oh Jesus. She isn't sick in a physical way at all, just crazy. She's really crazy now, Richard thinks. I will take her somewhere. A psycho ward, that's where she should be.

A chain of associations then goes off in his mind, leading him to think, Mount Zion Hospital. It's sort of Jewish. Jews, psychiatry. I'll take her to Mount Zion; they must have a crazy ward there. Out of the Castro.

In the car, Marina seems to forget how she looks, and she almost tries to flirt—to flirt!—with her former husband who met her in Paterson when they were both eighteen. Is that crazy?

"You know I do miss seeing you, old handsome, and it doesn't seem right, especially since you're not with that Claudia anymore. Don't you think we could, you know, try it out sometime?" Through terrible dangling hair, she leers up sideways at him. "For a long time I was with this other person, his wife was a cop, did I tell you that? And jealous? I'm here to tell you." She laughs, tossing hair from her face. Horribly. "But he's not around anymore, and so, Rickie, gee, why not?"

Minutes later, as they turn onto Divisadero, she asks him, "Rickie, where are we going?"

Clutching his arm as he drives too fast, she says, "Rickie, you know I never loved anyone but you."

He makes a fast right off Divisadero and onto Sutter, pulls into Emergency. Ambulances, attendants. Fortunately no big emergency going on right now, just some nurses and intern-looking people walking slowly through the revolving door.

But he can't just leave her right there, can he? Can he leave now, get out of there?

"Rickie, don't leave me, please!"

Not looking at her, and feeling the rise of panic in his veins, Richard parks beside an idling ambulance, calls "Be right out!" to the driver, and propels Marina through the doors. And into a scene of hell: old people, black people, middle-aged people, kids, lying there on gurneys or sitting in wheelchairs. Fright, anguish, despair or simple stoic rage on every face. Taking it all in, for one instant Richard closes his eyes.

He grasps at a man who must be a doctor—green scrub clothes, a stethoscope around his neck; he points over to Marina, now cowering by a water cooler. Her eyes are more scared than any other eyes in that room. Richard whispers to the doctor, "That woman is psychotic. Maybe dangerous. I've got to get out of here."

Hurrying out, passing Marina, he pats her arm. "You'll be okay now," he murmurs. "They'll take good care of you."

"But, Rickie—"

He is gone.

He wants to see Andrew Bacci. His Dog Shoes. He desperately wants to see Andrew, he does not know why. To fuck Andrew, or let himself be fucked by Andrew, at last?

No.

No, of course not. For one thing it would be dangerous, since Andrew tested positive.

He just wants to see Andrew, or just talk to him. If he gets Andrew's answering tape he will die. Explode.

"Dog Shoes? You don't sound like yourself, what's the matter? Did I wake you up? At three in the afternoon? Well, I envy you. But I might just go home and do the same. To my studio, I mean. I'm in a phone booth, and I've had such a day. Full of crazy women. I do need a nap. Well, it sounds like you're just getting up when I'm going down. So to speak. Well, I might. But then again I might not. But don't bother to knock."

"Just relax," says Andrew, close to Richard's ear. "I'll stop if you don't like it. I told you."

"It sort of hurts—oh!"

"But you sort of like it."

"Yes."

"Relax, darling boy. You feel beautiful."

"Yes. Touch me."

"Yes—"

"But did you put on—?"

"Yes, I'm wearing. Can't you—?"

"Yes. Oh Jesus—yes—yes—"

"Oh, Richard, great Christ! you're lovely—"

"Yes!"

18

Living Together

"How much rent do you pay for this ghastly dump anyway?"

That sentence, spoken by Andrew Bacci to Margot Carlisle, was in fact the first clear signal from Andrew that he wanted Margot to move in with him, but Margot conveniently manages to forget both that sentence and the ensuing conversation. In her later recountings of just how this move came about, and even in her own recollections, these negotiations are obscured in the soft, golden glow of affectionate, quasi-romantic feelings, like a cloud that hides sharp rocks. "Andrew and I have always cared most terrifically for each other," she may say, sometimes adding, with her slightly dirty laugh, "in our fashions." And then, rather piously, "I always somehow knew we'd end up together."

But at the time it actually went like this:

"Oh, far too much," Margot answered Andrew's very rude question. "I really can't afford it."

"Come on, babes. Don't play games. You know how much you pay."

"Well. It's just been raised." Margot lowered her voice. "Twelve hundred dollars. Is that a scandal?"

"It's a lot less than I pay. I'll tell you what, Mrs. Carlisle. You move into my place with me and pay me, oh, say seven fifty? That way, you can save some dollars, and I can afford to keep my pad. And you get me." He smiled at her.

"Andrew, really. What an idea. I have to admit, I'm quite startled." This was the literal truth. Margot's breath stopped, as her quick imagination whirled through rooms—his rooms, *their* rooms, filled with his-their furniture, and everywhere Andrew. She felt herself enchanted, even as a tiny mean voice within her whispered, Andrew is sick. He only wants someone to be around to care for him when he gets really sick, and he knows you will. He knows you'll do anything for him.

"Actually I thought it was your idea, our living together. A few months back," Andrew reminded her.

"Oh, but I was only kidding," Margot lied, remembering that occasion only too well. And she laughed, to prove what an all-round joke that conversation was. And then, flirtatiously, "But you really mean it, don't you, darling Andrew?"

"Yes, in fact I do. We'd get on, don't you think? Once we'd laid down certain ground rules. Like no conversation at breakfast, I can't bear chatter in the morning."

"Oh! nor I. In fact must we breakfast together at all? I'd much rather not. I like to make a cup of coffee and take it back to bed with me, with the papers, and that's breakfast."

"Really? Good. You see? We will get along. We might have been made for each other."

At this they both laughed very merrily, rejoicing in their mutual sophistication and in their sheer affection for each other— or so it seemed for the moment.

"And no pretty boys in your room," Andrew added. At which they both laughed again.

"She loves me, is the point. She'll do anything for me, in- cluding taking care of me when I get sick. I have plans to turn her into a very smart Mother Teresa," is how Andrew explains it to his friend Simon Daniels. "Besides, she's promised. She can never say to me, Look, you're too sick, get out. Well, I know Richard loves me too, sort of, but he's so unreliable. He also loves his dowdy little Stella, and God knows who else. Richard forgets about people when they're not there. No, Margot's my best bet, she really is. Besides, a lot of the time we have fun together. She's very smart, and she can be mean as a snake. I love it when she's mean. Simon, you don't really know her. Trust me. I do."

"How do you mean, Richard loves you too?" Simon thinks he has caught some odd pride in Andrew's tone. Something new.

"Oh, like a pal, unfortunately. You know how straight men are. Even the kinkiest of them."

The matter of furniture, private possessions, has worked out far better than anyone could have predicted, or even imagined. Margot's new bedroom is huge, so large in fact that most of her furniture is thus taken care of. A huge room, but it has no view. Andrew's bedroom has the famous bay view, with Angel Island, the bluffs and hills of Marin, and the bridge. Which is fine with Margot. She tells Andrew that she does not especially like views. "You don't like them because you can't decorate them," he teases. Pleased, she laughs, and does not tell him that nearsightedness prevents her from seeing more than a few feet out the window.

In the living room, their living room, the few of Margot's things that have been inserted here and there have added an interesting, slightly offbeat note: a tiny inlaid box here; a large, dim, heavily gold-framed family portrait over there, in the corner; two small French chairs in the entry hall.

Their domestic habits also seem to work out well with each other. Without telling her why (he hardly has to), Andrew has adopted Margot's lifelong nutritionist views; their kitchen now abounds in shelves of vitamins, and vegetables and fruits. Jars of grains, and beans and rice and pasta. And that is what they have for dinner, mostly. "This stuff is really quite delicious, you know. And it makes you feel so much better," they say to each other.

They separate early in the evenings, off to their private bedrooms for reading. But sometimes, in the middle of the night, or
early in the morning, Margot will hear a tap at her door, and
then, standing next to her bed, in a lovely striped silk robe, there
will be Andrew. Andrew saying, "Margot, babes, I'm lonely. I'm
scared. Why don't you tell me a story?"

The first night that he came to her in that way, Margot was
seriously frightened—first out of uncertainty that it was indeed
Andrew outside her door, rapping lightly. And, second, out of
some wild fear that they had misunderstood each other all along.
That Andrew might have crazily misinterpreted the nature of
her love, her passion for him. Which would never do.

But seemingly not.

Andrew, having murmured his name, comes in and arranges
himself, in his handsome robe, in the pretty (Louis Seize) chair
nearest Margot's bed, and asks for a story.

Sitting up, pulling ruffled sheets up around her gown, and
pushing her long hair back, Margot tells him, "But, darling Andrew, I'm not sure I know any stories. I'm not very inventive,
you know." And she laughs.

"Don't invent. Just tell me the story of your life. Tell the
truth. We've got forever now."

"Shall I tell you about the time I almost had an affair with
Picasso?"

"Yes. Tell me everything."

"*Well.* It was in 1947, just after the war, and I was sitting in
the Flore one afternoon, and I looked across the street—Saint
Germain was so beautifully quiet back then, just a nice neighborhood—and anyway there he was, coming out of the Brasserie
Lipp. I knew him right away. Those eyes."

"Even from across the street?"

"Absolutely."

"Go on."

"Well. I was with my friend Anne-Marie—a great friend of
Juliette Greco, by the way, which is a whole other story—but he
knew Anne-Marie, Picasso did, and so he came over to our table,
and he stared at me. And stared. That *look.* I almost fainted, so
intense. But worse luck, I already had a dinner date that night,

this enchanting boy from Morocco, and so I couldn't go on to the party they were going to, although he begged and begged, and when I couldn't he really seemed annoyed . . ."

And so on. (She did not see Picasso again, and soon heard that he had left for Spain.)

Andrew loves her stories, and Margot quickly develops an extreme sensitivity to his needs, in terms of narrative. He likes visual details, likes to hear about costume and decoration, furniture. Flowers. He is not especially interested in details of weather. He likes names, especially of course famous ones. Likes tales of social and/or sexual intrigue. He does not want any too-intimate details from Margot's or actually from anyone's life. On the whole he prefers humor to sentiment, and Margot can almost always make him laugh.

Every afternoon at precisely four they take tea together, an herbal tea, with cucumber or watercress sandwiches that Margot has carefully made. Occasionally some friend is invited in to partake of this very ceremonial rite, but more often they are alone, gossiping over their still fairly separate social lives. Their friends, their plans for decoration, or possible small trips together.

"It's turning out even better than I thought," Andrew confides to Simon, and to a couple of formerly dubious pals. "We have our own lives, and she's as clean as a cat, always tidying up or polishing something. She even irons the cocktail napkins, and she has some heavenly furniture polish. But the truth is, she keeps me amused."

"It's an almost perfect marriage," Margot says happily to Stella, on the phone. "Or maybe it *is* perfect. You know, I've never thought that living with the person you're having sex with was at all a good idea. So unromantic. Breakfast. I always wanted my lovers to get up and leave, and a lot of them really seemed to resent that."

"How different we are," is Stella's comment.

"Yes, darling Stella. Aren't we, though."

Fairly often, over tea, Richard and Stella are a topic of discussion, *chez* Margot and Andrew. What is not discussed, of course, or even disclosed, is the fact that Andrew visits Richard in his studio from time to time. Every week or so. Andrew would tell no one of this, not ever, although he can't resist an occasional hint, thrown out to Simon, say—which he will then deny. He believes that this is his first experience of true love. But he still finds that he is able to discuss Richard quite dispassionately with Margot. Or so he thinks.

"Richard is in many ways a very dependent person," Andrew pontificates; as always, he is vastly energized by the first shot of tea. "He has to be attached to some woman, and it's hard for him to become unattached. In many ways marriage is ideal for Richard. If Stella had better sense she'd insist on it."

"Maybe she doesn't want to marry him, darling. You know how feminists are these days."

"Well, I'll bet she'll somehow lose him if she doesn't. I think being unmarried makes Richard a little nervous."

"My dearest Andrew, Richard *is* nervous. Look how much he drinks. I know I sound like an old puritan, but that's never, never a very good sign. And of course one has no idea how he felt about that gorgeous German girl I saw him with."

"Just window dressing, probably." Andrew is actually somewhat piqued that Richard has never mentioned any large blond German girl; he would prefer to think that he himself is Richard's only infidelity to Stella.

"He certainly looked crazy about her," says Margot, as she has before.

"Drunk, probably," Andrew muses; and then he says, "This Fillmore job is really going to put Richard over the top. I wouldn't be surprised if he took off in a whole new direction after this."

"But suppose it doesn't work out?" asks Margot. "Al Bolling is very difficult. A troubled person, I've told you." After Stella and Richard's party, Margot had dinner twice with Al Bolling; in her view, an almost total loss. For one thing he is very cheap and takes her to rather dingy, unknown places. And he drinks too much.

Andrew laughs. "Richard's great with difficult people. It's his specialty, or one of them." He laughs again, in a pleased way that signals more to clever Margot than he intended.

"Stella's the success I'm betting on," says Margot. "I think Stella's going to be really rich and famous."

"Oh, you feminists."

"Me? Don't be ridiculous."

"But she is getting better-looking, don't you think?" asks Andrew. "I wonder if Richard's helping her with her clothes."

19

Justine and Bunny and John

Since deciding not to marry Bunny, and decisively turning him down, Justine has had occasion from time to time to wonder about her decision. "Friendship" has been their agreed-upon mode (non-explicitly meaning they don't make love), and although as a friend Bunny is very nice indeed, both a wiser and a more interesting man than she once thought, still, the truth is she misses the sex. Very much. And she thinks, This is ridiculous: does making love mean we have to marry? Crazy!

Furthermore, she has liked his son very much indeed, on sight. Young John Schmidt, a doctor. A smaller, much thinner man than Bunny is, John is also darker, a thin small dark young man with Collin's wide blue eyes, which on him, with all that dark hair and skin, look somewhat exotic. And to make all this still more attractive, John does not seem at all to know that he

7

is handsome; he has in no way the demeanor of a good-looking man. He is neither vain nor self-conscious—an innocent, Justine decides, and she wonders how this could be possible: whatever are young girls like these days? how do they manage not to spoil handsome men?

A young man like that would be very easy to spoil, she further thinks—and then flushes, seeing the direction and the full implication of her thoughts.

The three of them, Justine and Collin and John, are having lunch in Justine's garden on a sunny November day. It is almost too sunny; it is hot, in what should be the rainy season but that seems to mark, instead, the start of another drought. Collin is in shirtsleeves, his habitual blue work shirt, but buttoned almost to the neck; Justine has had to resist the wifely (or mistressly?) impulse to unbutton one or two. John, with only an hour to spare from the hospital, came in his lab coat (all starched and white, so handsome!). Justine is wearing an old pink cotton dress and wishing, at this moment of unruly lust (so unbecoming, so unwelcome), that she had worn something prettier, maybe sexier? maybe bare black? (But is she mad? bare black in November, for lunch in her own garden?)

"Fortunately I've been too busy to think much about it." John finishes whatever he was saying to his father. "I'm just a clinician, you know. I leave research to the scientists, the artists of our trade."

"But doesn't it interest you, research? I mean, with all that's going on in Africa? That's where I'd be, artist or not. Scientist or not."

"Dad, there's a lot of AIDS right here in town, or hadn't you heard."

His somewhat literal, slightly snotty tone has made Justine like him just slightly less, she observes with a certain relief. And from recent articles in the paper and elsewhere, she knows a fair amount about AIDS research in Africa; she also knows a couple of doctors involved in it, whom John must know? She names a few people, tells John that she has talked to them, and agrees with Collin that she finds what is going on in Africa intensely interesting.

Now in total control of herself, she sounds, she knows, just that: controlled. As well as intelligent, very. (Well, she knows she's exceptionally bright; that has always been among the givens of her existence, along with height and large breasts and a Texas accent. Gray hair. No money.)

"Well, damn, I've got to get back there now," says John, rising to his feet. "It's been great, Ms. Jones, uh, Justine. And, Dad, good to see you."

"I worry about that boy," says Collin, classically, once John has gone.

"Oh, why?" Because he's so attractive? But he can't mean that, not Bunny, who is possibly not even aware of his son's good looks. Because the boy has no sense of humor? (It has come to Justine that this must be the case with John; he almost never smiled.)

Collin surprises her. "For a good-looking boy like that, he leads such a narrow life. No dating, or whatever they call it now. Of course I'm proud that he's so dedicated, but he overdoes it. He's had only one serious girlfriend since college."

"What happened with her?" Justine is unable to control specific curiosity; she would like to hear all John's sexual history.

"She died. Estelle. Cancer. So sad; she was a wonderful young woman. I think John's a little like his old man. Monogamous. Serious. I think he overdoes it."

Maybe you do too, Justine does not say.

She is fighting off a fantasy in which John occasionally comes by to talk. (Her house is quite near his hospital, U.C.) A nice cup of tea with an older woman. Maybe she could make him laugh? A few laughs, and then, who knows?

And then she thinks, This is seriously deranged. Some midlife flash of craziness, such thoughts of this younger and probably uninteresting man. That small fling with Cats was quite bad enough.

This is what happened with Cats: After the celebration party, Justine went out with Cats exactly twice—a neat though unknown parallel to Margot's record with Al Bolling. She liked Cats, she thought; he was cute, sort of sexy. But then, the morning after their second date, on which they had kissed good night with some promising passion, Cats called to say, Guess what? Valerie's back, and I guess I have to let her stick around. I guess you do, Justine agreed, and she remained unmoved when he called three days later to say that Valerie was gone again, so couldn't they? wouldn't Justine? She said no; no, he was very nice, but she really didn't think so.

"But I'm a lot more worried about my old pal Richard than I am about my boy," says Collin, with a worried smile.

The remark seems sudden, or perhaps her own quite foolish self-absorption has made it so, Justine inwardly muses, even as she directs her attention to the question of Richard. "Why so?"

Collin's frown deepens. "I'm not sure. Just small things, here and there. He reminds me of a tightrope walker. Very good at his act, but it's risky."

This is so precisely Justine's own sense of Richard that she smiles, liking Collin very much for his perception. She asks, "But hasn't he always been like that?"

"Not so much. I don't know. He used to be a little closer to the ground. Just a regular sort of guy. Really good with his hands, with tools and stuff. A good workman." And then he says, "I wonder how Stella feels."

Justine laughs a little. "We know how she feels. In love. But how she sees him, I really don't know. I wonder if she does. I have no idea how clearly she thinks of him."

"She must be kind of worried."

"I don't know," repeats Justine. And then she says, "Would you mind a lot if I unbuttoned the top button of that shirt?"

He laughs. "Not at all. Unbutton away. I'm game." He leans toward her, very close.

They begin to kiss.

20

Crazy

Which one of them was crazy? That crude question, sometimes voiced, seemed central to all the conflict between Stella and Richard. "You're crazy!" one or the other of them would desperately, furiously, drunkenly yell at the other. It was as though craziness were a heavy black rubber ball (so Stella imagined it) tossed back and forth between them; thus if one of them had it, the other did not.

Richard thought Stella was crazy; he did not in a deep way think about himself. Certain of her opinions seemed crazy: if Stella seriously said, "Now that the Cold War's over, why can't all of everyone's weapons just be junked, so we can get on with some big new social program?" Richard would silently look at her in a particular way, an expression compounded of hopelessness and contempt, which meant, You're the one, you're crazy.

In a somewhat more complicated and illogical way, Stella thought that if she was crazy, as Richard said she was (and a long look at her history and her parentage might well support this view)—if she was crazy, then Richard was not.

Certainly at the start of their connection, on the face of it Richard had not looked especially mad. A handsome and healthy person, good both at his work and at various practical tasks that often defeated Stella (he could even fix his old car), he looked perfectly okay. Whereas she, in her offbeat clothes, with her makeshift job and her failing finances, looked at best eccentric, a person not quite making it. And she was prey to certain secret fears and anxieties; true states of panic could attack her in a drug-store, or at the approach of a friend. She had trouble making phone calls.

However, more recently Stella has felt less sure of who is crazy. Now that she is doing well in her work, even earning money, she feels less offbeat, less incompetent. Less fearful, more okay.

So does that mean that Richard is crazy? And if he is, Stella more or less for the first time thinks, I am crazy to stay with him.

But for much, perhaps most of the time, Stella and Richard do not seem crazy to each other. They do not talk about crazi-ness. They begin to take small trips together, and Stella even finds that she can work, travelling with Richard. While he is off sketching, she writes.

"I know this is sudden, but how about Squaw Valley this weekend?" is how Richard broaches one of those first trips, one January Wednesday. Hitherto he has mostly gone sketching alone, to places fairly near at hand, to Carmel or to Napa, the Alexander Valley, Mendocino. They have talked of Stella's going along, but so far that has not worked out; she has deadlines, commitments. (She has almost, but not quite, welcomed his ab-sence. Almost admitted to herself the relief that she felt.)

Which is another reason for agreeing to this trip, although it is late and she does have a lot to do.

Off to a late start on Friday night, they nevertheless drive up in high spirits, anticipating snow, a new landscape. Richard has managed to rent a condo for the weekend. Right on the slopes, he says.

In a roadhouse near Auburn they eat a large steak dinner, something they do not ordinarily have, but it seems appropriate to skiing, snow. They drink wine in a slow, controlled way; Richard is a little worried about driving in the snow, he says. "I'd better take it easy on the sauce." In moderation, the wine tastes so good, Stella thinks: why couldn't they drink like this all the time?

Richard, in his heavy dark sweater, fair hair gleaming, looks Nordic, a Viking hero, with pale sea-blue eyes. Animated and excited, but not at all drunk, he is very beautiful. Stella's whole heart yearns toward him. It is all she can do not to say, I love you, I love you more than I can bear. I will always love you.

About half an hour later, as they begin to wind up into the mountains, in the dark, it starts to snow. Traffic slows and thickens. Massed cars and trucks are ahead of them, and off to the side of the road are more stopped cars, and men in yellow slickers, flashing strong lights. A sign above the highway then spells out CHAIN CONTROL.

"I outsmarted those greedy bastards, I brought along chains. Rented them in town, and I know how to put them on," Richard mutters, getting out of the car with the package of chains.

The men in slickers can be hired to put on your chains, Stella observes, watching adjacent cars. She wonders how much they charge, and reasons that it could not be enormous: ten dollars? fifteen? So why didn't Richard . . . ? But then she understands that this has nothing to do with money; this is Richard the competent protector, braving snow and cold and oncoming traffic to do it himself. Which is foolhardy, maybe, but surely not crazy. Or only crazy in the sense that all men are crazy in their need to be brave. To take risks.

Later, as they roll along on their tightly chained tires across a broad meadow of snow, driving directly into the snow, it looks as though all the flakes were magnetized into their headlights, all whirling toward them, all the billions of flakes, all the white. As though there were nothing in the world but snow, and sudden light.

The condo is an A-frame, with a huge bed snuggled under low eaves, and floor-to-ceiling windows that face the white descent of snow, the slopes.

"Romantic, no?" Richard is ironic, but he is smiling.

"But, darling, it is romantic."

Making love to her later that night, Richard murmurs, "Oh, I love all your long tall body."

But I'm quite small, Stella does not say. Who are you with? she does not ask.

"Oh, I love you!" Richard murmurs, kissing her neck.

"I love you too."

Another trip.

In early February they go down to Santa Barbara, where it is suddenly as warm as summer. They walk barefoot along the beach, trying not to step on the black oil patches that have appeared here and there; they look out to sea to the oil rigs—so weird, extraterrestrial. And back along the shore to discreetly beautiful houses of the very rich, with lovely old overgrown gardens and glassed-in sunrooms.

"They have a sort of New England look, don't you think?" says Stella, of those houses.

"If you say so."

"How about sketching the oil rigs?"

"You've got to be kidding."

"As a matter of fact, I was."

"Oh. Good."

In this mood Richard is quite unreachable. Stella watches as he picks up a small stone and hurls it angrily against the sand. Mad that it isn't pretty enough to keep? Stella crazily thinks this, just then.

But she is unable not to try to reach him, still. "These houses remind me a little of my grandparents' house," she tells him. "Prentice's parents."

"Oh. The rich Communists. Right."

"Well, actually they weren't. Sort of liberal Republicans, actually. And not all that rich."

"Listen, by Jersey standards they were fucking rich. And Communists."

"*Okay.*"

Disliking him very much just then, Stella tries instead to think of those pretty houses. She supposes the lives lived within them to be unimaginably peaceful, sunny and light; she knows this to be total nonsense: surely those houses enclose their full share of quarrels and pain, loneliness and death. But from her present vantage point, walking along so silently with angry Richard, almost any house looks like a refuge. As indeed her grandparents' house was for her a refuge from noisily angry parents and all their furious drunken friends.

But actually, Stella reminds herself, most of her own life at this moment is not, viewed objectively, so bad. She is selling one long piece to *The Gotham* every month (she is now under contract to them, with a guaranteed escalating word rate and other nice features), and she just sold a small piece about a young Cambodian woman, a painter of Victorian houses, to *The Atlantic* (*The Gotham* said very nice but not for them). She is working hard, she is doing very well (she tells herself this, but it is true).

Having more or less forgotten Richard's mood in the course of these happier thoughts, Stella now asks him, "How are things going with Bolling, generally, would you say?"

Richard, who has been walking somewhat ahead, now turns and comes to a full stop, there in the now cooling coarse gray sand. "Well, as you know, he dinged the ski scene. Too much snow and too few skiers, he said. And he may be in the process of dinging Mendocino. And he's making a serious effort to drink himself to death. Anything else you want to know about Bolling?"

"Uh, I guess not."

"Needless to say, I'm not head-over-heels enthusiastic about starting the next new phase. Santa Barbara oil rigs, maybe. 'Great for a Sierra Club poster, old man.' Christ, I can hear that phony Yale voice. That man can't open his mouth without putting someone down, somewhere. Christ, no wonder his daughter hates men."

"I just don't think—" Stella begins.

"Christ, spare me your depth psychology on lesbians. Dykes. It's a wonder we're all not queer, is what I think. Christ, we all had parents."

Despite herself, Stella laughs. "Well, you're right there," she tells him.

Fortunately the laughter, or something in the cool salt air, works to defuse Richard, as it were, although all he says is, "I'm tired of California, you know that? Really fucking tired of this whole state."

"Oh, so'm I," agrees Stella; with all her new money, she has had a lot of Europe fantasies lately. Or Mexico. Canada? She asks, "Have you ever been to Canada?"

"Christ no. You know I've never been anywhere. This is not Liam O'Gara you're dealing with these days."

"We could go to Venice," Stella attempts.

He scowls. "I'm not all that sure I want to go to Venice. How about Germany? Castles on the Rhine, all that?"

"I'd really rather go to Italy," Stella tells him.

"Okay, okay, we'll go to Italy. If I ever finish this fucking job." But he smiles and takes her hand, as they walk along the beach.

On a long weekend in March, as a semi-vacation they go up to Richard's house, and at last, Justine and Collin-Bunny come along as guests. Stella has gathered from indirect remarks of Justine's that they have been "seeing" each other again, after what has seemed a hiatus. Justine would never in a direct way have described the intimate nature of their connection, any more than Stella would have.

And on Saturday night at dinner, Justine makes a startling announcement.

They arrived in the late afternoon, and Stella noted that Justine seemed keyed up, wired, laughing a lot and reckless in her gestures. "Oh, it's so beautiful," she almost instantly cried out. "Can't we all go for a walk right now?"

"But dinner . . ." Stella was making a somewhat complicated seafood stew, time-consuming in that mussels and shrimp must be cleaned and shelled, tomatoes peeled. Richard had offered to help, but she had quite deliberately chosen to do it herself, and so she had to. "Why don't you all go?" she suggested.

In the end it was Collin and Justine who walked, Richard having some urgent project in the basement.

Working there in the kitchen, alone with the spectacular view of the sea, steep wet rocks and cliffs of wet green ferns, and a molten, golden sky, thick and heavy with sunlight, Stella still thinks of her friend, of Justine, and she wonders, Is it possible that Collin and Justine have worked something out, like getting married? At the same time a reliable inner voice says, No, that's not it. On the other hand, what else? In any case, she thinks, as she scrubs at the mussel shells, Justine looks great, with her lovely gray-white hair. In her faded blue-violet sweater and narrow old faded jeans.

"Do we change for dinner?" Laughing, flushed from the warm outdoors, Justine asks this on her return.

"Oh no, you look super."

"Besides, it's time to drink," Richard cuts in, just then taking over as host.

"You know, old man, this house is looking better all the time," Collin obligingly supplies.

"Well, it's not so bad. A nice house." But Richard smiles with deep pleasure, with love for this house.

"Dinner in a minute," Stella tells them, after drinks.

"Time for a rammer?" Richard asks everyone. No one wants another drink but Richard himself, who gulps it down.

Stella gets dinner on, thinking as she does so how pretty the table is, with its vase of field grasses, the bleached wood-handled cutlery, pale-blue plates and bowls. All Richard's doing, all perfect. And she has quite suddenly, then, a curious thought: she wonders, If I were to live alone now, in some new place, could

I pull together a house that is beautiful? Have I learned that much from Richard? (Richard, who sometimes says, "I should have been a goddam interior desecrator. That's my true vocation, you know that?")

At dinner, while Stella busies herself with serving food, bringing in bread and salad, Richard pours out lots of wine, a nice Beaujolais, and he tells several jokes. Long jokes, and fairly good ones, and he tells them well, but Stella has heard them all before. Several times. She even says, soft-voiced, "But, darling, I've heard that one a lot."

He glares. "Collin and Justine haven't heard it. I'm telling *them*."

He tells the joke, and everyone laughs. Even Stella—dutifully.

And then Justine drops her bomb. With no preamble, she says to the group at large: "Well, kids, guess what? I'm pulling up stakes and moving to New York."

What? What do you mean? Do you have a job? When? Where will you live? *Why?*

They all ask all these things, or rather, Stella and Richard do; Collin presumably has been told before and must be more or less accepting.

Justine tries to explain, to defend herself. No, she does not have a job there, but she knows a few people. Things are tough back there, she's aware of that. Even worse than here. Layoffs on all the papers. She knows what she's jumping out into, but that is more or less the point, if they see what she means. She wants to jump, to see what happens. Her job here at the paper is much too easy; she is cushioned, not working hard enough. She wants to see what she can do. What will happen. Besides, more goes on in New York than in San Francisco.

To this last, only Richard takes exception. "Oh come on, Justine. You mean New York is where it's at? That's just childish."

He has said this more or less jokingly, but Justine chooses to answer him seriously.

She says, "I mean that things seem to happen first in New York. And almost simultaneously but with a difference in L.A. San Francisco often seems a sort of pretty side street, or a suburb.

And more to the point for me is the lousy paper, my silly job there." She suddenly laughs. "I'm fifty years old. I have to get into something serious."

I'll go with you! it suddenly occurs to Stella to say. Of course she does not say this.

"Justine is really crazy, you know that?" Richard mutters to Stella, much later that night. In bed. Fairly drunk, they have not made love.

"I don't think so," Stella tells him, adding, "I just know I'll miss her. Terrifically."

"No you won't. You'll write to her for a while, talk about how much you miss her and fill her in on what's happening here. And then you'll both forget you ever knew each other."

"Oh, Richard."

"Oh, Richard, nothing. You'll see. You're both crazy. Poor old Bunny," he gets out. And then is asleep.

The next day (unfairly) everyone but Richard is hung over, and it is Richard who cleans up the kitchen and produces an elaborate breakfast, popovers and sausages and scrambled eggs. "Your cholesterol fix," he tells them all, serving things out.

"This is so good, I don't even feel guilty about it," says Justine, as Richard beams. (And Stella wonders, Does he really think she's crazy—sane Justine?)

That day they talk less in general terms about Justine's large move than in specifics: how and when she will break it to the paper that she is leaving, where in New York she might live.

"I'd like to try some whole new area," Justine tells them. "Everyone I know used to be down in the Village, and now they're all Upper West Side. There must be somewhere else."

"Try Jersey; you'd love it there," Richard tells her.

Collin laughs. "Try Staten Island, baby. You might like it."

The day itself is ravishingly beautiful. Pure spring, the air light and pale and fresh, new wildflowers strewn everywhere, the broad green meadows above the sea all dotted with white and pink and blue and butter yellow, and the sea itself calm and flat, and shining blue.

Walking for a moment alone with Justine, Stella says to her, half facetiously, "How can you leave California? It's so incredibly beautiful here."

And again Justine answers her seriously. "But that's almost a reason I have to, don't you see?"

Stella does see.

"I'm so fucking tired of California. It's too fucking beautiful," says Richard, on the long drive home, exactly as though he had heard Stella's conversation with Justine.

"We could go somewhere else."

"Haven't we had this conversation a few times before?"

"How about Santa Fe?" she asks him. "We could go to the opera. I have some really nice friends there."

"Or we could go to Venice. I know. Or Germany. Now that you're such a big rich successful lady." His laugh is unpleasant, but then he (surprisingly) smiles, and he says, "Okay. Let's go to the opera in Santa Fe. At least we've never done that before."

21

Santa Fe

This house, toward which Stella and Richard and their hosts, Stella's friends the Fiegenbaums, have driven for miles out into the scrubby canyon country, out from Santa Fe—the house seems all windows, multiple plate glass just now ablaze with late-afternoon sunlight. A desert garden, an effusion of exotic cactus with spiky, wild-colored flowers, surrounds the house and spreads off at one side in the direction of some scrim-fenced tennis courts and an enormous oblong swimming pool.

I won't like these people but Richard will, is what Stella is thinking, as the four of them approach the house. And we'll all drink too much and maybe miss the opera, she thinks. And then she reverses to tell herself, Christ, Richard is right: I really am negative, a killjoy, a spoilsport. I haven't even seen these people, and already they're making me late to the opera.

The front door, high-gloss black with bright brass trimmings, then opens—and there is Richard's perfect woman, his type, the paradigmatic blonde. Tall, with long legs and visible breasts, in a pink silk T-shirt, white pants. Long fluffy fair hair and over-sized eyes, slightly wild, blue. Stella looks over at Richard for one instant, to see him beginning his warm killer-sexy smile. Stella has never felt so small, so dark. So Mexican.

But what the woman says is, to Stella, "Stella *Blake!* I can't tell you how glad I am, I'm such a fan, I've been dying to meet you. This is so *great!*"

"That's so nice, that's kind of you," Stella stumbles, glancing again at Richard, somewhat fearfully. His smile has gone blank, pale blue-gray eyes slate, opaque.

"Well, I've read everything you've written; those last pieces in *The Gotham,* so wonderful—"

"I hate to interrupt this love feast, but couldn't we all be introduced?" The husband, whose name they have been told is Gregory—does not like to be called Greg—is small, barrel-chested, with a heavy, jutting jaw. "I'm Gregory," he says, "and the blonde is Irene. Ma femme."

Tracy Fiegenbaum, also tall and blond and very thin (too thin for Richard, Stella has half-consciously thought), laughs un-comfortably and says, "Oh—I should have—Stella and Richard, Irene and Gregory."

"Richard Fallon," Richard says, just emphasizing his own last name, as in a manly way he shakes hands with Gregory (Baker, Banker? somehow the last name was lost).

"You're here for the opera?" Gregory too is very deep-voiced. (How odd men are together, Stella notes, sensing immediate Gregory-Richard bonds.)

"Mostly to see Jerry and Tracy, here." Richard gracefully backs up to stand next to (very close to) Tracy, who looks sur-prised and then smiles, going faintly pink.

In a gradual way, then, those six somewhat uneasily linked people begin to move toward the pool, rather than into the house. Stella has hoped for the house; it might be cooler there, and also she is curious: how could any two people fill so much space? But they walk along a path among marvelous gaudy flowers, to an area of white gravel, white wrought iron—lacy-looking, nice—beside the very long black pool. They all arrange themselves across the furniture.

"Anyone care to swim?" Puckering her forehead, sure that no one will swim, blond Irene still asks, adding, "I'm sure it's warm enough."

She has spoken mostly to Stella, who is thinking that in fact she would have loved to swim, if only there weren't all that business about bathing suits. She does not like to think of herself in a suit that belonged to perfect Irene.

"Honey, for Christ's sake, we all want a drink. It's drink time, not body-dunking time. That bloody pool," he tells his guests. "Costs its weight in uranium, or truffles, maybe. Don't know why we put in the damn thing."

"You can't beat a custom pool, though," says Richard, instantly a pool expert. "And that black, that was really a smart move."

What Stella likes best, so far, about Santa Fe is the sky, the giant wafting clouds, now tinged with pale gold from the slowly setting sun. In the two days that they have been here, she has observed the most amazing cloud shifts and changes, from fleecy sheep clouds to thunderheads, in minutes. Yesterday in the afternoon there was a terrific thunderstorm, reminding her of New England thunderstorms, with her grandparents, in the summer, which she managed not to say: Richard much dislikes these reminders. ("He's very threatened by New England," she once remarked to Justine, but they could not work out why, and they laughed a lot instead; it did sound silly, once you got away from Richard and his aura of scariness.) And after the thunderstorm yesterday, a perfect clarity, a lovely cool clear evening. Today, though, is still hot at sunset: perhaps it will storm later? For some reason the notion is ominous, although generally Stella likes rain, and thunderstorms. And their opera seats are sheltered.

The morning was cool and breezy, clouds moved swiftly across the sky, and along Canyon Road the poplar leaves rustled, as merchants hovered nervously about their wares and scanned the sky, as though eager tourists might be coming from up there. Stella and Richard had been heading for—or, rather, looking for—a store that San Francisco friends had said was "marvelous." But it had a name they could not remember. Something about an owl, they both thought.

"On the other hand," Stella pointed out, "do we really want to find a store that Margot recommended? Her taste is so precious, so predictable. You used to say that every time."

"Yes, but she really knows Santa Fe; she's been here a lot. Andrew told me."

They both ignored the slight illogic of this; in fact Richard much dislikes "logic," seeming to feel that it is some female trick. Unlike most men, he believes that women, and especially Stella, are highly, punitively rational, whereas he, with his instinctive grasp of everything, is right, and not only right but more in tune, more a part of the world, the universe.

Unfortunately a new idea along those lines, rational lines, occurred to Stella at just that moment. "We do take advice from odd people, have you noticed? Remember the restaurant in Capitola that that dopey girlfriend of Cats's told us to go to? and the hotel in Mendocino? It's as though we think almost anyone knows more than we do."

Richard scowled—though beautifully. This is precisely the sort of speculation he most dislikes—and Stella knows how he dislikes it, but still, sometimes, she finds herself going on and on in that vein. Speculating. Rationally.

"Write an article about it," said Richard. "Tell it to *The Gotham.*"

"Oh, that must be the store." Stella was grateful at that moment for a hanging sign that swayed in the stiffening breeze, announcing *The Unstuffed Owl.*

"My God, pure Margot," Stella whispered, as they entered.

Antiques: tiny fruitwood tables crowded with amethyst paperweights and filigreed silver frames; carved mahogany tables; heavily framed oil portraits on the walls, the canvas dark and cracked.

The owner, though, looked purely Sante Fe: a plumpish blond woman in a starched ruffled blouse, a denim skirt, and the requisite silver conch belt (hers somewhat larger and heavier than most, Stella and no doubt Richard also noted). A woman of un-identifiable age, and little manifest charm or attractiveness— whom Richard, ever quixotic, decided to win.

"I can certainly see that you haven't limited your travels to the Southwest," he began.

"Oh no. Actually, England. And New England. Sometimes France." She beamed, showing large tobacco-stained teeth.

"We travel quite a lot too . . ."

Stella at that point began to disengage from them, and from that conversation, and to wander, though much impeded by sheer clutter, through other rooms, to which she paid minimal atten-tion. More of the same, everywhere. She had recently been asked by *The Gotham* to do some travel pieces, with emphasis on women travelling alone. ("But mostly I don't travel alone." "Try it, you might like it." They both laughed, she and the editor.) It might not be a bad idea, Stella thought, as ostensibly she exam-ined a grandfather clock (are there grandmother clocks? she won-dered). She could take a few trips alone, let Richard fend for himself occasionally—but at that thought the familiar net of anx-ieties in which he kept her bound descended again, and she thought, Oh, if I go on a trip he might do . . . anything.

Just at that moment she heard the voice of Richard, who was saying, "Stella has a contract with *The Gotham;* they want to see everything she writes. Stella Blake, maybe you've read her?"

"No, actually we don't, I don't subscribe to *The Gotham* yet. But I'll certainly . . ."

And as Stella came back into the room (no choice: she saw no other way to exit from the store, much as she would have liked to), she heard the woman say, "My, your husband is cer-tainly proud of you," beaming, with all those dirty teeth.

Furiously embarrassed, Stella would have liked to set her straight, to deny both assumptions: they are not married, Rich-ard is not proud of her. Instead she smiled and touched Richard's arm, reminded him that they were due back at the Fiegenbaums'.

"I'll certainly look for your name!" called out the woman from behind them, as Richard flashed her his warm-wonderful smile and called back, "See you again!" then muttered to Stella, "Christ, she really gets the ugly-teeth prize, did you notice?"

She would not get angry, Stella decided; it never worked. Anger was only estranging, and always in the long run it made her look worse. And so, linking her arm into Richard's arm (why? such an out-of-character gesture, that), she began, "Darling, I know you meant really well, but you embarrassed me . . ."

"Why should it? I don't see that at all."

"Well, you know I'm shy, and I just didn't see the point. I mean, such a big deal . . ." She was floundering, she knew she was, not saying what she meant.

"You're the one making a big deal. Shy. *Shit,* that's your problem."

His sentences never quite connected, Stella not for the first time thought; or it seemed to her that (maybe) Richard's responses did not quite make sense. Or am I the one not making sense? This too was a familiar question.

The air that had been cool and lively a scant half hour before, as they searched for the store, was heavy then, and hot, and still. And the other tourists looked heavier, and slow. As Stella felt herself to be: dowdy, shamed, small, and powerless.

Now, in the dying, blazing sunlight, beside the long black oval of the pool, Richard is telling a joke. "This is guaranteed to offend almost everyone," he announces, pale blue-gray eyes wide and barely moving, but taking in (Stella can see this) group reactions. Checking his hold on everyone there.

And he must sense some lapse, or some degree less than the welcoming, full attention he generally commands, for his voice rises aggressively as he continues. "This happened in the days of Jesus Christ. The living Christ, out riding around on his donkey."

This is Richard's currently favorite joke, one that Stella has heard approximately twenty times in the past four or five months (Richard sticks to jokes for quite a while). But he also told it that morning to the Fiegenbaums, who laughed appreciatively enough, although Stella sensed that Jerry too had heard it before and that Tracy was not especially fond of jokes. Is it possible that he has forgotten already, forgotten that he told the joke this morning? or does he remember but simply not care, not think it's impor-

tant that three people out of an audience of five have heard it
before? Stella does not understand Richard, she decides for the
thousandth time.

It is, unhappily, the beautiful Irene whose attention is flick-
ering off—who is looking, in fact, at Stella, with a questioning
semi-smile. Can she be going to interrupt Richard, wanting to
ask Stella something? This possibility is suddenly terrifying; Stella
must prevent it, and so she does: she turns dismissively away
from Irene, giving all her own full attention to Richard and his
joke, not hearing the words but admiring, adoring, as always, his
most incredibly beautiful face, the bones and planes of his forehead, his strong nose, flat cheeks and deeply cleft chin.

"Let you who is without sin cast the first stone," says Richard, with faintly leering emphasis.

What Stella attempted did not work: Irene has leaned forward
to whisper, "I'd give anything to know what you're working on
now."

"Not much at the moment." Not looking at Irene, Stella has
expelled these words on a single breath, a very soft one.

But Richard of course caught the whole exchange. "If you
ladies wouldn't mind," he says softly, with a menacing smile.
"Maybe you could tell your stories later?" And he turns back to
the audience whose sympathy he assumes, two fellow men.

Irene and Stella, thus linked, exchange a look, in which much
is contained: men are crazy, aren't they? but we mustn't make
too much of it, must we?

"And Jesus said, 'You know, Mom, sometimes you really
piss me off,' " concludes Richard, his punch line.

"A guy in our office, he gets these really good new jokes all
the time," says Jerry Fiegenbaum, with what Stella takes to be
unconscious wistfulness.

Richard, though, takes it otherwise. "Well, I can't compete
with fresh sources," he says with his angry smile. "But maybe
you haven't heard this one. About the contest between three
samurai swordsmen? the fly-slicing contest?"

Pleasant Jerry says, "No, I don't think I know that one."
However, he does glance at his watch. "Say, if you kids are going
to make it to the opera, you'd better think about moving along."

"Well, these three top expert swordsmen—I suppose you girls would say swordspersons?—they got up to test their skills, and the first one . . ."

Richard is crazy.

Stella has never before thought this so simply and clearly. As such a pure statement of fact. Richard is crazy. It is not *her* craziness. So often he has said to her, You're crazy, that she has come at least half to believe him. He even has a certain facial expression that signifies exactly those words: *You're crazy.* An expression of fury and impatience—and fear: he is deeply afraid of madness.

"That fry will never fruck again," says Richard, amid laughter from the men.

"You guys had really better move it along if you want to get to the opera," says Jerry, again.

Consulting his Rolex, Gregory disagrees. "I calculate precisely the time for one more drink."

Richard grins. "Now, there's a man after my own—"

"Actually the overture is what I almost like best in *Figaro*," Stella murmurs, to no one.

Richard turns on her. "Then maybe you'd rather not go? Since we might miss the fucking overture?"

In fact, some twenty, twenty-five minutes later, as in their rented car Stella and Richard swing into the parking lot of the opera house, miles out of town, up on the crest of a very long, circular hill, the overture to *Figaro* is what they clearly hear, and despite herself, despite everything, including Richard, Stella is cheered, exhilarated by the music.

Their seats, good ones that Stella ordered from San Francisco, are just under the sheltering roof. Out beyond the stage set, all that eighteenth-century scenery, they can see the dead or dying embers of the sunset, the faint red burn line, above the black New Mexico horizon.

Events onstage proceed, choruses and arias, stiffly costumed people move about. It is all familiar; Stella has probably seen this opera five or six times before; but tonight she is following none of it. She is only hearing the music, responding to the music, resonating to the lovely strains of Mozart.

It is almost without forethought, and astoundingly without excitement, fear or anger, that she turns and whispers to Richard, "We have to separate. Not live together anymore. You'll be much happier this way, and so will I. We have to."

Some tiny motion of a muscle in his face, a vein, a nerve, tells Stella that he has heard her. But otherwise nothing. No words.

Even, later that night, in bed, as Stella clings to Richard's back, as she always has, and she whispers, "You'll be much happier without me, you'll see . . . ," even then Richard says nothing at all, although of course he has heard her.

Will I ever tell anyone about this? Stella wonders. Could I ever possibly say, We broke up while listening to *The Marriage of Figaro*?

The next morning, though, seems problematic to Stella: should they, as planned, drive up to Taos and spend the night there? or should they try for tickets that would take them immediately back to San Francisco? Stella rather thinks the latter: surely some major change should be instantly apparent, to themselves as well as to the Fiegenbaums?

She almost instantly reads from Richard, though, from his face and his every gesture, that his plan is to carry on as usual. He is his usual self, or one of those selves; he is mildly cross, a little remote, and hurried. Enclosed.

By the time they are clean and dressed and out in the kitchen, Jerry has gone to work and Tracy is about to go off to one of her classes. "Coffee," she points. "Eggs and fruit and stuff in the fridge. Take anything, please. And tomorrow I'll expect you when I see you, okay?"

"Did you get the idea she wanted to get away from us?" asks Richard, once Tracy has hurried out to her car.

"A little. Maybe."

"I can't think why, such happy, attractive guests." His irony, so familiar, is still so wounding, and scary.

The drive to Taos is through canyon country: vast vistas of sand and eroded clay, weird rock formations, deformed gray cactus. Emptiness. Space. A huge river gorge. It is a nightmare landscape, the earth after nuclear disaster. And at the same time it is beautiful. Very beautiful. Unreal. As unreal as death.

As the end of love.

Somewhere, in some town, they stop for lunch. A pleasant small restaurant. They order margaritas. On the small banquette, in the room full of white wrought-iron furniture, they sit side by side behind their green glass table with its woven blue straw mats. Stella sips at her drink and thinks of Mexico, of the good margaritas there. Although actually this one is excellent. She begins to cry, small quiet tears falling down her face.

"Well, I guess we should order lunch," Richard tells her. "What do you feel like?"

"Oh. Anything."

After lunch, for no reason that Stella can later remember, they go into several stores in the town.

Where Richard buys things.

In a shop full of stamped tinware he buys belts and picture frames and some large tin trays, three or four of each, all charged and sent to himself in San Francisco.

Feeling herself to be withdrawn, not entering into this sport that Richard enjoys, this shopping, feeling that she is indeed a spoilsport, a killjoy, Stella fingers a belt; it was all right from a distance, mildly pretty, but on close inspection it is shoddily made, not pretty.

"Buy it!" Richard encourages. "You won't find it in San Francisco."

"I don't really want it," Stella tells him; she did not mean to have said this, it simply surfaced: the truth.

He gives her a steely look.

In another store, an art store, they find some posters by an artist whose work they saw in a gallery in Santa Fe, with the Fiegenbaums. Mostly landscapes, large skies and clouds, and small adobe houses. All in pastels. Very nice, and undistinguished.

"I have lots of time. Sit down if you'd like, and I'll show you," instructs the storekeeper, a tiny, wizened, very dark woman, laden with turquoise jewelry, earrings, necklaces, belt; she looks like an overdressed doll, a grandmother Indian doll, with shining, emphatic eyes. A little like Stella's own grandmother, Stella thinks, except that Serena was poor, not jeweled.

Richard and Stella sit down on the camp stools indicated, and the doll-woman opens a portfolio and begins to leaf through. At almost every poster Richard stops her. "I'll take one of those. A dozen. Eight of that one." And so on, until he must have bought a couple of hundred posters.

Watching him as he sits there, noting the look in his eyes, which is both greedy and frightened (someone might find him out), Stella also observes his increased weight. He dresses so well, in such beautiful clothes, and generally manages to sit or stand in positions that make his paunch unobtrusive—and naked, it simply does not matter. But his posture there on the camp stool, which must be very uncomfortable for such a large man, shows his girth. He looks heavy.

And quite crazy.

And for the first time Stella thinks, He is having some sort of breakdown. He is going mad. How can I leave a man who is going mad?

Their motel in Taos is large and extremely plain, a sort of barn construction. And the upstairs room to which Stella and Richard are shown is barnlike, oversized and bare, with raw pine beams and unstained pine-slab walls. Unadorned. Two beds, both medium wide.

Stella sprawls across one of those beds. This is not a position in which she usually works, but there is no desk or table, and she has chosen to stay in the room and work, or try to work, while Richard goes off to a museum.

She is writing about Serena, the vendor of flowers, in Oaxaca. Serena, whose feet were as brown and gnarled as roots, toes swollen and bent from a lifetime of walking barefoot over harsh rocks and pavements, of exposure to cold and broken glass and thorns in the flower market.

Stella is thinking about Serena; as she writes, she is seeing Serena's feet and her terrible clenched hands; she is not really thinking of Richard. Of whether or not they will continue to live together. Of whether or not he is truly crazy. Mad.

22

Germany

So *great,* the greatest thing that ever happened. The luckiest chance: Richard is going to *Germany.* To an international food conference in Cologne. Cologne, Germany. Where she is. Eva. Eva, who laughed that slow deep laugh of hers as she told him, "Well, my darling handsome Richard, this is indeed great luck. My grandparents live in Cologne, they always keep a beautiful house there, and they retire to the country. Cologne is marvelous. And in October—perfect."

Perfect. Cologne. The rivers. Germany. Eva.

And all this came about because of that craphead bubble party he put on. Webster Wines. God, before he even met Eva. (Or Stella either, come to think of it.) His bubble days of innocence.

(Before Andrew Bacci.) But that dumb party is what got him invited to this conference. International, on food and wine.

Clothes. Surely he has enough?

He makes lists, coordinating blazers and slacks, sweaters and shirts and ties. Shoes and socks. A couple of suits. Scarves. He draws small pictures of some favorite outfits, imagining himself wearing them there. With Eva.

He may need some new things, after all.

But he doesn't really have the right luggage for this stuff. Doesn't even know who carries the very best luggage in town.

"Oddly enough, Magnin's does," Andrew tells him. "Still. And have you thought about a passport, old man? I mean, you've got some time, but those things can take a while."

Jesus! A passport; he hadn't thought of that at all. No one said. Jesus, they just assumed he would have one, like everyone else, everyone who goes to Europe all the time. "Oh sure," Richard says to Andrew, and he gets off the phone as quickly as he can. (First telling Andrew yes, to come over a little after five.) He rushes out to his car, dashes for the Federal Building. The passport office.

"Your expired passport, please?" A heavy black woman, wearing what looks to be layers and layers of clothes, all colors and fabrics, says this to Richard just as, breathless, he arrives at her counter in the crowded office.

Expired passport? For Christ's sake, he doesn't have a passport; if he did he wouldn't be here. For Christ's sake. This is his first trip abroad (you fucking bitch!); is that some kind of a crime? "I don't have an expired passport," he says to the woman. "Is that some kind of a crime?"

"No, sir, but in that case you belong in the other line. You really do." In rap time: is she putting him on?

"You segregate the first-timers, is that it?" Yes, I said segregate, you fat black mother.

"That line. Right there. Sir." She glares; she probably has a gun stashed somewhere in the folds of all those clothes. Christ, she even has a mustache, a heavy black one, just visible but he can see it clearly. He stares at her upper lip before moving over to the other line. The back of the other line.

Leaving the Federal Building, directionless, Richard fast and skillfully drives over the city, heading nowhere. Observing, and thinking of Eva, of Germany—and in another part of his angry mind he thinks still of that fat black snotty dykey bitch in the passport office. He nevertheless sees everything, and his inner eye records: a pack of tiny black-haired Chinese children, in some sort of school uniform, probably Catholic, all holding hands and jabbering to each other. A small, very shabby white Victorian house, its intricate eaves and cornices so sadly gray and dingy, and the house itself all alone there, pitifully sagging in its yard of rangy bright weeds and orphan flowers. A hideous cheapo apartment building, all glass and pink tile—in which some low-rent couples who got married just to fuck will be entirely miserable, no money, for several years, until it's trashed into a slum.

He sees late-afternoon sunlight on the gray bay waves, all those dirty depths, descending down to mud and sludge, dead fish and human bodies. And sunlight on the bright hard flat side of an unpainted billboard, just flat white, and sunlight, which in its way is a hell of an advertisement for something. For nothing? Maybe. He looks back to the bay, sure that he never before saw just that shade of gray. Well, of course he didn't; there never was today before. (Would Stella laugh if he said that? She never has, but he is always in secret afraid that she will. Laugh. The over-educated bookish bitch. And most of her friends are too.) Gray, in which there is blue and green, and yellow and purple too, when you really look at it.

Christ, it's time to go meet Andrew!

"You would not believe what they're hiring in government offices these days," says Richard to Stella that night. "I got this big black woman at the passport office. Christ, she really hated me on sight. 'Get outta here, blond honkie!' I could hear the words in her head. 'Outta here!' " He laughs; he is feeling very tired but good, very good. For the moment.

Stella says, "You're really getting into it, aren't you."

Didn't she even listen to his story about the big black woman, didn't she hear what he said? "Yes, I am," he tells her. It sounded more angry than he had meant to sound, but what the hell, she should listen when he tells a story, even if it's only a little story.

"I'll see about dinner," says Stella, getting up very quickly from the sofa, where they were sitting some distance apart.

Finally, at dinner (not one of her best efforts: the chicken is underdone, the rice a little gluey), Stella gets out what he knows she has wanted all along to say. She takes this big gulp of wine and swallows it down (he is almost sorry for her, watching so much effort), and then she says, "You know, I really could come to Europe too. At the same time, I mean. I've never even been to Germany, and then we could go on to Paris, or—"

"Christ, Stella," he cannot help bursting out. "Are you crazy? This is business. Business! Don't you have the least idea how busy— This is *my* trip, my work, don't you get it? Jesus!"

"Richard, I only said."

"But you've been wanting to say that ever since I first mentioned it. Well, haven't you? All this time getting your nerve up—" Oh Christ: is she about to cry? She looks odd.

A surprise. Stella gets to her feet, and what she says is, "Okay, Richard. But I'm tired." She is wearing a new expression, which he already hates. "And I don't feel like hearing a lot of shit from you. Do you think you could clear the table?"

Well, what the hell? He clears, and for good measure he does the dishes too.

23

Stella and Marina

"It was like being on a roller coaster, you know? I was scared to death, and thrilled but not really having fun, and much too scared to jump off," says Marina Fallon, former wife of Richard, to Stella Blake.

"Yes. it's just like that," says Stella, and she gives a small laugh. "My problem is that I'm still on the ride. But it may be slowing down, I think. Or else I'm getting up my nerve to jump."

They are seated (a somewhat wary settling down, on Stella's part) in the most totally chaotic room that Stella has ever seen, much less entered. This is Marina's "studio apartment," her one room in the basement of a building on Bush Street, near Van Ness. The windows, just below street level, all are barred, which apparently does nothing at all to keep out dust, or noise; there is dust on all visible surfaces and no doubt too on all the clothes that are strewn everywhere about, the bras and panty hose, shirts and *things*. And from the street the rush of cars, trucks, fire engines, emergency vehicles, is constant, loud and distracting. "They call it Lower Pacific Heights," said Marina, telling Stella how to get there. "It's pretty goddam lower."

"They've sprung Marina; she sent me this postcard. She says she's okay, but Jesus, she's never been okay."

"Do you think you should go to see her, see how she is?"

"Are you nuts? Why on earth would I do that? God knows what she might pull this time." He laughs. "You might never see me again."

But he left the postcard (by mistake?) conspicuously out on the top of his dresser. It said, "I'm out, on Lower Pacific Heights. Is that near you? I need to see you. Or someone." With a phone number.

Finding the card, Stella felt no guilt at reading it (did he want her to call Marina?). And she realized that she had often, if half consciously, carried on fantasy conversations with Marina, of course concerning Richard: Has he always . . . ? What makes him . . . ? What do *you* think . . . ?

How, though, was she to introduce herself; as whom? Nothing worked, none of the pretended roles that she was able to imagine; not social worker, or even reporter, for who would send out a reporter to interview Marina Fallon? And she probably had an assigned social worker. And so Stella settled on a partial truth: she was a friend of Richard's, she said; he was busy and had asked her to come by.

But this small ruse was instantly and correctly assessed by Marina. "Oh, the new girlfriend," she said, with a level, unsurprised look. "Claudia told me. I sort of thought you'd show up sometime."

"But how did Claudia . . . ?" Stella was unable to prevent herself from asking this.

"Richard brags about you," said Marina. "I guess you're his first intellectual." She adds, "Claudia used to call me all the time." And then she says, "You're not exactly his usual type, are you.

I guess I am, or I used to be. But Richard's smart, he really is. I guess you know that. I think he's some kind of a genius. It must be nice for him to be with somebody smart like him." This last was said ingenuously, indeed musingly—as though Marina had given the matter some thought and had come to this positive conclusion.

Marina: her hair is dark, but it is the cloudy, indeterminate darkness of a formerly blond person, and her white-shadowed skin is blond skin. Her mouth is wide and unpainted, puffy and vulnerable, opening to disclose very small, uneven teeth. Her eyes are large and empty, sky eyes, a no-color blue. Her voice is a little hoarse (she clears her throat a lot, as though it were strained) and at the same time curiously sweet, and delicate. Her clothes are all black and shabby, hanging loosely from her terribly thin body. Her bones.

But once she must have been a tall, terrific blonde. Richard's type.

"When we were in high school he was mostly shy," Marina has said. "I think he was embarrassed about, you know, his parents. He'd moved to Paterson from Jersey City. But he always had these terrific clothes. It was funny; the other boys all began to copy the way he dressed. The pastel cashmere sweaters and gabardine slacks. Dirty white bucks. If he hadn't been so thin, such a scrawny kid, and tall, he would have looked like a movie star."

"What did he want to do, back then?"

"Oh, he was always drawing stuff. Little funny drawings. Cartoons, I guess they were. He wanted to be a cartoonist. A cartoonist for *The New Yorker,* he used to say."

Suppose that somehow we had been in high school together, Stella wonders, as in her mind she sees broad brown crowded dusty corridors, tall boys in letter sweaters and jeans. The girls with curled hair and cashmere sweaters and pearls. And one tall boy, too thin and very blond, in a pale-blue sweater, his look both shy and disdainful, haughty and eager to please. A very conflicted boy, hiding desperation. Hiding.

Would Richard have liked me then? she wonders.

But we wouldn't even have known each other, Stella next

thinks. He wouldn't have seen me: I was far too small and too dark for him to notice.

She has been moved and touched, though, by this early view of Richard.

"But his face is so beautiful," next says Marina, dreamily. "Isn't it. I used to look at him, so perfect, and I'd think, how could a person who looked like that be mean or bad or evil, ever? I know that's silly, or something worse, but that's what I really thought."

"I've sort of thought that way too," admits Stella.

"He made me feel bad about myself. I've been finding that out, talking to all these shrinks," says Marina. "Like he was so beautiful I had to be this ugly person. And I think while I was with him I got to be a lot uglier. I remember the two of us standing in front of the mirror in the bedroom, getting ready to go out somewhere. And Richard looking terrific, and so pleased with how he looked, but not especially pleased with me. Not really looking at me, or seeing me, even. But I think a lot of it was my fault. I don't know. . . ." She trails off.

"He's confusing, all right." Stella adds, "And scary. What you said about the roller coaster, it is like that."

"How can you be afraid of him, though?" asks Marina. "I mean, with your work and everything. I mean, you're almost famous."

"I'm less afraid of him than I was. I was always mostly afraid he'd leave, rush out the door. And he actually did that a few times. Quite a few times, in fact."

And then Stella begins to say what she almost feels that she came there to say, and what she has so far said to no one else.

"We were in Santa Fe a few weeks ago," she tells Marina, "and Richard seemed so, so, uh, terrible." She had been about to say *crazy*. "Wild. He kept telling the same jokes all day and buying stuff—buying just to be buying things. And making these speeches to people he didn't even know, some about me. Anyway I told him I didn't think we could live together anymore. That we shouldn't. But—this is so peculiar—it's as though I hadn't said that. But I know he heard me. Of course he heard. We were at the opera. *The Marriage of Figaro*." She laughs a little.

"Men don't hear—haven't you ever noticed that?" asks Marina. Her mouth twists down. "They don't listen. *Doctors* don't listen. And Rickie doesn't. He never did."

"No." Stella considers, and then she adds, "So I don't exactly know where we are now." She pauses. "But it doesn't feel so much like a roller coaster anymore." She recognizes for the first time that this is true, that some new process has at least begun between her and Richard.

Marina says, "This policeman. I've got all mixed up with him, and now I don't know how to get out of it. Or if I want to, even. I guess he'll be coming over soon." Not furtively, she looks at her watch.

It is time to go, but before she leaves Stella feels that she must find out something about Marina's "situation." What she will do now. What she thinks will happen to her. And so Stella simply asks, "Will you be okay now, do you think?"

At which Marina chooses to laugh. "Okay? As okay as I've ever been, I guess."

Would it have been better if they had struck up some true intimacy, some instant accord? Stella is not sure; she is only sure that Marina needs much more help than she is getting, or is likely to get, from any visible quarter. It is not my problem, Stella tries to tell herself, I don't even know this woman—and yet she feels that somehow it *is* her problem.

And whether it is or not, she resolves to help, or at least to try to.

"God knows I shouldn't be telling you this," says the social worker whom Stella, through infinite red tape, finally contacts, and whom she has conned with most of her reportorial bag of tricks. "But I just don't hold out too much hope for a woman like Marina Fallon. With her background, those parents . . ."

"Abuse," murmurs Stella, as though she already knew, as if Marina had told her.

"That too," says the social worker mysteriously.

* * *

"He used to beat her up for going out with me. Her old man. That's why I married her, actually. I was a regular Galahad in those days." Richard laughs. "Sir Shining Armor."

"But why? I mean, why didn't he like you?"

"Oh, some stuff about my parents. I guess he'd heard rumors. He didn't like it that my mother worked, hired out, and that my old man drank. But he should talk. Jesus, fucking old bastard. I always thought he had the hots for his daughter."

Stella has so far not told Richard that she went to see Marina, and she now decides not to tell him at all, less from cowardice than from a sense of sheer futility. He is all locked against Marina; he would burst out angrily—and why? Poor Marina!

Instead Stella says, "That's a beautiful shirt. Is it new?"

"Sort of new. Part of my trip trousseau." And Richard begins to talk about his trip—again.

And they do not discuss Marina any further.

24

Richard

Reeling from bad news—the worst—Richard makes quick decisions:

He won't tell Stella.

He won't tell Eva.

He will go to Cologne anyway.

These are all sentences that clatter about like dull plates in Richard's empty mind as he sits in his studio chair. Transfixed. Dumbfounded. Having just been told that the conference is cancelled. All off. No funding, no Cologne.

No Germany. No castles. No passport needed.

But Richard has his passport, his clothes and his bags. He has everything. He is almost packed.

And so he sees what he will do: he will finish packing and go ahead with all his plans—how can he not, after all? And it will work, he knows that, for isn't that how most people operate, most of the time, as though their fantasies were true? Most highly successful people, that is.

The only difference will be that no one will pay for him, and what does that matter? He can pay for himself, subsidize his own trip. God knows he owes himself a trip to Europe, a man of his age, who has worked hard all his life—and for what? For a bunch of ungrateful women, it sometimes seems.

But below all this clatter of words and plans, of bravado, another area of Richard, perhaps his heart, is deeply and terribly wounded, and sore. And frightened: is this how life will be from now on, things falling apart? Promises turned bitter in his mouth? It could kill him, a life like that; he could just dissolve, as though in an acid bath. His heart hurts! He longs for someone, someone warm and loving and unquestioning. Someone to kiss his cock— oh, infinitely.

He feels like taking a shower, beating off there. But he does not.

He is so, so battered. He can't believe it. This is like a cancelled birthday party, or the Christmas your parents forgot. (Is that possible, could anyone actually ever, ever forget it was Christmas? He knows it is, that it happened to him.) Poor Richard, he thinks, and he thinks, I would like to cry. Or to die.

No Cologne. No Rhine, no castles. No wild, wild lovely Eva.

He can't believe it.

He won't.

He telephones Andrew.

"Well, how nice to hear from you, big Rich. How's tricks? Well, I'm about the same. Margot's busy as a flea, all over the place, making everything what she calls perfect. And worrying over my so-called bloody health. Well, it isn't perfect, whoever said it was? I've got this flu, and it won't go away. And no one loved my blood count, but shit, it could be just that. Flu and a low blood count. And I'm tired. Christ, I sound like a girl, don't I, though. I'd like to come over, Rich, and fool around some, but I've got this flu and I'm tired. Next thing I'll be saying I've got the curse. Well, I do—what I've got is the curse, all right."

Richard forces himself to laugh, and decides not, after all, to tell Andrew about Cologne. He wonders, Is Andrew dying? He really can't bear it. He can't bear *anything*.

He sits there in his beautiful studio, and he wonders who else to call.

He suddenly feels as though he knows absolutely no one in the world.

25

Margot and Justine

"I wonder how you'd look if you went, say, pale blond?" In a speculative look, in what has been a small pause in an intensely animated conversation, Margot asks this of her teatime guest— who is Justine. "You do understand that that's not a suggestion," Margot adds.

Justine laughs. "Well, of course in a way it is, and I have to say it's been made before. Especially by hairdressers. Actually I tried blond once. I didn't like it."

"Touché," murmurs Margot.

"Anyway I really like gray hair. It seems more original than blond," says Justine, in a serious way. "And more like me. Margot, I will have some more of your marvelous tea." It occurs to her to speculate on how Margot herself might look with gray hair, instead of her constant very dark black-brown, but something, perhaps small-town Texas good manners, prevents her.

"It is good," says Margot, pleased. "I get it from Cost Plus, of all places."

There is another pause—during which Margot fusses with tea things, adding hot water, pouring—before Justine remarks, "Well, we've certainly covered a lot of ground."

"Indeed." With the pleased smile of a mischievous child, Margot passes the teacup. "I can't tell you how glad I am that you came over."

They have indeed discussed a great deal, in the hour or so of Justine's visit so far—and there seems in the air between them an aroused suggestion of more to come.

This visit came about, as one might imagine, through the agency of Stella, their bond, the mutual friend. Stella told Justine that Margot knew everything about living in New York, how and where to find apartments, all that, and Justine really should call Margot, Stella said. And so Justine did; she made the call and to her mild surprise was invited to tea. She had always imagined herself in Margot's mind as a somewhat suspicious, definitely not chic friend of Stella's—and she had to admit that she, Justine, had always thought of Margot as a somewhat ridiculous, pretentious friend of Stella's.

But today they have indeed got on, perhaps simply because of the tea, which was indeed good, and plentifully poured by Margot.

And they have covered a lot of ground; it would be hard, if not impossible, for either of them to recall just how each topic and person discussed was arrived at, but arrive they did, discovering some quite remarkable areas of agreement.

They began, oddly enough (but quite possibly because of that day's headlines—more transparent lies, Iran-*contra* diaries), with a rather personal discussion of the President, whom neither had met but about whom they both had strong and surprisingly convergent views.

"What a jerk," they almost in unison say.

And Margot adds, "You could certainly call my taste in men catholic, but one type I've never liked is that preppy Brooks New England wimp. So sexless, don't you think? Basically? So cute-little-boy. So *mean.*"

"Absolutely," agrees Justine. "And me neither, I've never gone for those guys. Although I didn't exactly meet a lot of them in Texas. I wasn't hanging out in Midland, around big oil. But last year in Cambridge there were still some around. Old preppies."

"The worst," Margot tells her. "They don't age well. The ones you meet around Harvard are lots, lots better than Yalies, though. The only nice men I ever met who went to Yale were gay, and they had an awful time of it there, poor dears."

"I'll bet," Justine muses. "Lord, when was the last time we had an attractive president, not to mention an honest one?"

Carter was fairly honest but not too attractive, they agree. Roosevelt was the last really sexy president, though neither woman can remember him. Jack Kennedy seems not to have appealed to either Justine or Margot.

"Didn't Richard's pal Al Bolling go to Yale?" asks Justine.

"A perfect example. There he is, terrifically rich and successful, and what does he do with it all? He drinks and gets married a lot, and goes on and on about his daughter, who's probably a perfectly happy lesbian."

"He sure looks depressed. Did you go out with him?" asks Justine.

"Twice, and believe me that was enough. I always think that if sometime during dinner I begin to long for the book at home that I'm reading, that means I'm out with the wrong person. Or I shouldn't be out at all. I wanted to get away from Bolling before he decided to drive off the bridge, or ram his car into something solid, or something."

" 'Marbles.' Wherever does Richard get these names?"

"God knows, but they all sort of fit, don't you think? Didn't you go out with the one he calls Bunny for a while?"

"Well, I sort of still do. Collin Schmidt. He's a contractor. Very nice. Not Yale or drunk or a possible suicide, nothing like that." And the greatest lover, Justine does not say—although it is what she thinks of, thinking of Bunny. And what Margot, she knows, would like to hear. But Justine doesn't talk in that way. She says instead, "He has this terrific handsome son."

"Oh?" Margot's eyebrows rise.

"Just a kid. A doctor." Not wanting to talk more about Collin Schmidt, or his son, Justine surveys the room, and then says to Margot, "It's really beautiful here. I don't know, is it you or Andrew?"

Very pleased, Margot laughs. "Well, very much both of us. It's so funny, isn't it? It's as though we were meant to live together." A shadow passes over her face then, the visible shadow of Andrew's illness. And then she says, "We seem to have covered everyone but Stella and Richard."

"Yes, we do."

Justine has spoken neutrally, but as she speaks she feels some dim foreboding, dim but dark, so dark that she almost begins to prepare to leave, to gather up her things and commence the polite words of parting (in her case all this is elaborate, the remnants of southern girlhood). And later she is almost to think that she should have left just then.

"This awful thing happened with Richard," Margot begins. "To me, I mean." She whispers, leaning toward Justine. "I've never told anyone this, not even Andrew. You know how he is about Richard." And then she relates her dinner with Denny ("my hairdresser, but he's really adorable. And if you ever change your mind about color . . ."), her seeing Richard with this huge but very beautiful blond German woman. "They were all over each other, I mean literally. I've never seen anyone so in love as Richard looked; I'll never forget it. And so imagine how I've felt all this time, with Stella so in love, and so trusting. And especially now, with Richard all worked up about his trip to Germany. I just know he plans to see this woman. I mean, of course he does."

Justine's first reaction has been one of annoyance at Margot, not only for telling this tale but for quite possibly (it seems at first) having made it up—from God knows what combination of malice and boredom. And so she asks, as gently as she can, "But, Margot, are you sure? And how on earth did you know the woman was German?"

"Well, Denny said he could tell by her hair. I know that sounds nuts, but then we walked out near their table—Richard was still too absorbed to notice. But her accent, really, pure

Kraut. I remember girls like that around Paris in the Sixties. When they all started to get so rich."

"Even so. They could have been just drunk. Getting a little sloppy." Even as she says this, though, defensively, Justine is quite suddenly assailed by a small, sharp, urgent memory: she recalls several minutes of a phone conversation in which Stella said, quite worriedly, "I don't know, Richard seems to have this strange new obsession with Germany. He keeps mentioning it so oddly. German this and that. Cameras. Castles. And he says someone told him they have the most beautiful women in the world. He goes on and on—it's so peculiar." And Stella made a short, despairing sound, something between a hopeless laugh and a little cry of pain.

At the time, this behavior of Richard's seemed no worse than odd to Justine—one more oddity from very brilliant, admittedly difficult, eccentric Richard. But now, recalled, it fits much too perfectly with Margot's story.

"Even Andrew thinks he's up to something," Margot continues. "This thing about a food conference in Cologne. There's more to it than just going to Europe for a conference."

"But I read that that was all off," says Justine heedlessly. "Didn't you? I mean, in the *Times* business section."

"Oh, I never read any business news. Too deeply depressing. Remember Bush saying that now is a good time to buy cars and houses. *He* should have read the business news."

"You're right there," says Justine. "But I'm sure I read an item about the Cologne food conference. Cancelled for poor attendance, and no corporate funding. But maybe I've got it all wrong." But she does not have it all wrong. Justine knows she does not. Her memory for the printed word is exceptional; not quite photographic but nearly. Extremely useful for examinations, not to mention day-to-day newspaper work.

"Odd," says Margot. "When I spoke to Stella she just mentioned Richard's going to Cologne. He's apparently made the most elaborate preparations." Margot pauses. "She certainly does not sound happy about it, and she definitely did not say it was all off."

"When did you talk to her?"

"Yesterday. Or maybe it was this morning. No, I think yesterday."

Justine hesitates, before saying, "Well, maybe I am wrong and I read something about some other conference."

"Or else Richard's really nuts and he's going to a conference that isn't there."

Justine tries to laugh at this (they both do), although she really finds it a little scary: she has suddenly seen the possibility that Richard is in fact more than a little crazy and that he might indeed have chosen to go to a nonexistent conference. Or, more plausibly, somewhat more sanely, have decided to go to Cologne, to Germany, conference or not. Especially if there is indeed a beautiful German woman out there for him.

She says, "I really do have to go now," and gets up. But then she stops, and she laughs as she says to Margot, "What we haven't talked about at all, you know, is what I supposedly came for. Your advice about New York."

"Then you'll have to come back. I hope you will. Andrew would love to see you." The Andrew shadow passes across Margot's face again. "Do come," she says. "You'll cheer us up. Andrew loves to talk about New York. Maybe I can persuade him to take a trip there."

26

Stella and Prentice

The very few lies that Stella has told to Richard, in the course of their knowing each other, have been quite minor in nature and mostly to do with shadings rather than hard facts. About Liam O'Gara, Stella has been discreet rather than dishonest; as she has been discreet about a couple of other men, not spelling out the nature of the relationships involved. As why indeed should she do so? No one else has anything to do with her and Richard, she reasons.

And so it is with her grandfather's house (of all the minor issues). Stella has not exactly lied about that house; however, walking on the beach that day at Santa Barbara, she more or less implied that the Blake house was similar to those houses but indeed somewhat simpler. Whereas, in fact, the Blake house was closer in style and in scope to the Bush mansion in Kennebunkport or the Kennedy compound on the Cape. Prentice Blake was exactly what Richard so angrily, scathingly called him: an upper-crust Communist. But Prentice had grown up richer and more upper-crust than Richard had any idea of. The Blake fortune, a New England amalgam of leather goods and lumber, had been immense. (And whatever had happened to all that money? Stella wondered. She supposed that Prentice squandered his share on marriages and good causes and the Communist Party. And that his parents, with whom he had many times quarreled, left the rest to charities and to Harvard.) In any case, the gray-timbered pile of a house on a large lake in southern New Hampshire was truly immense—and frightening and very confusing to a small half-Mexican child on her infrequent visits there with her father. Delia never came to New Hampshire, by whose wish or by what edict Stella was never sure.

It was in New Hampshire, one hot green June afternoon, out on the sun porch, which was Stella's private jungle, her retreat—it was there that as though for the very first time she saw her father and she fell in love with him.

The event was extraordinary, as was its memory. As a young child, a year or so after that memorable day—when she was three or four instead of only two—she would think, That was when I first saw Prentice. It was not of course when she first saw Prentice, actually: she had lived with him in New York and in Mexico, with Prentice and Delia.

Still later, recalling her sense of his newness, and her delight, she thought of it as falling in love.

There she was, on the floor beside the faded floral chintz settee, playing with a little painted wooden train that her grandmother had found for her up in the attic, where the books and toys from the childhoods of Prentice and his sisters were all kept. The dolls were considered too fragile for further use, as were the oversized and delicately furnished dolls' houses. Stella was given a host of stuffed animals, building blocks, balls and cars and trains, with which she was dizzily happy, such an abundance. But in the way of children, which is so often viewed as perverse by the adult world, she especially liked this simple, workable train. She liked to pull it along through the large bright squares of sunlight, on the high-gloss parquet floor—under chairs, between the spiky bamboo legs of tables, carefully around the wicker frames of plant stands and the trailing strands of ivy.

There she was, looking up at the sound of grown-up footsteps creaking across the uncarpeted library floor (there were Oriental scatter rugs), adjacent to the sunroom, where she was. And then he came in, her father, Prentice, whom of course she knew, had recently lived with, but he seemed to her, just then, a brand-new person.

As she must have seemed to him—for looking down, and then bending toward her, her father exclaimed, "Well, hello. My, you are a cute little thing, aren't you now?" And he sat right down beside her, with his dark leather skin and blue eyes, the smell of his pipe, his knees in gray flannel, his long, thin feet in ragged white tennis shoes. He picked up the train and smiled. "It's very satisfying, don't you find it so?"

"Yes," Stella told him. "Wood won't break like plastic."

He laughed. "You're a smart little kid. You must get that from me," and he laughed again.

That was their encounter. No more to it than that. A couple of minutes for Stella to remember, always—minutes to which in later years she would attach new meaning: falling in love.

The rest of that visit with her grandparents and her father passed unmemorably. During those years the grownups were using the same words over and over: McCarthy. FBI. Witch hunt. Russia. Communist menace. Her father did most of the talking; his parents, who were very old, were quiet, sad-looking. At the dinner table and then again at breakfast, and lunch, her father ranted on: Red scare. HUAC. The Smith Act. McCarran. Treachery. Friends. Loyalties. Frida, Diego. Lillian, Hammett. Miller. Kazan.

In the daytime they swam in the lake and took small excursions in the long green canvas canoes, Old Towns, that were tied up for the summer to the heavy dock pilings on slimy green ropes. Out on the water, passing an enclave of smaller, cozier-looking houses along the lakeshore, Stella used to think, but did not quite dare to say, that the three of them, she and Prentice and Delia, could have lived all together and alone in such a house. Lived happily ever after, maybe.

Later on there was a period, dimmer and more distant, more

confused in Stella's mind than the summer when she discovered and fell in love with Prentice—a long period in which she was mostly in Mexico, in Oaxaca and sometimes Cuernavaca, sometimes Mexico City, with Delia. During that time she rarely saw her father; she saw him only in New Hampshire, where he seemed to be living with his parents, and a new blond woman who sometimes seemed to visit.

Hiding out, she later supposed him to be doing, as she grew older and understood something of the atmosphere of the Fifties. When she understood at last that "witch hunt" had nothing to do with black costumes and pointy hats.

In a sense it was surprising, Stella later thought, that they took him in at all, those old super-rich entrenched Republicans. But that surprise lessened as she grew older still and understood a little more of the complexity of human affections, especially those in families.

She gathered that later, though, Prentice quarrelled in a final way with his parents, and that on their deaths his rich sisters, the very right-wing and proper aunts whom Stella had never met, were made richer still, whereas Prentice received what must have been for his parents a mere token, and his half-Mexican child was unmentioned in the will. As she was, in effect, in the will of Prentice himself. A chain of disinheritance.

27

Richard and Bolling

"But I'm not going to Cologne. There is no Cologne!" Richard bursts out, to his own surprise and shock and horror. He has been sitting in this shabby terrible bar forever. With Al Bolling, who likes it here. He has been saying a lot more than he ever meant to say, Richard has, at the end of this horrible day. And so, having said everything else that he did not intend to say, it is not surprising that he should explode with this news of Cologne.

News that he has not told anyone. Not Stella. Or Andrew. Or even Eva.

The day began, or it seemed to begin, with the phone call on his office tape. About Marina. Who was found dead in that place where she lived out on Bush Street; it seemed to have taken them a week to find his address. The female voice on the tape did not announce her identity. A neighbor? an official? Richard is not to know.

Marina was bruised and "pretty much banged up," and lying beside her was an empty bottle of Halcion, which is certainly not supposed to kill you. The person left a number at which she could be reached.

Richard turned off the tape and began to think of Marina, so beautiful that she took his breath away when he was eighteen and flunking out of high school, smoking dope and drinking Gallo Hearty Burgundy. In New Jersey. There she was, so tall and fair and frail; all blue veins, she seemed more blue than blond. His blue girl: he named her that right away. Blue.

She always cried a lot. That is how he remembers Marina, crying, wiping her eyes and her nose, shredding Kleenex. Thin shoulders shaking as he held them. And why? why did she cry so much? Even crying he could always make her come, at first with his fingers and then with himself, his cock. She always came. So why wasn't Marina happy?

At last he dialled the number that was left for him (it must have been a neighbor), getting her after many rings. Wasn't there an investigation? he asked. For instance, who beat her up? That's not something that even unhappy Marina could do to herself. The woman gave him some crazy routine about friends on the force, some cop that Marina knew, so there wasn't any investigation. And Richard remembered Marina boasting about this cop she knew, who no doubt beat her up.

Sitting there at his studio table, in the room so crammed with *things*, all things that he used to find so beautiful, that he coveted and bargained for, Richard longed to weep for poor Marina. He could like himself so much better if he cried, if he could think of himself as a man moved to tears by the death of a woman he used to love. He lowered his face into his hands, as though to cradle sobs, but it didn't work; the smooth vibrant familiar fresh-shaved feel of his skin on his hands reminded him crazily of Claudia's hands. He remembered Claudia stroking his face (they were hiding in a bathroom, at someone's party up at Tahoe, during ski season). And then he remembered crazy jealous Marina, making scenes at a party. So that instead of weeping for

Marina he remembered how he had hated her sometimes. And he thought, What a shit I am, what a total shit.

The next thing that happened, on that awful day, was that Cats came by, just a knock at the door and there he was, small and dark and cute. Richard's Cats. But totally down; Cats was down: Richard read deep depression in his friend's walk, his posture, even before Cats had come across the room to Richard's desk and slumped down into the chair.

"It's her, of course," Cats told Richard. "Fucking whore. She's getting married. To this old rich guy. Whom she's been seeing *all along.*"

"Jesus," was all that Richard could think of to say. "Oh Jesus." And then, unhelpfully, "Are you sure?"

"Of course I'm sure, you asshole. It's not something I'd make up. She came out and admitted it, finally. 'How come I've got all these great clothes that you like so much?' She asked me that, like I was really dumb."

"Jesus," said Richard again.

"I know, there could have been other explanations. But then she smiled in this particular way and she said, Presents. Well, shit, man, I know what that means as well as you do."

Hating to be called "man," and by cute little Cats, who ordinarily didn't talk like that, Richard was reduced to saying, "Well, I don't know."

"Hell, you do know, Rich. You know what she's like. Just look at her."

"But." But you were in love with her, Richard did not say.

The two of them stared at each other across the crowded table, glum and helpless. Richard considered telling Cats about some of his own problems; it would be the friendly male-bonding thing to do, but then he thought, Fuck it, why should I share my head with this stupid dago furnituremaker? Who will walk out of here and find another Valerie in the next bar he walks into? And so, instead of acting like himself, like warm charming Richard, Richard made a small speech. "You've got to pull yourself together, old man," is what Richard said. "Stiff upper lip, all that sort of thing." (Why on earth was he sounding like Al Bolling? So Yale, so incredibly stupid.)

Cats of course looked unhappier yet. He frowned, his small

dark face deeply lined with misery and incomprehension. "Ah, Rich," he pleaded.

"I mean it, Cats Pie. Be a little tough with yourself. Give it a try."

"But, Rich, I loved her."

"Christ, don't be so fucking silly."

"Shit, man, you really know how to hit a fellow when he's down."

"And for God's sake don't call me man! I can't stand it." By the time he had said that, Richard was standing up, shouting.

So that Cats could only scramble to his feet and stand up too, giving Richard one last look as he said, "What a shit you are, Richard Fallon. Just one pretty shit."

Richard watched Cats's receding back, leaving the studio very possibly for the last time. He noted both the slump of those small shoulders and the jaunty effort that Cats was making to get out of there as quickly as possible, and he almost called out to him, Cats, dear old Cats, come back. I didn't mean it. That wasn't me talking.

But he did not call out to Cats. Instead he put his head down on his desk, the cold wood pressing his forehead, and he sobbed. Sobbed, crying for Cats and for poor dead Marina. For poor Al Bolling, so deeply troubled. And for himself, poor Richard, who is, as Cats said, just a pretty shit.

An hour or so after lunch, Stella called to say that she had won some sort of prize. Some literary deal. Not much money but really an honor, she said. Richard could tell that she was playing it down, pretending that it was nothing much; she just thought she'd mention that she got it. But that really, really, she thought it was the cat's pajamas. Whatever the hell it was she got. What prize.

Richard could hardly respond to what she was saying. As usual, her timing was terrible. Not her fault, but shouldn't she really have some sense about things like that? Shouldn't she know how he feels?

He managed, though, not to put her down too much. He just said, How great, and he told her, again, that he's not exactly an expert on literary prizes but it's great that she got one. He wishes they could go out to celebrate tonight, if that's what she had in mind, but he has this thing with Al Bolling, and it could be late.

She sounded disappointed, but not as though she couldn't handle it. Stella is not Marina, thank God.

Richard actually did not have any such plan with Al Bolling, but now he called and fairly readily made the date. Al never seemed to have much to do these days, poor old Marbles. But he insisted on his favorite bar, Al did: this awful place out on Geary, all dark green and black and shabby, so *shabby*. The pure ugliness of the place literally hurts Richard's eyes: the wax flowers in a false-flute vase behind the bar (and anthuriums, for God's sake; bad enough when they're real); the sunset-on-black-velvet painting, framed in nail-studded brass; the bar itself, with its cheap cheap black Formica; the fat cracked Naugahyde barstools; and the fucking floor, dirty linoleum, with black and purple Art Deco swirls. A bar from hell. Richard has never been anywhere so ugly. (But in fact he has: his mother's living room was almost this ugly, and sort of in the same way. She even liked anthuriums. Odd he never remembered before.)

Al likes this bar because he thinks it's a real *bar*, whatever the hell that means.

First off, for no good reason, Richard told Al about Marina, which seemed to open a can of worms for Al.

"My first wife, uh, killed herself," Al said, looking straight ahead at the velvet sunset and the anthuriums. "Did I ever tell you that?"

Well, he had, a couple of times, but Richard politely shook his head no, in an interested way.

"Well, she did. Slit her wrists in the bathtub with a razor blade. Imagine finding a thing like that. Your naked wife, in all that blood? Christ, what a thing to do to a man! And our daughter—it was Alexis who found her, you know. Explains quite a lot, I think. But what anger! When I think about it, I could kill that woman. Killing myself would be more like it, I guess." He paused. "A lot Alexis would care if I did." Another pause. "Lucky for her, I guess."

"Marina's killing herself would not have been a big surprise to me," said Richard.

"But that's actually not how she died, now is it?" Al Bolling pointed out. (Helpfully? Not exactly.)

"No," Richard agreed. "But she still could have, and Christ, for all I know she really provoked this man into beating her up."

"You're not supposed to talk that way these days," instructed Bolling. "When women get beat up or raped, it is not their fault. It's all our fault, fella, and we'd better face it."

The irony was so heavy, leaden as clouds, that Richard realized how drunk Bolling was. He had no doubt been drinking since lunch, and lunch was very likely liquid too. Well, shit. There were a couple of things Richard really needed to say to Al Bolling. Things to get straight.

As though merely changing the subject and introducing a more pleasant topic, after a small pause Richard, as brightly as he could, remarked, "I'm really happy about the way my sketches are shaping up. If I do say so myself, they look *good*."

"What sketches?"

Richard's heart dropped, although there was no way that Bolling could be serious. *No way.* He managed to laugh. "Only the greatest drawings ever made. The northern California coast, in all its dramatic glory. The redwoods—"

"Oh, that shit. Jesus, sometimes I could tie a can to that whole project."

He could not be serious. Although Richard felt that his stomach had risen to his throat, that he was being strangled, choked on his own inner organs, still he knew that this was not the time for pressure. That the last thing he should do, the very last, was in any way to force the issue with Bolling. To force it now. (But holy Christ, how could he have said that, even half drunk and half kidding? How could he have made that remark about tying a can to the Fillmore project? Doesn't he know that that would ruin Richard's whole life? Well, maybe he does know that. Rich people generally do know things, in Richard's experience.)

"How's Stella these days?" was Bolling's next (somewhat surprising) inquiry.

"She's terrific, doing just terrific. She just won some really important literary prize—can't remember the name of it. But she's terrific."

"Well, that's great. I'm glad to hear it. That way you can take early retirement and let her support you."

Was Bolling actually saying that Richard was almost out of work? Before Richard could even think along those lines, Bolling came up with another killer question.

He asked, "How's Stella reacting to your going off to Cologne? She doesn't mind not going too?"

"But I'm not going to Cologne. There is no Cologne," is what Richard then bursts out with.

People whom he has barely noticed in his peripheral vision, sitting near them at the bar, turn now to stare, and Richard stares back, for several horrified moments, and then he tries to laugh. "What's the matter?" he says, more or less to the room at large. "A person can't make a joke around here? What'd you think I meant, the start of World War Three? Cologne has been cancelled, not bombed."

"I more or less thought that might happen," says Bolling to Richard, very quietly.

Richard tries another laugh, with even less success. "Well, I wish you'd told me about it, old man," he said. "If you had this inside information. Where'd you get it anyway? The Skull and Bones Gazette?"

Unsmilingly, Bolling tells him, "It's just in the air. Everything's fucked. Can't you smell the rot?"

"I guess I can," says Richard.

No Cologne and now, from the sound of it, the sound of Bolling, no Fillmore chain project. No heavy money for the next few years or maybe the rest of his life. Richard experiences a surge of depression so profound that it is peaceful. Like drowning, he imagines, and for one wild instant he wonders, When you jump off the bridge, is that what happens, you drown? Or does the water break your back first, or your neck? Or your heart?

He is suddenly a ruin. The wreck that he has always known that he would be, eventually, when everyone caught on to him. Eva caught on a long time ago, he now thinks; she never really loved him. Stella will be the last to get it.

"Well, how about dinner?" asks Al Bolling, with a big sloppy smile that does not include his eyes.

"I think I'll pass on dinner," Richard tells him, feeling cruel. Knowing that Bolling wants, *needs* company tonight.

"Okay then, old man. Whatever you say."

Driving across the city very slowly, with his leaden heart and his dizzy squeezed-out stomach, Richard pauses to stare at a couple of hookers on Polk Street. Tall, pretty black girls, in miniskirts, with those nice high hard asses that some black women have, and very long skinny legs. Richard watches as a car pulls up and one of them goes out to the curb, and after no time at all she gets into the car, and they pull off, while the other girl just stands there, smoking and smiling and contemplating the empty street.

For one insane instant Richard is tempted to go over to her, get her into his car, and drive somewhere and get blown. Well, he's never had a whore; why not? It's what the big boys like Bolling do, he thinks. But then he thinks, Jesus, no. AIDS, herpes, God knows what all. Besides, the shape he's in, he probably couldn't even get it up.

He thinks about whores. Romantic, legendary San Francisco and her whores, with their big gold hearts. They're what the city smells of, Richard thinks. A hundred years and more of whores and pimps and their grimy loot, their putrid beds all covered over now with pretty parks and cable cars and clean white rows of curly Victorian houses. But underneath all that the city stinks. It's getting old and broke and it smells, smells of homeless people and AIDS and poverty and loneliness and cancer. And suicide.

The night is terrifically black. Richard has never seen such a thickly black night, so heavy and quiet, almost no traffic. Dead. A dead night.

Out on Lake Street, almost home, a fast-speeding long black car, an old Jag, comes up behind him and passes, looping far out into the oncoming lane to do so. Some drunk, and then Richard has the sudden idea, next the near conviction, that that was Bolling, who drives an old Jag like that one. Al Bolling on his way to the bridge, where he will start across and then stop in the middle, look both ways to see if other cars might notice him.

Get out of the car and hurry to the railing—and then what? Will he pause for an instant, maybe reconsider, maybe think about his life? No, old Bolling will just lurch on over, over, over the railing and down, down much faster than thought to the black cold slap of water.

Oh God! Poor Marbles.

Richard considers driving on to the bridge himself, following Bolling—but how could he be sure that was Bolling? But it was, he is almost sure it was Marbles, and maybe he could manage to stop him. Look, old Marbles, he could say, we're both in the soup, but you're still rich, and I don't really give a fuck, and so why don't we pool our resources and run off to Mexico?

Would that save either of their lives, running off to Mexico?

Drunk as he is, Richard very much doubts it, and pulling his own car over to the curb, he sits there and, for the second time that day, begins to weep, for Cats, for dead Marina, and for poor wet cold dead Al Bolling (probably).

And for Stella, big feminist, big success.

And for himself.

28

Richard and Stella

"Of course my father didn't kill my mother. Did you believe that? I was just trying to make myself more colorful. More interesting to you. I thought you'd like me better."

"Oh." And then, "How could I have liked you better?" murmurs Stella.

This somewhat unreal conversation takes place on a brilliantly sunny day in early February, up on the northern California coast. Not far from Richard's house. Having taken a fairly long walk, a couple of hours, along the grassy bluffs, they are now seated some feet apart on a sort of hillock, overlooking the bright spreading azure sea.

A little earlier they stopped at what was to Stella a terrifying sight: there suddenly, cut into a dip in this billowing green land, was an enormous crater, a huge round hole, looking far down to a circle of water, tunnelled in from the plunging, churning sea. Interior cliffs of steep sharp rock lined this treacherous cavity; ferns and small flowers sprouted here and there from their tiny crevices. But down below was always that dark flooding water, waiting. Horrifying. Stella quickly stepped back, not liking to see Richard standing there on the edge, peering down; she closed her eyes, and as, together, they left that place she said to Richard, "What a frightful place. Shouldn't there be a fence or something?"

Unexpectedly docile (this is a new and alarming mood in Richard), he said, "I suppose."

And then they walked on some more, now in the direction of Richard's house. And sat down in the sun to rest and to begin, somehow, to talk about parents.

"They fought a lot," Stella said, of Prentice Blake and Delia. "Drank and fought, the way people did in the Fifties. The other side of togetherness. They both had filthy tempers. It's odd that I don't, I guess, or maybe that's why," she mused. "I was too scared." And then, "Did yours fight much?" She paused, "I mean before . . ."

The pause was her first reference, ever, to Richard's early confession: "I've never told anyone this. My old man killed my mom." (Of course at the time she believed him.) And Richard, understanding that pause, getting the reference, then tells her, "Of course my father didn't kill my mother."

And Stella answers, helplessly, "How could I have liked you better?"

This past month or so, Richard has seemed at least twenty years older than his actual age. An old man, terrifically sad. His posture and his walk have perhaps shown it most of all. He once walked with such confidence, a big man, quick and certain, flaunting his marvelous body before the world. Now he slumps and seems to sag. His movements are slow, uncertain.

Stella is sure that much more is oppressively on his mind than she knows about, but she can list at least a few of the causes of his sorrows: the conference at Cologne, which he was so excited about and which then seemed to dissolve and disappear. The death of Marina: "I should have stayed married to her, I know I could have saved her," Richard has ranted, drunkenly, crazily. And the suicide of Al Bolling. Richard: "I *could* have saved him. Christ! I had a chance to. Dinner, we could have really talked for once, I could have talked him out of it. I know I could have. And then he drove right past me! I knew it was him, I could have followed him. Saved his life. Jesus, it is my fault! It's what I get—holy Jesus!"

Somewhere in all this, along with his other panics, Stella senses that Richard is terrified about money. The loss of Bolling also means the loss of the Fillmore job; Richard has said that this was so, but he has not, so far, said that he is worried about money. (It is so like the two of them, Stella has thought, not to mention money.) But she knows that it is something that they have to talk about.

Now, in response to what Stella has said about liking him better, Richard tells her, "You love me. I'm not so sure that you like me very much. But that's the story of my life. I'm loved but not liked a lot."

Struck by the (probable) accuracy of this, Stella nevertheless assures him, "Of course I like you. A lot of people do."

"No they don't. I make them feel sentimental, or I make them laugh. Or I sex them up. But that's not the same as liking." He laughs a little. "You're the one people like, Stell."

And you don't love me, or like me, she thinks but does not say. She only says, "I suppose," aware that this conversation is bringing her close to tears. In fact Richard's sadness penetrates to her bones, like a wind. She has even in a conscious way to control her way of walking, so as not to slump and lag as he does. His sorrow is truly contagious; she fights succumbing to it as best she can, while at the same time she is desperate to help him.

Partly to shake this mood, she gets to her feet. "Let's go," she says. "I'm hungry, aren't you? Let's have a real lunch with some wine, okay?"

* * *

Richard drinks very little of the wine and eats only part of his pasta. No salad. Stella gulps down what are for her unusual amounts of all these things.

In the afternoon, in Richard's large and beautiful sunny bedroom, which is open to views of the bluffs, the grass and sky and sea—in his broad white linen-upholstered bed, they try to make love. With good intentions, some passion and much tenderness, and at last some desperation, they try everything they know, and nothing works. They can't make it, they can't make love.

And afterwards Stella can't fall asleep.

Beside her, Richard sleeps heavily. He breathes in long gasps, like someone dying. In his sleep, where is he? Stella wonders. Is he at home in New Jersey, with very ordinary, embattled, but not murderous parents? Or is he off skiing somewhere? Or in Cologne, where he longed to go, with such strange and unsettling intensity?

They decide to go out for dinner.

And there in the slightly garish, very Fifties-looking roadhouse, Italian style, over bad roast chicken they finally talk in a practical way about Richard's problems.

"I'm much worse off than you think," he tells Stella across the blue-and-white-checkered oilcloth tablecloth. "I'm in too deep. It's hopeless. I'm hopeless."

"How do you mean? Richard, please tell me."

"I've robbed Peter to pay Paul. It's all fucked, completely." He says this with a curious enthusiasm, though. Stella has an odd sense that he is rushing out to embrace his fate.

"But how?" she asks. "Just tell me."

He glances about the room and seems to decide that the other people there, mainly locals in work clothes, are safe, won't hurt him. Although he still lowers his voice as he tells her, "I've taken money for work I haven't done, and now it's too late. I can't. There's too much. And so some of them want it back. I was counting too much on the Fillmore job. You know, actually Al tried to tell me it was over."

Stella asks him, "You mean you owe a lot of money?"

Richard is very pale. Even his blue eyes seem to have paled, and his perfect nose is sharper, whiter than usual. He looks wildly around the room. He says, almost whispering, "Oh Christ, you can't imagine. I could go to jail. What I've done is like embezzling. Taking money I shouldn't have. I had no right—"

"Richard darling, how much money?" Stella feels very adult, very in charge as she asks this, and she thinks, How odd and terrible that having money should be required to turn you into a grownup.

"Oh, a lot. Maybe thirty or forty thousand. I haven't had the nerve to add it all up."

"Richard, I could so easily lend you that," she tells him. "I have much more than that, just lying around in the bank."

"No."

"Come on. My crazy *Gotham* money. I haven't even thought about what I'd do with it. I thought some trips for us, but this is more urgent."

"You're an incredibly wise woman, Stella. Do you know that?"

"I don't feel very wise. Or not often."

"You are. You're a marvelous woman."

He is looking at her as though she were enormously tall, and powerful. And distant. I'm not any of those things, she would like to say to him. I'm small and unwise. And I love you. Oh, how I love you!

"And you're getting beautiful," Richard tells her. "It's amazing. In a couple of years you'll be a really beautiful woman."

"Well, thanks." But he has sounded elegiac, as though mourning a beauty that he will not be around to see, so that Stella shivers, terrified.

He says, "My whole life is shot. Down the tubes. Everything. You're probably just wasting your money."

"It's what I want to do."

"You're a very great woman," he says again, but distantly, as though from somewhere very far away.

Thinking suddenly of that crater, that dizzy plunge down to rolling, ravening black waves, the dark cave of water, Stella shudders—as though Richard had fallen there, in the night, and were lost to her, for good.

29

Richard

The shrink, recommended by Justine, to whom Stella goes to talk about Richard (from whom to possibly "get help") is younger than she expected. About her own age, in fact. Blond and boyish-looking. Handsome, she supposes—although, not looking like Richard, not *being* Richard, how could he be handsome?

He lives and works in a comfortable small Victorian in Lower Pacific Heights, on Pine Street. In his study are all the requisite book-lined walls and leather chairs. The couch with its Oriental rug, its discreetly napkined pillow.

"Well, of course I agree that he sounds depressed," says Dr. Perle. "But as you can imagine, I don't diagnose at a distance. And I certainly can't prescribe."

He says in his rather cold voice these obvious things—as Stella thinks, Of course. And she wonders what she expected. What possible help. Magic pills to take home to Richard? Even brilliantly illuminating words? She says, "Of course. Of course you can't," as her own cold heart sinks lower in her chest.

"What are the chances of getting him in to see me?"

"Not so good, I wouldn't think."

"Well, you could give it a try."

You don't know Richard, Stella starts to say; then only says, "I will." A lie. Richard would take the very suggestion as some further accusation.

Dr. Perle then asks, "But how about you, Miss Blake? All this must be pretty hard on you. I know it's not easy, living with a very depressed person."

"Oh, I'm okay. It's really not so bad—" But having said that, Stella to her horror bursts into tears, a seizure of tears and sobbing from the depths of her body, it seems. She weeps helplessly, powerless to stop.

Mercifully, after several very long minutes (during which she thought she might cry for the rest of her life), she is able to stop and to reach for his handy box of Kleenex. She even smiles as she says, "I feel like a patient." She blows her nose, and she tells him, "I guess really I'm not in the most wonderful shape in the world. It's sort of getting to me."

"I'm here if you want to see me. Either of you. Or both."

"You do that too? Couple therapy?"

"A little. I don't make a specialty of it. Too difficult." He smiles, and although Stella has not been there for the full fifty minutes, she gets up to leave. She says, "I guess that's all I can say right now," and she thanks him. For almost nothing.

Outside in the balmy April air, a pale sky with innocent small fleecy clouds lying over the darker, peaceful bay, despite all that she knows of Richard, Stella has a sudden vision of herself and Richard at the doctor's office. Together. An ordinary couple, perhaps a little more "high-strung," more "creative" than most, they have simply been "having problems." As everyone does. And there in the bland and tasteful office of the shrink, Dr. Perle, they will talk about these problems. Bring dark things to light, expunging anger, guilt, resentments, black frustrations. They will have a perfectly rational three-way conversation.

Instantly of course she knows that they cannot do that, not she and Richard. They are not like that, neither of them is, or could be. Whatever is wrong is blackly rooted around their hearts, their brains and guts, requiring surgery that would kill them in the process. Ah, Richard, she thinks, through tears that have suddenly returned, as she starts up her car. Richard, we were truly made for each other.

Tenderness overcomes the small wave of irony as, driving home, she thinks of Richard as he is now, his utter despair. His slow, slumped-over walk. His new hesitant smile. How she loves him, after all! She will do anything, will do everything, to save him.

But at the sight of his car, parked near their house, she is frightened, and aware that her emotions are sliding about like marbles: what color will come up next? Some red of passion, or maybe green for fresh grief?

Richard is supposed to be at his studio: her fear informs Stella that she thinks he could wretchedly, angrily kill himself at any time.

Still and terrified, she forces herself to walk into the apartment.

There is Richard, in an old gray robe; has she seen it before? She does not remember. It could be a costume for depression. He is watching television. "That's right," he says, to everything on her face, all that she has not said. "I'm here, and I'm watching soaps." He turns back to the screen, where an adolescent couple in matching sweaters is walking toward a white-pillared house, hand in hand.

But you've got all that work to do, Stella does not say. Nor does she remind him of promises: you said you would.

She only asks, "Can I make you some lunch?"

"No, thanks." His voice is cold and dead, and his eyes too, so cold and blank.

How he must hate me, Stella thinks. And she wonders, Has he always?

She says, "I think I'll go down to the office. I've got a lot of stuff to do down there."

"Can't stand to be around me, right? I don't blame you."

She goes over and puts her arms around him, as he sits

there. "Darling Richard, you're sick. This is called being depressed. But you don't have to feel like this. Doctors—they have pills." His body as she holds him is as stiff and unyielding as an angry child's body.

He says, "I'm not depressed. I've just got myself in a lot of trouble. I have to figure out what to do."

It is true: she cannot stand to be with him. "I'll see you later," she says. "Dinner here? I'll get some stuff."

"Where else?" He adds, "I'm not very hungry."

Justine is in New York, looking at apartments. Looking around. Stella feels her absence keenly; she needs her friend. As she drives in an idle way across town, it seems to Stella that all her friends are out of town. Gone somewhere. Unavailable.

On an impulse, and partly because she sees a place to park right there, she stops in front of the building where Margot and Andrew live, on Russian Hill. She parks and, in their lobby, rings their bell.

Margot's voice says, Hello? And then, as Stella identifies herself, "Darling, come right up. You're an answered prayer." But over the intercom her voice is ghostly, strange.

And at her door, Margot warns, "You must take me as you find me. I'm the most total wreck. I look ghastly." She has in fact a white linen scarf tied unbecomingly over her hair, and her trim jeans are dust-spattered, stained. "I'm cleaning house," she explains. "Since Andrew's away. But you're my excuse to stop for tea. Just don't mind how I look. Do you want a sandwich?"

"No; no, thanks. Tea would be wonderful. But where's Andrew?"

"Oh . . ." A pause. "He's off to Mexico. So foolish. He'll only get sick. Or sicker." Margot is almost tearful as she says this.

"Lucky Andrew. I'd give almost anything to be in Mexico," says Stella, with conscious foolishness—but realizing as she speaks that she would love to be almost anywhere, away from San Francisco. Even away from Richard, and so much trouble.

"I'm afraid he thinks it'll be some terrific help to him, going to Mexico," Margot explains. "He'll get all healthy, he thinks. He's at some beach place I never heard of. Escondido."

"South of Oaxaca," Stella tells her. "It's getting popular."

"Yes, but I'd feel safer if he went to some normal place. Like Vallarta or even Acapulco. If he did get sick they'd have good doctors."

But even good doctors can't do a lot for people with AIDS. Stella of course does not say this, although she feels that her ensuing silence must speak, must imply her true hopelessness, and so she breaks it, saying, "He could get a lot of sun, and exercise, and come back at least feeling better."

Margot frowns. "Yes, but infections. Any infection, don't you see?"

"Yes, I do see."

Stella sees too, or begins to see, the extent of Margot's panic. Like a cloud, like weather, it fills the room, infecting the air.

Margot continues. "What's that terrible phrase they use? Opportunistic infections—is that it?"

Stella tries a small laugh. "I think so. Sounds right. I wonder if doctors ever think of metaphors."

"Oh, they can't have time. Excuse me, I'll go make tea. Sit down. Why are we standing about like this?"

We're standing because we're both much too agitated to sit. Stella could have told her this but does not. Partaking of Margot's concern for Andrew, Stella has pushed Richard to some invisible depth of her consciousness, but still he is there, an enormous ache. A longing. A terrified premonition of loss.

"Well," says Margot, returning with their tea sometime later (it has seemed an hour but cannot have been more than ten minutes). "How is gorgeous Richard these days?"

"Oh, I think he was sort of disappointed at not going to Cologne." Why did she say this? Stella cannot imagine. Nor does she know why she then goes on to say, "This food conference there, you know. He was invited and all set to go, and then it was cancelled." She emphasizes, "He was really looking forward to it."

Meaningfully Margot takes this up. "I'll *bet* he was disappointed."

"Well, he was. I guess he would have mentioned it to Andrew?" But why ask Margot this? What on earth does it matter, Richard talking to Andrew; who cares what they say? "And then there was that man who jumped off the bridge," she hurries on. "Al Bolling. Richard knew him pretty well; he was doing some work with him."

"I knew Al Bolling," Margot reminds her. "I met him at your party, remember? We went out for dinner. Twice. I can't say I was surprised that he did what he did. I mean, of course I was sorry to hear it, but what a drunk, and you know those drinkers get really depressed."

After the smallest of pauses, during which Stella and possibly Margot too considers Richard's drinking, Stella says, "And then Richard's poor wife. His first wife, Marina. Getting killed like that. So sad."

Ignoring poor Marina, Margot next says, "I think Richard must be *really* worried over Andrew."

"Oh, do you?" Somewhat surprised that Margot would claim such intimate knowledge of Richard, Stella for the moment only grasps at this further (possible) explanation for Richard's being so terribly depressed: of course, he likes Andrew, and Andrew, who is HIV positive, will almost certainly die of AIDS.

"Yes," says Margot, and with what later strikes Stella as undue emphasis, she adds, "Very worried."

At the time, as Stella sips her tea and considers where to go next, the knot in her stomach that is worry over Richard tightens, so that it is hard to breathe, much less think. Or respond to what is being said.

They talk very little more, and Stella leaves as soon as she can.

At the paper, amid all the good, reassuring, familiar and sometimes intolerable clatter, the clacking and humming machines, the talk, endless talk, and laughs, screeches, noisy sighs— there Stella at last is able to work. It is as though the part of her mind that has been focussed on Richard, anxiously whirling in circles around the problem of Richard, is now taken up or absorbed by the sounds of other people, leaving the rest of Stella's attention for her work.

* * *

What to have for dinner.

By late afternoon this looms as an enormous problem for Stella. And it is one that has always been so easily resolved: Usually at some point during the day, if this has not been discussed at breakfast, Stella and Richard will talk on the phone, telling what happened to each of them so far in his and her day. And then one or the other will say, Shall we go out for dinner, try that new place, Suppers? It sounds good. Or, I feel like cooking, okay? I'll make a surprise. (Either of them might say this, since they both really like to cook.) Or, shall I pick up something in North Beach?

But tonight she has not talked to Richard, and she knows what he will say if he calls: Nothing, he will say. Don't bother. I'm not hungry. And so it is important that she get something good, and she cannot, cannot think what to buy.

Walking through the familiar market, believing that she will somehow be inspired there, Stella stops and pauses, stops and pauses, staring at food displays that are no more tempting or instructive than cardboard pictures of food would be. And as she looks at the faces of other women shoppers, the occasional man, it seems to Stella that they are all similarly paralyzed; all the faces that she sees show anxiety, indecision, sadness. No happy lust for food, healthy appetites.

"I think Richard must be *really* worried over Andrew." That sentence of Margot's, with her particular stress, replays itself quite unexpectedly in Stella's head, and she suddenly understands what was meant: Margot believes, or conceivably she knows, that Richard and Andrew were lovers. At this thought, which is quick and graphic, Stella shudders, aware of a sudden heat in her own loins and a chill of fear in her heart.

Blindly, she buys halibut steaks and some things for salad. But surely they need something else? She cannot think.

Lemons. They are out of lemons, she remembers halfway between the store and where they live, she and Richard. She considers going back for the lemons, and then does not.

With increasing apprehension, her heart almost choked with dread, she drives on toward Lake Street, to her (their) apartment.

She parks and gets out with her package. Scanning the street, she does not see Richard's car, but that really means nothing; he could have parked anywhere. With her key she opens the door, and she finds what all day she has deeply known that she would come home to: black space. No lights. No sound. Nothing. No Richard.

Unless he is dead.

He could be stretched out on their bed, having taken pills. Or cut his wrists. Or suffocated in a plastic bag.

Paralyzed by these pictures, Stella waits a long instant before turning on a light. An instant during which she thinks, No, if Richard were to kill himself he would jump off the bridge, or drive his car into a train, or leap down a cliff. Down into that crater near his house. Into the sea. It would have to be something dramatic—something that he could in fact be doing at this very moment, somewhere else.

Stella stands there in the dark, in panic, more and more believing that Richard is dead. Her chest has been hollowed out; she feels a large cold cavity where her heart was.

She reaches for the light switch, flicks to bright empty rooms, through which she begins to search for signs of Richard.

And finds nothing, except that he is gone.

His toilet things are all gone from the bathroom: is that a good sign or a bad one? does it mean that he plans to live, though not with her?

The fact of his absence from herself is most horrendously powerful to Stella, almost overriding the question of whether or not he is still alive.

At last, on the kitchen table, she sees a scrap of white paper. Where she might not even have seen it. A very small scrap, among the canisters and notepads, near the telephone. In Richard's familiar flamboyant childish printing, it says:

STELLA, I'M GONE. PLEASE DON'T COME AFTER ME. I'M SORRY. R.

30

Richard

Driving north in the pale late-April sunshine, Richard figures it will be dark before he gets there, and he wonders if he will have trouble finding the place. Probably he won't. His sense of direction is terrific still. He has always had this magic sense of where things are, like a bird. Even places where he has never been before, and this is a place that he must have been to several dozen times. He takes people there, to scare them.

The last time was with Stella, and she was really frightened. But then Stella is scared of so much. Scared of making money and being famous. Scared of him, Richard, of what he might do: fuck other people, leave her, and now this. Well, Stella's been right all along, the intelligent bitch. He did everything she always feared he would do, and maybe a few things more.

The light at this hour is really strange, more green than gray, as though the air held a reflection of all the grass and leaves, the thousands of shades of green from everywhere. From spring itself, which is no big deal in northern California; not like in the East. Even in Jersey there was spring. Electric. Bursting. Waterfalls and rainbows. New colors. New clothes. New girls.

The light makes it hard to see. And maybe that would be better, easier; he could just take advantage of this lack of vision. Ram right into another car, some huge cross-country truck with a load of gasoline, maybe. Less driving involved, and everything over with several hours sooner. And making news in all the papers.

But actually even now he does not have to do this; does not have to go through with this plan, this dire determination. At this very moment he could turn right around and drive back to Stella. She would be there, he knows she would. Having read his note, at this very moment she is lying there, across their bed, probably crying. She is terrifically upset, of course, not knowing what to do, what to think. What will happen. She does not know where he is. And in an hour or so he could change all that; he could turn around and head straight back to the city, to their house. He could open the door with his key and just walk in, just say, "Anybody home?" like a joke. And then take her in his arms and talk about love. Make love to her. Be comforting, reassuring. Make promises.

Stella would take him back today, or even tomorrow, he is sure of that; even without much explaining she would take him back. Take care of him, pay off his debts, and support him as long as he would let her. And always be faithful to him: that's Stella. But if he waits another month or so, even several weeks, it might be another story. Even Stella has her limits, he thinks, and she is getting stronger all the time. God knows she is.

But what is he talking about? He won't be around in another couple of months, or weeks. Nor even tomorrow. Christ, how could he slip like that and forget what he is doing?

Richard is wearing an old brown tweed jacket and a brown-and-white-checked shirt; it is what he was wearing the first time he came to see Stella. Dowdy small Stella, then, in that hideous apartment, both now so magically transformed. Even if he can't take all the credit for Stella's transformation, he can take some credit, surely some. And the apartment is gorgeous now, if he does say so. And Stella; Stella is almost beautiful. Buying good clothes, and her face has changed. Another year or so and she'll be there, a beautiful woman.

He can see himself, though, in these clothes, tonight, standing in that living room, and hear his own voice, *Anybody home?* And then see Stella rushing out to him with tears and kisses. Embraces, passionate words. This vision is so real and so appealing that he automatically slows the car and almost stops. And then does not.

He has reached the coast now and is driving along a high bluff, where rocks are strewn all over a grassy meadow, like flocks of sheep. Or maybe they actually are sheep; impossible to tell in this crazy light. This non-light, this green. On the other side, his left, darkness falls across the sea, a shroud of clouds, purple-black, with ragged edges. Richard shudders, thinking ahead. Thinking, It's too late now to go back. Too late for everything and everyone, for Stella and for Eva, for Claudia and poor Marina. And for Andrew, his darling boy, his lovely Andrew, dying of the plague.

(Which he could have too. Although it doesn't much matter now. No one will do an autopsy on him; why should they?)

An hour or so later he has parked his car where he planned to park, where he remembered that there was a lookout area, with no cars there at the moment. He gets out and locks the car. Eventually of course they will break in and find the envelope marked for Stella; he counts on that.

He begins to stride across the meadow, feeling a terrific excitement in his chest: he is actually going to do it! How brave he feels—he *is* brave. He thinks, This should all be on video: a man who is reasonably young, and handsome (well, everyone says he is, and women in the street still stare, and some men). This handsome brave man walking with such resolution, walking toward his own anonymous extinction. His death march.

He breathes in the salty, misty cool air, and he thinks, Ten minutes from now I won't be doing this, won't be walking, won't breathe. There will be no more me. No more Richard Fallon in the world.

31

Stella

Words hurt.

Unbearable. Stella thinks this word repeatedly. But what do you do if you can't bear something? You bear it anyway.

Loss. The anguish of loss. This word makes her very blood hurt.

Never. Never to be with Richard again. Ever. (Probably.)

The words themselves make her cry, crowding her brain, as they do, with their echoes. Alone, she weeps disgracefully, incontinently. She cannot stop. Tears flood her eyes, seeming to rise from the actual, literal pain in her chest. The unbearable pain of loss. Of alone. Of never.

It is not, though, as if Richard were dead. Or is it? His death is surely possible, an unthinkable that must be thought about.

He could be dead, and there is no way for Stella to find out, immediately. If she called the highway patrol, for example (the obvious, sensible thing to do), and if they should find Richard and his car, he would be even angrier, more desperate than he is now. Probably.

She has telephoned to his house up the coast, many dozens of times, but if Richard is there, he is not answering.

She is always seeing his face; it lives in her mind.

Curiously, she finds it most moving at its least beautiful. For example, when they went up to the snow, to ski, on most days Richard wore a purple-striped knit cap that made him look funny. The whole shape of his face, that angular perfection of planes, was somehow altered to comic effect. So amazing: a silly-looking, laughable Richard, whose red nose ran. He thought he looked funny too, and he laughed at his own face, mugging in the too-large, awful gilt motel mirror.

Which, now remembered, is worse than his beauty. Human Richard with a runny nose, laughing at himself. Laughing at her.

With other people, at work or out with friends, Stella manages to behave fairly well. Even to speak of Richard with some analytic distance.

To Justine she speaks perhaps most intimately (but she would not cry around Justine). "In a way it is sort of a relief," she says. "I always had to be so *up* for Richard. Even at best he was never easy. I couldn't relax."

"You sound so sure you won't see him again."

"Do I? I guess I think that, a lot of the time. Or I expect him just to walk in. That's a big problem for me, always expecting him. He has a key, of course."

"You don't feel like putting some agencies to work?"

"No, not yet. If ever. You know, if anyone found him he'd be so furious. I think I'll hear from him sometime. One way or another. And he did say not to come after him."

"Well . . ."

A long pause ensues, during which Justine looks about and seems to concentrate on Stella's rooms, this flat in which, on this late-April afternoon, they are having tea. "Well," says Justine at last, "he certainly was—I mean is—a genius, in his way. This place is fantastic. When I remember how it was before." She sighs.

"Was. In his way," echoes Stella. "I just don't think he'll come back to working again. If he does come back. He was so burned out. But yes, he is a genius." And she too looks at the beautiful space around her—the rich stripped wooden floors, muted Oriental rugs, sofas and chairs and tables, vases and plants—and it comes to her (so strange that she had not thought of this before): she thinks, This is not stuff that Richard "had around," as he said. In the first place it isn't "stuff." These are first-rate, expensive pieces. He bought them, of course he did. How stupid I was not to see that, she thinks, and she adds, to herself, Poor broke extravagant Richard, so generous. So crazy.

Keeping these thoughts to herself, she says to Justine, "You know, that business Richard was in was so crazy in itself. Advertising. The keeping up, the killing trendiness. Even staying out of it for a couple of months, you're probably gone. It seems some Eighties holdover that's got to change, don't you think?"

"I suppose." Justine pauses, and then some moments later she says, with a small smile, "You know, I think I'm developing a crush on Collin's young son. John. So disquieting. A real sign of old age, I think. Young women don't get crushes on younger men."

"They don't? Probably some of them do." Stella finds it hard to focus on this topic—for that matter on any topic other than Richard.

"If there's anything I don't feel like, it's going to Margot's party," she says, moments later, in this somewhat disjointed conversation. Of course she is thinking: Richard just might be there.

"She was so insistent: a sort of command performance," says Justine, as she laughs. "My new best friend. But she's really not a bad sort."

* * *

This constant possibility of Richard, which she feels as his imminence, is both frightening and deeply unsettling to Stella. He might be anywhere at all, she feels. Wherever she goes she might find him. Any ring of her phone or knock at her door might be Richard. Going anywhere at all seems unsafe: suppose, in some restaurant, Richard just happened to be there? (With a tall thin Nordic blonde, her polar opposite and Richard's true type, Stella believes.)

Or just Richard by himself, on the street.

Richard, anywhere.

She is haunted by the possibility of Richard.

She manages to get herself to Margot's party, and she instantly feels, even from outside the door, that Richard will not be there. He simply won't; he could never turn up at a party, to see old friends, and so for a couple of hours she is safe. Among friends.

Laughing her silent wild laugh, almost choking on her own laughter, and whispering to each person, Margot greets her guests. In a shimmering pale-blue silk dress, very tight; her sharp bones protrude here and there.

"Guess what we did this afternoon?" she says to everyone who comes to her party, at the door. "Andrew and I got married! We actually did, we're married. I'm Mrs. Andrew Julio Bacci, if I should choose to use that most improbable name." And she laughs once more. "This is our wedding reception."

And so people generally laugh too; they accept this act, this marriage, as simply too ridiculous (as Margot herself might put it), as hilarious—and so what might have been a real tear-jerker of a party (as Stella and Justine later describe it to each other) is fairly funny.

Justine is there with Collin. Her move to New York, which is imminent, has improved their connection vastly, Justine has said. Collin, at first disapproving, even (it seemed) reluctant to release her, has now come around and is looking forward to visits—his to New York ("Shows! Restaurants! All your new friends") and hers back there, to San Francisco: Justine will stay with him when she comes out, he will see her more than ever. At the moment, as a couple, they exude a happy sensual rapport—for Stella, painful to observe. What a shit I am, she thinks, increasing her misery. Can't I even bear to see a favorite friend happy?

Andrew, very thin, faintly tan from Mexico, looks luminous, intense. As their eyes meet, Andrew's and Stella's, Stella in that flash of darkness sees . . . too much. She sees a look that she can almost but not quite read. A look that is an acknowledgment, but of what? Love of Richard? Death?

They approach each other and exchange routine social greetings. How *are* you? You look *great*! Stella somehow manages to neglect to mention the new marriage, which for that moment she has actually forgotten. And the next thing Andrew says is not about Richard at all; he says, "Oh, I heard from our friend Simon Daniels. He's terribly excited; he's had some sort of first word on his book, and it's really good." He pauses. "The one on your father." (As though Stella might not know what book he meant.)

"That's great," she says, and then adds, "It's odd, though. You know my father wasn't all that famous."

"It could be just a good book, then. Good on its own, I mean."

"Of course. I hope so."

They stare at each other in a helpless, floundering way for a moment or two, before Stella says, as lightly as she can, "You think we'll ever hear from Richard?"

Still staring at her, seeming to search for what to say, Andrew at last tells her, "I don't think so somehow. He'd be holed up in his house, don't you imagine?"

Stella has indeed imagined Richard at his house (has continued to call him there, to no avail), but not "holed up." That phrase has for her a suggestion of coziness, of a perhaps needed vacation. Whereas she has thought of Richard as being in a state of desperation, hiding out. She asks, "You mean you think he's okay?"

"Oh, probably." But Andrew's eyes have gone vague, almost glazed. And anyway, how would he know? Why is his guess any better than Stella's?

Quite unreasonably, though, Stella feels a small spurt of cheer: Richard is okay, probably. He just needed a sort of rest. Even a rest from her.

Though at the same time another part of her mind insists: Richard is not okay. He is desperate. Sick.

To Andrew she says, with a sudden uncontrollable brightness, "I'm so glad you got married. That's so nice."

"Do you think so? We were trying to be funny."

Obligingly Stella laughs. "Well, it *is* funny," she tells him. "Nice and funny."

When she goes home, Stella begins what is not exactly a letter to Richard but rather a sort of journal that is headed in his direction. She is to write many pages of this sort, which, for the moment, she simply saves, in a corner of a shelf.

"What I think is," she writes, "although I know this is impossible, and wrong, I think you could just walk back into this house. Anybody home? in your announcing voice. And you could just be here. Ordinarily. And sometimes I think that is what I most miss, the daily words, the small connections. The continuity. The silly jokes about Legs.

"You could just walk in, we could casually kiss, as though nothing, none of this, had happened. It is very hard for me to believe that you can't or won't do that. And that I am alone for good, with this screaming loss.

"My dreams are still full of trouble, darkness and panic. But in all my waking fantasies you are here. Friendly, jokey. Ordinary, or as ordinary as is possible for you, for us. Strong and warm. You are here, and busy, and mostly in motion.

"You are very beautiful.

"You love me."

32

Richard

Richard is not all right.

He can't even do a decent job of killing himself. Those are the words that he repeats, and repeats, lying across his bed in the fogbound, cool spring night, the damp air resounding with waves. Over and over, to himself but aloud, he says, He can't even do a decent job.

On the brink, on the very cold edge, the slippery cold rim of that cauldron, that churning, deathly hole, at the crucial moment, that night in the dark, Richard became some other person. He became a cowardly person who flung himself headlong down on the long wet grass, the scratchy weeds. He was suddenly someone afraid to jump, to die like that.

He remembered Stella, how terrified she had been at that place, that edge. As though he were inhabited by Stella. As though he were Stella, a frightened woman.

His bowels felt tight and hot. Unmanly.

Eventually he got up from the grass, and he slunk back to his car at the side of the road. That is how he saw himself, a slinking, dishonored person, a sneak and a thief. God knows, a liar. (And at least half queer, to boot.)

In his car he headed north, partly because he saw no point in turning around. No point in doing anything. But he drove and drove, beneath the thick black boring desolate sky. Past motels where people were probably not even fucking anymore.

He was hungry, he knew he was. On the other hand, why should he bother to eat? He did not deserve food, he knew that. But he stopped at an all-night coffee shop kind of place, where he knew beforehand that the booths would be cracked red vinyl and that there would be a round plastic-covered display of cakes and pies, all yellowed, sick.

He did not know, though, that in one of those bulbous booths, slumped over a cup of coffee, he would suddenly see the most beautiful boy: a young man, maybe eighteen or nineteen, with stringy blond hair and the loveliest mouth, with a pouted lower lip. And a perfect nose. The nose in fact was very much like someone's: whose? And then Richard saw that the nose was exactly like his own. It was enough to make him smile, almost. The mouth, though, was not his, he was sure of that: the mouth was Eva's, her pouted lip, so sexy. This boy could be their son, his and Eva's. Tears stung Richard's eyes at this thought, this dream of a son with Eva.

He sat down in the booth right next to the boy's, sat so that they faced each other, and he imagined himself as this boy must see him: an old guy, middle-aged or more, in his silly checked shirt (the clothes he had meant to die in).

How he longed for that boy! Not sexually, nothing like that. He longed just to sleep with that boy in his arms. His son, his child.

The waitress was fat and dark. Mexican. Unpretty. Richard ordered scrambled eggs (why? he hates them), and as the woman left his booth he caught the boy's eye, and they exchanged the slightest, smallest possible smile. Anything more, Richard perfectly well knew, and the boy would think he was coming on to him. Which, looking like that, with that mouth (and that nose!), must happen fairly often.

In Richard's car there was still an envelope of bills for Stella, the almost five grand. (Actually, $4,987.31.) His last money, or nearly; it had taken three IRAs to pull that together for her. The least he could do, since he owes her forty thou. The least, but all he could do.

But on a quick, frenzied impulse, in that ratty all-night place, Richard got up and left his booth, his coffee, his cooling, coagulating eggs. He rushed out to his car for the envelope, just lying there on the seat. Back in the restaurant, breathless, he worked for a moment at obliterating Stella's name and address with a marker pen. And then, pushing a ten onto his table, getting up and casually passing that lovely boy's booth, he flipped the hidden money in its fat envelope onto the table, only saying, "I guess this is for you," with a small hand salute.

And then Richard was out of there, gone. Still hungry and now without money. Almost.

At least for the rest of that night he had good thoughts, though. Dreams, although he never slept. He dreamed of that lovely mouth, all surprised and smiling, as the boy counted out the bills. Maybe took a few to the bank the next day to see if they were okay. Smiling, making plans.

Five grand is enough to change your life for at least a little, if you're very young. Make a down payment on a certain kind of car. Take a trip to Mexico or even Europe; you could make it to France or Germany with that much money. Maybe the boy would go to Cologne? Or Venice; he had a romantic look to him, with his fallen hair and wild blue eyes. He could be a boy with a secret itch for Venice, and how easily Richard can imagine him there, in a gondola, his amazed young eyes lifted to the sight of an arched stone bridge, or to some magnificent palace, all beautifully dank, rotting into the depths of the Grand Canal.

*   *   *

Now, though, alone and cold in his own decaying house, Richard is not imagining Venice. That boy could just as well have been some young hooker, on his way down from Seattle to give glamorous San Francisco a try. Or he could be all mixed up with some dopey girl who needs an abortion, or needs a house, or a diamond ring, for Christ's sake. So that he, Richard, has paid for a ring for some young bimbo. With Stella's money.

How low can you sink without actually dying of it?

He has no money, almost none, for anything. Not the PG&E, much less the mortgage. It isn't his house anymore, not really, and his credit at the grocery store is getting thin. He'll be lucky to get through the summer up here.

His landlord at the studio in San Francisco, Mr. Caruso, has said he would try to sell all Richard's things. But so far no action on that—and a secret that Richard knows, and no one else would guess, is that most of that stuff is junk. It looked good, was probably worthless. Like himself.

He still sometimes thinks of just driving down to the city, to Stella. Just walking right in, the way he always did. But he's almost sure that it's much too late for that.

He has waited too long to go back to Stella.

Besides, he owes her all that money.

He is actually a homeless person now. And that is where he will have to go, eventually. He will have to go someplace where there are shelters for the homeless. Shelters and soup kitchens. Feeding stations.

Probably it really won't be too bad. Less lonely than now. Guys to talk to, everyone with his story. No more middle-class consumer-competitive shit to cope with, all day every day. Just down-and-outers like himself.

He'll grow a beard and dye his hair dark; he wouldn't want to run into anyone he knows. Used to know. Who would believe that dark-haired and shabby man, in dirty clothes, was him, handsome Richard, former clotheshorse, former hotshot lover?

Poor Stella would die if she saw him like that. It is almost tempting to see that she does, somehow.

But all in all it won't be too bad, Richard thinks. Soup and muscatel. In many ways an improvement. Less stress. At least until it gets cold.

33

Stella

In Stella's mind, all that long and cold fogged summer, Richard is almost anywhere, although she now knows that he is actually in his seacoast house. Collin Schmidt went up there, and after what sounded like a considerable search he found Richard.

"We didn't talk long," Bunny reported back. "He wouldn't. Didn't want to." He added, "I think he feels bad about not getting in touch with you, Stella."

(But: did Richard *say* he felt bad, or did kind Collin-Bunny simply assume that he would—or should?)

"I think he's sort of embarrassed," added Bunny.

This seemed plausible, and a wave of pity flushed through Stella's veins, as she thought of Richard's humiliation. His fall from every grace. His diminished self.

Somewhat later, though, another reaction set in, and with

some anger she thought: How cruel of Richard to send me no word at all. He knew how I would feel. How I loved him.

A month or so later Bunny went up again and this time could not find Richard. "But I think he's still living there. Stuff lying around. Sort of camped out. You might say hiding out, I guess."

But is he still up there? Sometimes Stella imagines that horrifying crater in the earth, the unholy hole, up on that bluff: the roiling, crashing surf down below, and the sharp wet rocks all the way down that long descent. Could Richard have fallen there, accidentally or purposefully?

She thinks not, she does not believe that Richard is dead, but still—still, she is haunted.

Or could Richard indeed have abandoned his house and come back to town? Could he be a homeless person? Walking anywhere in San Francisco, past shabby, huddled men slumped down on sidewalks, Stella feels a terror that one of them could be Richard.

(Very few homeless men have pale-blond hair, she notes.)

Sometimes she can make up stories about him, stories with happy endings. In the most convincing of these (to her), Richard has gone off to some very small town, someplace off in the valley, say, and there he has got work as a gardener. From time to time he used to say (she can hear him saying this): "What I do is such shit, as shitty as money is. I should have done something honestly dirty, like working in gardens. I'd be good at it, you know how I love flowers, and I really know quite a bit. I'd get tired and eat a lot and drink less, and sleep well." Richard said that, and so why not? Why couldn't Richard be living that life right now, working in gardens, maybe even with some young tall blond country girl that he had found along the way.

(I must be getting much better, Stella thinks, if I can wish for a girl for Richard. I must be a nicer, more grown-up person than I generally think.)

Somewhat later it occurs to her that most people in small towns tend their own gardens; especially in these depressed days, they do not hire new fancy gardeners from the city. And so that small fantasy explodes.

*   *   *

From her own desk, looking out into the woods, Stella watches the summer strollers there: couples, people with dogs, with children. Occasionally a man alone, a man with blond hair who turns out not to be Richard.

One day, at last, she thinks, This is crazy, out of control. Self-destructive. I am making a career of the loss of Richard. Ridiculous. I already have a career.

The next day she rents an office in a downtown building—very expensive, because she wants it right away and because it has a very small postcard view of the bay, the Bay Bridge, Treasure Island. Cars, sails, freighters. Lost seagulls. No people.

Expensive, but to Stella entirely worth it; her strategy works. In this room where, God knows, Richard has never been, and where the version of herself who loved and lived with Richard has not been either, Stella does not think of him. She works, and she is slowly aware of the emergence within herself of a saner, stronger person.

34

Richard

Standing in a phone booth on a corner in downtown Mendocino, as he scolds an operator and mutters, out of her earshot, "Bitch. Retard. Jesus Christ!" Richard also observes the passing parade of late-summer tourists, all misshapen, fat, or scrawny or somehow twisted, in their awful, awful clothes. He does not look across the street and down across bluffs to the water, the beach, and the wide green mouth of the river—which he used to find breathtaking, mind-stopping, beautiful.

"My darling man, why on earth are you calling collect?" says Andrew, in an unfamiliar voice. A thin voice, faintly rasping.

"Because I don't have any money. Why do you think?" But Richard laughs; of course he is joking. And then he asks, "So how's by you?"

"Not great. Fucking plague. I'm going, Rich. I really am."

"No," says Richard, as though a question had been asked. "Guess what, old Dog Shoes? I won't let you go."

"So what'll you do to save me, Dickie Bird?"

"Anything. Far as that goes, I may have it too, you know?"

"You may, but I doubt it. Safe sex, remember? But all my fault, right?"

"Well, I liked it, you know." Saying this required an effort, but if he can make Andrew feel any better at all, Richard somewhat vaguely thinks, things will improve for them both.

And Andrew's voice does sound a little stronger as he says, "Well. Thanks."

A long, probably expensive pause ensues, during which Richard watches a fat family. Mom and Dad in matching purple sweatshirts, fat kids with sticky faces, and the baby wearing glasses, already broken and mended with Scotch tape.

Andrew says, "Well, old man, you certainly did a vanishing act."

"I guess I did." They have, collectively, the biggest asses he ever saw, that family. The poor baby will grow up not only nearsighted but heavy-assed, poor child.

"So." Andrew pauses, and then, in his increasingly confident voice, he asks Richard, "Feel like doing it again?"

"How do you mean?"

But even as he asks this, Richard too feels a surge of confidence, of hope. A clear instinct told him to go out and call Andrew this afternoon, and now Andrew sounds as though he had been waiting for this call. Richard was right to call—in the sense that he is always right. His inner voice is right.

Andrew begins to explain. "There is this place in Mexico, near Guymas. They do this cure there, and I've been thinking about it. But I needed someone, I guess I needed you. Of course Margot doesn't think it will work." He pauses. "Don't worry, I've got plenty of money for us both. For almost forever."

Richard is in love with Mexico City. The whole insane polluted overpopulated gorgeous mess. Walking along the streets and boulevards, he is time after time stopped in his tracks by some marvel: a small pale-green plaster house, with curling white oversized scrolls around all the windows and the door. Or the dull gray and crazily carved wildly irregular facade of a church, with its entering courtyard of trees, now all leafed out. So beautiful! It almost makes him weep.

He walks all day. He walks until he almost drops and his eyes are strained and dizzy with seeing so much, and then he comes back to the hotel, and to Andrew. Poor pale exhausted Andrew, less beautiful now, who lies by the pool on a long pink plastic lounge chair, covered with towels.

They are staying in a large commercial hotel, down by Chapultepec Park (where the castle is! and the museum of carriages). In a few days, or more (Richard is secretly hoping for much longer), they will leave for Guymas. Andrew calls the clinic every day, but so far there are no vacancies. They're really crowded.

"I guess that's a good sign?" Andrew has asked this several times.

And Richard always reassures him: "Of course it is. The word's got out." Although privately he doesn't think it's such a great sign, necessarily; it only means more desperate people, clutching at what might be a little more life.

When they do go to the clinic, Richard himself plans to be tested, or he might even take the cure—prophylactically, as it were. Although he feels okay. Just tired. Not quite his old energy level, but it's probably just the altitude. And so much walking.

He loves Mexicans, all those lovely dark-eyed, dark-haired people, many with brownish skins. How blond he feels, and how tall! How they stare! I would not have liked it in Cologne, he decides; I would have looked too much like everyone else there. Eva and I looked too much alike. No wonder Stella loved me so much, he thinks.

He is seeing bits of Stella everywhere. Stella, in all the faces in Mexico.

I was never so beautiful as when I was with Stella, Richard thinks.

In a way that's really too bad.

Maybe someday he'll go back to Stella.

35

October: Stella and John

"I love you! Oh, how I love you. Your body, all of you, so beautiful . . ."

Moved by these words, murmured close to her ear (how could she not be moved?), Stella, in another part of her mind, is registering a question: Who does he sound like? This is John Schmidt, her young lover; of course it is John who is speaking, she knows that. But those words have a ring of someone else.

Surely not Richard. He never talked like that, was never so reckless. And not Liam; his avowals were edited, were faintly literary, always.

And then in a rush it comes to her that John sounds like herself. Herself with Richard. Herself quite crazed, quite crazy in love.

John sounds like her, although she wonders, did she actually say those things, or is that simply how she felt? But John is neither crazy nor out of control. He is simply an openhearted, generous young man. In love.

They are in a motel on the Oregon coast, high up on a bluff, overlooking a rocky beach and now, in late fall, a turbulent sea. The motel itself is simple, utilitarian; plain and clean. The view is the room's main feature; one wall is all glass, all view. But the wall that faces the king-size, low-slung bed in which Stella and John now lie is papered over with a large, sepia-tinted photo-mural—incongruously, of snow. Snow-laden boughs, a narrow path cut through deep banks of snow. In the distance, a snow-peaked mountain. So that Stella has thought of Richard, Richard in the snow. Richard with his silly hat and runny nose, not beautiful but human. Entirely loved.

Earlier that morning, John got up to run, down on the beach, and Stella, looking at all that snow (and wondering why a snow scene, in an Oregon coast motel?), thought so powerfully of Richard, more strongly than for some months now, that she thought it must be Richard who would come back into the room. Richard out on some car errand, who would tap lightly on the door and then come back into the room where she lay waiting for him. Casual Richard, coming in as he had to their condo at Tahoe, or anywhere. No momentous return, for nothing momentous had happened; they had always been together.

But there was no knock, and of course it was John who came in, grinning, throwing her a kiss on the way to the shower. Who after a lot of rushing water came back into bed with her, all clean, and breathing, "I love you, oh, how I love you." And touching her firmly, expertly.

"I love you too," says Stella, more matter-of-factly. She believes this to be true.

Certainly she loves his openness, his willingness to be vulnerable, exposed. He seems to have no guile, no calculation in these matters. He is about five years younger than Stella, but she feels him to be of another generation, and she wonders, Are all young men like that these days? She very much hopes so.

And certainly in a sexual way she is drawn to John; although she would never say this aloud, not even to Justine (and although she is ashamed, even, of these unbidden thoughts), Stella does make certain sexual comparisons. John and Richard. And by any reasonable standards, in a technical way John comes off much better. He is both livelier and more generous than Richard was; he makes love to her with an energetic, strong competence, and with love. Whereas with Richard, Stella had an occasional lurking sense that he and she together made love to him; they were joined in this essential enterprise of loving Richard.

But she is not in love with John. Although it is true that she loves him.

Young John Schmidt. Or sometimes "young Dr. Schmidt." That was how Stella thought of him when they first met, about a month before this trip. Kindly Collin-Bunny called to ask Stella out to dinner, and then called again to ask, would it be okay to bring his son along? He could guarantee good behavior. Stella did not think, then or later, that Bunny had intended to fix them up; more likely he shied away from the idea of an evening all alone with Stella, who might (he might think) talk too much about Richard (actually she talked rather little about him these days, even to Justine).

As it was, the three of them, Bunny and Stella and John, ate an enormous amount of calamari and pasta, somewhere south of Market Street, and they drank a lot of wine and generally had fun.

Stella was much struck by the unlikeness between father and son: Bunny's genial affability, John's dark shyness. And struck too by their mutual honest good spirits and pleasure in each other's company. That was what Stella mostly made of the evening: two exceptionally nice men, who seemed more friends than father and son. But then, she thought, I'm hardly an expert on families.

Partly they seemed unrelated biologically, because of physical dissimilarity: plump and rather florid, gray-bald Bunny—and smallish, dark, lithe John, with intelligent, wary gold-brown eyes. Only their mouths were very similar, both wide and firm, strong and shapely mouths. Sexy mouths, and she remembered Justine's saying, "It's his mouth that gets me. It's so—so competent." With her laugh. Stella did notice John's mouth, that first night.

John took her home, and he called the next day, and the next and the next, and he took her out to dinner on those nights. At her door, each night, he would kiss her, a light brush of his mouth against hers.

They had several such dinners, and kisses, and had a week or so apart when John was on call at the hospital. And then John asked if she had ever seen the Oregon coast. No. Would she like to? Yes.

"I think it's too soon after Richard for anything serious, and he's a very serious young man," is how Stella put it to Justine, on the phone from New York.

"Is he? I just remember how attractive. I was quite bowled over."

"Well, I'm not. Thank God. Who'd want that again."

During that early dinner with John and Bunny, Stella heard several references to someone named Estelle—a friend of John's, she gathered, but she noted that both John and Bunny spoke the name with a touch of sadness, of reverence, almost. And so it did not seem a matter for teasing questions, even were Stella given to that sort of thing. At a later point, though, when they began to discuss the trip to Oregon, John told her, "I did go up there with Estelle."

"Oh. Estelle?" as though she had not heard the name before.

He must have been wanting to tell her, for then a great deal came out: Estelle had been John's girlfriend ("We were very serious, going to get married"). And Estelle had died at twenty-five, of breast cancer. Terrible for Bunny too, John said; Bunny had been crazy about her.

Romantically, John and Stella waited to make love until their trip away. Stella also felt a strong superstitious fear of someone else in the bed she had shared with Richard—as though Richard, still, might sense this alien presence and suddenly in the night return.

When at last they were together, in the first motel, which was still in northern California (not far from where Richard probably was), when John exclaimed his love, and spoke so fervently of passion, Stella was sure that she heard a longing in his voice that was not for her alone. He loved and longed for poor dead Estelle, as, when Stella returned his kisses, passionately, the passion and the longing were also for Richard.

Now, in the Oregon motel, John asks her, "What about it— shall we push on up north, or stick around here for another day or so?"

Stella laughs with pleasure at their indolence, their leisure. Pulling back her hair, she tells him, "I don't even know where we are."

"It's called Port Orford."

"Well, we do like it here." She hesitates. "But maybe we should try farther on? Weren't there supposed to be wonderful sand dunes somewhere?"

His husky voice: "I think so." He hesitates. "I think I'd like it anywhere with you."

"Let's not put that to the test, okay?"

"Okay, lady. Whatever you say. But first, here, let me touch you."

"Oh yes." She closes her eyes, she moves to him.

36

Stella and Justine

Justine has come out to San Francisco to interview Stella. That is how she speaks of it, with a wondering small laugh. "I've come all the way out here for an interview with you!" in her special Texas-Harvard voice. Although the truth is that of course she wanted to come; she would use any excuse for a visit to what she now thinks of as home. "Back home in San Francisco" is her new joke. Still, both women are serious about the interview, which was commissioned by a new magazine, *YOU*, that Justine says looks very good so far. Competition for *The Gotham*.

Justine could use more free-lance work; life in New York is both more expensive and more difficult than she imagined; simply getting from one place to another seems difficult. And Stella is serious both out of helpfulness to Justine and because she has not been interviewed before simply as herself: she has been part of a group of women reporters, or, with Simon Daniels, there to talk about her father. She now has some sense of stepping out onto a stage.

Since what they are doing together is unfamiliar (an interview?), they have chosen unfamiliar grounds for it, Justine's hotel room, courtesy of the magazine. Large and pale, its furniture and fabrics of an even, nondescript pastel (probably called "sand"), the near-opulent room could be in any city, any country, except for the view, which is almost identical to that from Stella's new studio workroom: same bridge and boats, same seagulls.

Although Justine has her tape recorder turned on, it soon becomes apparent that this is a conversation that cannot be contained, or controlled. They digress, and digress—until it becomes silly for Stella to say, each time, "Of course you can't use this," and for Justine to agree, "Of course not."

Ostensibly there to discuss Stella's new project, her *Mexicans in San Francisco* tome (for which agent Gloria got her a whacking advance, even in these parlous early-Nineties times), they have not exactly given that topic short shrift, but certainly they have wandered from it.

One immediate but minor (very minor) problem, at which they nevertheless seem to stick, has to do with dinner: should the four of them, Justine and Bunny, Stella and John, go out together? Possibly not; on the other hand, *why* not? They all like each other, in various ways, and Justine is not here for long; she presumably wishes to maximize her time both with Stella and with Bunny, with whom she is now carrying on a bicoastal romance, which, as she more or less predicted, he loves. But so does she; it works.

However, the very idea of this foursome makes the two women laugh with embarrassment. "For one thing there're these neat age gaps all around," is Justine's comment, or one of her comments. "You're older than John—"

"Thanks for reminding me," Stella cannot help saying.

"And Bunny's older than I am, and of course I'm older than you."

"I think there's just this hint of incest." Stella laughs.

"I sure can't see myself as your mom."

"But it's okay, none of us are getting married."
"No, it's just a dinner."
"So what are we fussing about?"
"Okay, let's go back to work."

"There is just so much I have to learn." That is Stella's
strongest sense of her project, which she sometimes sees as literally beyond her, a mammoth bulk of facts, a monolith, that she
can neither move nor comprehend. "So much," she repeats to
Justine. "Hundreds of thousands of Mexicans, all kinds of Mexicans, coming to San Francisco. And all their sisters and brothers
and aunts scattered around in the valley towns, or down in L.A.
Mexicans often think California is still part of Mexico."

Speaking (recorded), there in the bland, expensive and char-
acterless hotel room, with her friend Justine, Stella is thinking
less of Mexicans in San Francisco than of Mexico City itself, how
she both loves and hates it there, the smog and smells and flowers
and lunatic architecture, the teeming crowds of dark large-small
happy mourning people. Who remind her of herself. She now
sees that she has always felt more Mexican than New England.
She is more Delia—and Serena—than Prentice.

A couple of days ago Margot called to say that she had had
a card from Andrew, in Mexico City. "He said, 'R. and I will be
pushing on to Guymas,' " Margot told Stella. "Could R. be Richard, do you think?"

"I don't know. I suppose. I guess it could."

Since then Stella has been sure, at times, that Richard is indeed in Mexico City. She can see him there, so tall and blond
among all those dark people. As handsome as Cortés.

But at other moments she very much doubts this: how *could*
Richard be in Mexico City? He could be a homeless person in
San Francisco. He could be dead. (But if he were dead she would
know it, Stella believes.)

* * *

For most of the afternoon, though, they manage, Stella and Justine, to talk about Stella's project. Her plans and even her working habits. ("I know it's boring, but I have to ask you this, people like to hear this nuts-and-bolts stuff.")

And from time to time they digress.

"Well no, I'm not," says Stella, in answer to a later, personal question. "Not at all in love with John. But I like him a lot, we mostly have fun, and I guess I'm lucky he's around." A pause. "I don't see it lasting very long, though. He'll get restless. Or I will."

"How long were you with Richard, in all?"

"Almost two years. I was just thinking, I met him the day I'd been interviewed by Simon Daniels. I was supposed to interview Richard that same day, remember?" She suddenly smiles. "On the way to Simon's, there was this little black girl who asked me what I was going to be on Halloween. Of course I didn't know." Stella laughs.

"Two years. It sure seems longer."

"Especially to me," Stella tells her friend. "But you know, Richard was so complicated. He was so many different people that it was like having a lot of love affairs." She says, "When I think the words 'in love,' I think of Richard. But it has less and less to do with the actual Richard Fallon. If you see what I mean."

"I think I do."

"Richard is the name I give to a certain set of emotions," Stella attempts. Like music left in the air when a concert is over, she thinks. The bright reflection of peonies in a mirror.

The scent of roses in a room where no flowers are.

"I just don't give it much time anymore," she says to Justine, with a small smile. "I'm really busy."

A NOTE ON THE TYPE

This book was set in Garamond, a typeface originally designed by the famous Parisian type cutter Claude Garamond (1480-1561). This version of Garamond was modeled on a 1592 specimen sheet from the Egenolff-Berner foundry, which was produced from types thought to have been brought to Frankfurt by Jacques Sabon (d. 1580).

Claude Garamond is one of the most famous type designers in printing history. His distinguished romans and italics first appeared in *Opera Ciceronis* in 1543-44. While delightfully unconventional in design, the Garamond types are clear and open, yet maintain an elegance and precision of line that mark them as French.

Composed by Creative Graphics,
Allentown, Pennsylvania
Printed and bound by Arcata Graphics/Martinsburg,
Martinsburg, West Virginia
Designed by Dorothy S. Baker